UNSTOLEN

TONY BATTON

*To Melissa
Very best wishes
Tony B
June 2018*

TWENTY-FIRST CENTURY THRILLERS

Jake Moro is a modern day Robin Hood. Almost.
He returns stolen items to their rightful owners.
For a price.

A man has to make a living, and Jake more than most.
Because he's still paying for mistakes made a long time ago.
And they weren't even his.

Unstolen - First Edition v1.0

First published in 2018 by
Twenty-First Century Thrillers

Copyright © Tony Batton, 2018

Cover photographs © Shutterstock
Cover Design by Books Covered

All rights reserved. No part of this book may be reproduced in any form or by any electronic or mechanical means, including information storage and retrieval systems, without written permission from the author, except for the use of brief quotations in a book review.

The right of Tony Batton to be identified as author of this work has been asserted in accordance with Section 77 of the Copyright, Designs and Patents Act 1988

This book is a work of fiction. Names, characters, places, incidents and dialogues are products of the author's imagination or are used fictitiously. Any resemblance to actual people, living or dead, events or locales is entirely coincidental.

This book is sold subject to the condition that it shall not, by way of trade or otherwise, be lent, resold, hired out, or otherwise circulated without the publisher's prior consent in any form of binding or cover other than that in which it is published without a similar condition, including this condition being imposed on the subsequent purchaser.

Find out more about the author at:
www.tonybatton.com

For Alex and Nathan

ONE

My name is Jake Moro, and I may not have long to live. As I stand here in the shadow of overhanging trees, contemplating that unpalatable thought, I can't help wondering, 'Is it my fault? Was my planning not good enough? Or is this simply some kind of bizarre justice for all that I've done, however much I believe I'm on the right side of things?'

I certainly present myself as the good guy. If you met me, you'd probably buy me a drink. We'd have a pleasant chat. But five minutes later you would have forgotten me. And who'd blame you? Everything about me is average: middling height, medium build, brownish hair. My clothes are, in the words of my friends, unremarkable. When we talked, I wouldn't have said anything noteworthy. Even if you did remember me, it wouldn't matter. Because everything you saw and heard would have been a lie. Including, most likely, my face.

Of course you shouldn't take it personally: I lie to everybody. My business is all about blending deception and truth, and using whichever is most effective. I'll be straight with you: by some definitions I am a criminal. However, as with most things about me, it's a bit more complicated than that.

Right now things are particularly complicated. I'm confident that staring down the barrel of a semi-automatic pistol warrants such characterisation – especially when that weapon is being held by someone who, until moments ago, I called a friend.

I *should* be scared. I regularly deal with some pretty unsavoury people, but they rarely feel the need to point a gun in my face. The fear *is* there, but my brain is smothering it with questions, as if this is all some puzzle that can be unlocked. Why is this happening to me? Why tonight? Do I deserve it? I've always had the best of intentions: like my father; like my somewhat erratic cousin. But when a billion pounds is at stake, intentions of any kind go out the window, off down the street and on the next plane to anywhere.

So, a more interesting question is this: *when* did it all go wrong? The day that car bomb exploded? Long before that, when a promise was broken by an inconsiderate rich man? Or some other moment during my descent into a world of deception?

And then I remembered a day in a cafe, a meeting with a stranger, and a story that was not what it seemed.

That was when things really fell apart.

TWO

It was mid-morning on a January Monday and I was sitting in a London cafe I had never been to before, wearing a face that was not my own, waiting to meet a stranger, all while trying to solve other people's problems. London was not quite freezing, but the kind of crisp where you feel the cold biting in your mouth. I preferred the bite of quality espresso, so I'd picked a coffee shop on Neal Street, only a few minutes' walk from Covent Garden. The place was quiet, but not too quiet: three tables away a woman with wire-framed glasses and short grey hair sat reading a paper; tucked in the corner next to the venue's sole power outlet a be-suited man in his thirties was hunched over his laptop, nodding along to whatever was playing over his cheap headset.

I glanced at my watch. Not exactly a fashion statement, it looked like a Casio G-Shock digital. Originally it was, but I'd made some significant modifications, any one of which would have voided the warranty. Among other things, it now served as a low-power voice recorder: something that often comes in handy in my line of work. It also still showed the time: my prospective client was late. When you're wearing a face full of rubber and make-up I can assure you timeliness matters.

The grey dossier in front of me contained initial research on the individual I was meeting, and I'd now read it several times. It was a starting point, but I never took someone on as a client without meeting them in person. The phone in my pocket – a temporary handset to which only three people had the number – buzzed silently: the signal that my meeting was on.

I adjusted my baseball cap and smiled at the waitress, who began busying herself with the coffee grinder. On cue a small, well-dressed man wearing a bowler hat walked into the cafe. He looked around, eyes flickering to the dossier. "Mr Smith? Restitution Consulting?"

I indicated the seat opposite mine. To my left came the clanging and roaring of the espresso machine, the aroma of coffee flooding the air.

"Gerald Meeks," he said as he sat. "We spoke on the phone." He removed his hat and placed it on the table.

The waitress hurried over with two steaming espressos, then quietly retreated behind the counter. We both ignored her. "The materials?" I asked.

Meeks reached into a briefcase and produced a plain brown oversized envelope. "Printed out, as per your requirements."

You might think it odd that I had not requested the documents electronically, but I've learned from experience that certain information should never travel over the net. For one thing, there's always a record, and that is rarely convenient. More importantly, it's the only way to truly ensure something is not hacked or intercepted, particularly when the person sending the data is not a professional who understands encryption.

I opened the envelope. Inside were two densely printed pages of text and a series of photographs. I felt a brief twinge as my eyes landed upon the image of an oil painting: *Afternoon Sun on the East Wing* by an artist named Josephine Courteau. There were also photos of an old English house. I knew this to be Mr Meeks' residence from earlier research. "When was the painting stolen?"

The man's eyes tightened. "Four weeks ago."

"You involved the police?"

"Of course, but they haven't got anywhere." He gave an exaggerated sigh. "Hardly their highest priority."

"Anything else taken?"

"No. Why? Is that relevant?"

"It suggests the theft was targeted, rather than opportunistic. Any theories as to who could be responsible?"

He raised an eyebrow. "That's why I'm talking to you. You're the expert, or so I've been told."

"Most clients are happy with my results."

"What about those who aren't?"

I smiled and ignored the question. "I presume you've claimed on your insurance?"

"The painting was not insured."

I put the photos down. "Why not?"

"What difference does it make?" He folded his arms. "Do you want this job or not?"

I leaned forward in my chair. "That's what I'm in the

process of determining. Part of that is checking all the facts. The *fact* that it was not insured is unusual."

Meeks shrugged. "I'm in finance. I'm used to assigning values to everything. But sometimes the monetary value isn't the point." He picked up his espresso and knocked it back in a single motion. "You probably aren't familiar with the artist as she wasn't widely known. However, she happened to be my wife, and it was the last thing she painted before she died."

I nodded slowly. His wife had been mentioned in the dossier – I recalled that she had died from leukaemia. So he wanted to recover an item of strong sentimental value: *now* this was starting to make more sense – which was a good sign, because if things didn't make sense, I would not accept the job. I pulled out my phone and took photos of each of the documents before placing them back in the envelope and handing it to him. "I have what I need." I prefer not to retain hard copy evidence from a client: it's simpler to keep things clean. It also means I don't have to worry about anybody placing a tracking device on me, as I usually do on my clients.

"So you'll help me?"

I put my hands in front of me, fingertips spread, resting lightly on the table. "We will do some poking around. See if we can get a location on the item, and whether it can realistically be recovered. If we decide that it cannot, we'll let you know. Whatever happens we keep the deposit you have already paid. But if we decide to proceed to recovery, I will notify you. You will then wire the full amount I specify, based on the difficulty and risk, to a new, numbered account. We also accept payment in Bitcoin or a number of other cryptocurrencies. Once we've received cleared funds we will commence the recovery operation. We will not tell you where the item is, nor exactly when we will recover it, which could be any time over a three-month period. If circumstances change after you have paid, or if we do not wish to go ahead, then we will refund your money, less any expenses incurred to that point."

Meeks shook his head. "Whatever you decide, I'd like to know who took it."

"Providing that information is not part of the service."

"Why not?"

"It adds a layer of unnecessary complexity and risk to an already sensitive situation. Restitution Consulting is not only the name of our business, Mr Meeks. It is the spirit in which we operate. If you want 'revenge' you need to go somewhere else."

"How do I know you aren't just going to spend the money on expenses and I end up not getting my painting back? What guarantees do I have?"

"None, except our reputation. If you feel that's not enough, you can walk away." I paused. "We will not hesitate to do the same if at any time we find ourselves doubting the authenticity of your motivations. Am I making myself clear here, Mr. Meeks?"

"I just want the painting back."

"Then we are on the same page. It is precisely your type of problem that Restitution Consulting is set up to rectify – quietly and effectively." I picked up my espresso and downed it.

Meeks gave a slow nod as he slipped on his bowler hat. "I look forward to being suitably impressed."

We stood and I shook his hand, patting him firmly

on the shoulder. "We'll be in touch soon."

THREE

I waited in the coffee shop for precisely five minutes after the departure of Gerald Meeks. No one spared me any attention as I nodded to the waitress and stepped outside. Standing in the doorway, eyes sweeping the street, I tried not to scratch at my itchy face. Everything looked as it should. Just a regular weekday morning, Londoners going about their business. I adjusted my cap in preparation to blend with the morning commuters, when I heard a raised voice.

To my left was a woman with a pushchair. She stood next to a worn-looking Volvo, remonstrating with a traffic warden. Two toddlers clung to the woman's legs while a younger child in the pushchair worked himself up into a scream. The traffic warden did not appear moved by the woman's arguments, or the children, and was continuing to type into his handheld ticketing machine.

I held my breath, torn between intervening and the wisdom of invisibility. Now was not the time to get involved. My phone was already vibrating: the others were expecting me. I didn't have time for distractions. I started to walk the other way.

"Come on!" the woman shouted. "I just went to get change for the meter. Then my son was sick."

The traffic warden shook his head. "Your car has been here for five minutes. It's the same for everyone."

"Have you got kids?" The child in the pushchair began to howl. "You don't have to do this."

He carried on pressing the buttons. "I've started processing the ticket now. There's nothing I can do."

Damn it, I thought. Why today? I puffed out my cheeks. I would just have to be quick. My hand was already reaching into my backpack, pulling out a small, phone-sized device. Sid calls it a negative ion static-charge generator. I call it a problem solver.

"C'mon," she said, "I can't afford to—"

I strode purposefully in their direction, raising my voice. "Excuse me, mate. What time do the parking restrictions start around here?" The woman spun, throwing me a look of confusion, perhaps wondering who would dare interrupt her altercation. I ignored her. "I don't want to get the next ticket."

The warden stared at me, confused. "It's written on the meters." He looked back down at his screen. "And there are clear signs."

"Really?" I said. "Couldn't see them."

"I'm sorry, sir, I need to finish what I'm doing."

"Of course." I held up my device and pressed the single square button expectantly.

Nothing happened.

"What are you doing?" the woman asked me. "Can you see I'm talking here?"

I rolled my eyes. "Just trying to get my phone

working." My fingers ran over the case and I felt where the battery had clicked out of place. I forced it back in and pressed the button again, holding it up, as close to the handheld ticket machine as I could reach, until they were almost touching. There was a hissing crackle in the air. "Can you point on my map where the nearest sign is?"

On reflex the traffic warden looked at my device, which didn't have a screen. "I think your phone's broken, mate. What kind of a phone is that, anyway?"

"Oh right," I said, pulling it back, feeling the heat from the static discharge. "Not to worry then."

He looked back at the ticket machine, then blinked. "What the—"

"Problem?" I asked innocently.

He jabbed at the buttons. "Something's gone wrong." He peered closer at the screen. "It's never crashed before…"

"How odd." I gave a cough, glancing sideways at the woman.

She stared at me, a smile creeping across her face. Her three children looked at me too, trying to work out what was going on. The oldest gave a chuckle. "I'll be getting along then," she said, unlocking the Volvo. "You have a nice day."

"Good plan." I nodded to the traffic warden. "Hope you sort out your IT problems."

Before he could reply, I walked away.

FOUR

My own phone only took a minute to recover from the problem solver's static discharge, but it had been much further away. The traffic warden's ticket machine might never recover. What a shame.

The van was parked a five-minute walk from the cafe, but despite my itching face, I spent nearly fifteen additional minutes looping back on myself to make sure I wasn't being followed. Finally I arrived and saw a familiar, if impatient, figure: a slim woman with long dark-red hair was leaning against the vehicle, chewing gum as usual. Although she could blend in if she wanted to, Meg was usually deployed in roles opposite to mine: she was meant to get noticed and had the walk, attitude and confidence to do it. On my team she was the catalyst: the one who made things happen, either by action or distraction.

"Took your time," she said between chews. "Even more than usual."

"I got delayed."

She tore out her gum and flicked it expertly into a

nearby bin. "Really? I thought we made it clear you weren't to start messing around in the middle of an op."

"I'd done my part. What's the big hurry?" I glanced at my watch. "Is there a problem?"

She shrugged. "Calum wants his breakfast."

"We're in central London. If he's hungry there are probably fifty cafes in spitting distance."

"He says he's been too busy working the mission. Personally, I think he was waiting until you arrived to pay." She tapped sharply on the side door of the van, which was painted a colour most people would describe as 'ugly grey'. There was a grumbling from inside then the door slid back. I climbed in and closed the door behind me.

"Morning, Jake," said Sidney Karl, in his perennially high-pitched voice. His unkempt brown hair pulled back in an ugly ponytail, he sat with two laptops open in front of him, cleaning a pair of glasses that were either very fashionable or very old.

"And I suppose you're hungry too?"

Sid held up a large paper cup. "Got my wheat grass smoothie. All the nutrition I need."

"And none of the taste." I reached up and peeled off my prosthetic nose overlay and eyebrows, along with the sound-box that subtly altered my voice. "Any update on our client?"

"Nothing unusual to report. Meeks looks clean. Calum followed him onto a bus, then to the mainline station. The micro-tracer's working fine: looks like he's heading home."

"You didn't need to use the drone?" Past experience had taught us that bogus 'clients' typically drop character the moment they believe they have travelled a sufficient distance from the meet. Our goal is to make that distance further than they realise.

Sid shrugged. "I had it ready to launch in case Calum got blocked but we didn't need it. Anyway, it's too likely to be seen and heard in town during the day. I've got some ideas for a less reflective exterior shell, plus I need to work on those rotors: see if I can baffle the sound somehow."

"Hey," said a voice from a speaker attached to the laptops, "what about the guy doing the actual legwork?"

"Calum," I said. "Did you think we'd forgotten you?"

"Wouldn't be the first time. Are we done?"

"That depends. Did you have any problems with our client?"

"What do you think? A guy in a bowler hat is hardly the most difficult target to follow."

"Great. Then we'll see you at the rendezvous."

"I'm looking forward to it." But something in his tone indicated otherwise.

Twenty minutes later we were sitting in a motorway service station, tucking into bacon, eggs and hot coffee. All except Sid, who was eating a lentil bake and sipping at something like green tea, only far more pungent.

I raised my mug. "Good work, all. Looks like our new client is a go."

Meg slurped her fruit smoothie loudly. "I didn't like him."

"You never like any of them," offered Sid. "I thought he was fine, for a city type. A little distant, perhaps."

"Maybe he's just mourning his wife," I replied. "Look, we don't have to like them as long as their loss is legitimate."

Calum ran a hand over his blond, closely-cropped hair. "I don't care whether he's legitimate or not. How much is he going to pay us?"

"Easy, Cal," Sid said. "Jake will have it covered."

Calum kept staring at me. "How much?"

I shook my head. "You know the process. We do a full analysis before we even get into how much is the correct—"

"You must have an idea or you would never have committed us this far."

"I've still got to review the new data. Give me until tomorrow: I should have something by then. Now, the next important order of business: who's for pancakes?"

Calum growled. "Screw your pancakes."

Meg sighed. "Cal, give it up, will you? Sid's supposed to be the dramatic one."

Sid snorted on his tea. "Oh really? Well let me tell you—"

Calum banged his coffee mug down on the table. "Did you hear me, Jake?"

I knitted my fingers together, then leaned forward and whispered, "I'd say £100k. Possibly more."

Calum's eyes flickered. "That's not much once we split it four… sorry, *five* ways."

"We need to set aside funds to pay for the right tech. It's a fair split." In fact, I spent a fair chunk of my own share on kit as well. I had an unfortunate habit of wanting the best.

Sid picked up his tea and slurped at it. "Jake's right -

the tech we use needs to be constantly updated. Plus he finds all the jobs."

Calum gritted his teeth. "I've brought several possible clients to the table. Jake wouldn't even talk to them."

I looked around the café. Nobody was paying us any attention, but I really hated arguing in public; it was amateurish. "Cal, what is it that we do? Do you actually recall?"

"We steal things. We find them, then we steal them. For money."

"Seriously?" Meg asked, draining her drink. "You know what we do is a lot more complicated than that."

I forced calm into my voice. "We *recover* stolen items. We find what is difficult to find and we return it to its rightful owner. We do it quietly and without a fuss."

"We're not a damn charity," Calum said. "I thought we were all in this for the money."

Sid gave a hesitant nod. "Robin Hood stole from the rich to give to the poor. We kind of right wrongs in a different way, but I guess—"

Calum slapped his hand on the table. "£100k isn't enough."

I leaned back. "I'll set the price at what is right."

"Then tell him it's £500k."

Normally I encouraged my team to voice their opinions. Today that didn't feel like such a good idea. "Even sentimental value has its limits, Calum."

"Then test it. And remember, he didn't even insure it. He doesn't care about money."

"He's a businessman, not a wealthy dreamer."

"You won't know unless you ask. So ask."

"That's simplistic," I replied. "If we're perceived as

money-grabbing, we'll lose our referral business. And attract the wrong kind of attention."

"What are you talking about?"

"We want people who just want their stuff back. If a client is driven by revenge, anger and greed – if they think we will do anything for a price – well, that makes them dangerous and unpredictable. I will not put the team in harm's way for more money."

Calum laughed. "What would you know about that type of thing?"

Actually I knew a great deal, but I didn't want to share that with my team. I shrugged. "It's basic risk management."

"Well these jobs are too risky not to be charging more."

"Our 'projects' are as low risk as it is possible to make them."

"Really?" Calum stood up sharply. "With our skills, we could be making serious sums if we could forget this nonsense about making things get *unstolen*… The real crime is that we don't use our set up to make more. If someone wants something, and they're prepared to pay for it, we should do it."

"Theft for hire?" I frowned. "We're not going down that path. We are not criminals."

"Keep telling yourself that," he replied. "Meanwhile we all stay poor."

"Look," Meg said, "no one is holding a gun to your head, forcing you to be part of this team. You're free to leave at any time."

Calum scowled. "Is that right, Jake?"

Sid looked down at the table. Meg folded her arms. I

placed my hands on the table. "We have to be of one mind—"

"Say no more. I'll see you around, losers." Calum turned and walked out.

We all stared after him in silence.

I drummed my fingernails on the Formica table-top. "I'm not sure if the ultimatum was a good idea."

Sid was eyeing Calum's half-eaten plate of food, perhaps keener on bacon than he might admit. "Think he's coming back?"

Meg shook her head. "He'd made up his mind before we got here. If that's how he wants to be, then good riddance."

I scratched my head. "He complained about the money a few times recently, but I thought he was just whining. The big question is, what will he do now? Can he hurt us?"

Meg frowned. "That idiot? Why would he do that? He just wants more money. If he can't get it here, he'll try somewhere else."

"What's to keep him from going to the police?"

"He never had proper system access, so what could he tell them that wouldn't get him arrested along with the rest of us?"

"OK." I puffed out my cheeks. "Let's reset all the system passwords, and do an audit of recent activity, just to make sure. Assuming that produces nothing, we move on."

"I agree," Sid said. "But while Calum was a bit of an idiot, we had him for a reason. I know we don't hurt people, but what if they want to hurt us?"

Meg nodded. "We will need a replacement. Unless Sid wants to step up and be our muscle."

"Very funny," Sid replied. "Why don't you do it yourself?"

"Don't think that I couldn't. But I prefer to keep my nails unbroken. And I know a couple of people: one in particular might be perfect."

"You seem to know lots of people," I replied. "Is it anyone we can trust?"

She gave me a hard stare.

"Fine, fine. Get us some profiles. Set up some interviews. Sid and I will start looking into this stolen painting."

She tipped her head. "At times like these, I bet you wish you listened more to your father."

I nodded. Fine art always seemed like both the cause of, and the solution to, my problems.

FIVE

IF I CAST MY MIND BACK, IT WAS PROBABLY THE ART gallery where the problems started. The clues were there, in my father's words and actions, if only I'd cared to consider things. But I'd been too young and blinkered at the time to notice.

I remember the first time I visited the place. It was 2008 and I was 14 years old. The visit meant I had to leave school an hour early and my maths teacher was less than cooperative, even though I was already way ahead of the class and finding lessons boring. Strangely, telling my teacher that hadn't helped my case.

The gallery was a small faux loft-space on a side street in the centre of Richmond-upon-Thames. My father unlocked the door with a heavy key, tapped a long code into a security alarm, then let us in to a single open space. It was all bare floorboards, white walls and bright lighting. Five large paintings hung along the walls, each bathed in its own spotlight.

"Do you like it?" he asked. "I hope so, because we open tomorrow."

I shrugged. "It's fine, I guess. What does Mum think?"

His smile tempered. "She's not been able to… Well, you know what she's like. She doesn't approve much of art as a business."

"What is up with her at the moment? She never wants to go anywhere. And both of you seem so secretive."

"Secrets are a part of life. Sometimes they shock you, sometimes they protect you."

"What are you going on about? You're being weird, Dad."

My father looked out the window then sighed, gesturing to the gallery. "Is '*fine*' all you have to say about all my hard work? I really thought my surprise would have more impact."

I looked around. "OK, I did actually know about the gallery already. Sorry."

He frowned. "How… wait, don't tell me. It was your damn cousin, wasn't it? He saw me here a few days ago. I *asked* him not to mention it."

"Kieran said it was a boring shop with a bunch of boring pictures in it."

"He'd probably think differently if I told him how much they'll sell for. He knows the price of a dollar, that boy. Not unlike my brother."

I pointed at the paintings. "Why are you doing this? And where did we get the money to pay for them?"

"We've had some… unexpected new expenses, so we had to find a way to earn more money." He tugged at his lip thoughtfully. "As with any new venture, you usually have to spend money to make money. But the paintings didn't cost me anything."

"Why?" I frowned. "Did you steal them?"

He laughed. "I'm a broker: I sell them on behalf of other people. I display each work here and, hopefully, the right buyer will come along."

I frowned. "I didn't think you knew much about art. Isn't that Mum's thing?"

"True, but she just wants to enjoy art, not buy and sell it. Plus I'm not basing my business on my knowledge of art: I'm basing it on my knowledge of people. I just need to connect the right person to the right painting." He gestured around. "Any catch your eye?"

I tried and failed to hide my lack of interest. "Sorry to agree with Kieran, but they're just paintings. It's not like they *do* anything."

"A lot of people say art makes the world a better place."

I frowned, then noticed heavy metal bars across the windows. "What are those for?"

"Security, unsurprisingly." A smile crossed his face. "Because they're worth a *lot* of money."

"Oh?" My curiosity piqued. "How much is a lot?"

My father walked over to the nearest picture and lightly stroked its frame. "This one was appraised at a hundred and fifty thousand."

"Pounds?" I stared in shock. "That's more than a car."

"I know. Although, for the calibre of customer I hope to get in here, that may not be the case."

"What do you mean, *appraised*?"

"An art expert has looked at it and said what she thinks it's worth."

"And how does she know?"

"Excellent point." My father smiled. "The truth is,

it's worth what someone is prepared to pay for it to secure it for their collection, which could be a lot less," he paused, "or a lot more."

"Aren't they insured?" I asked. "Why bother with the security?"

"Insurers usually require security measures like this, or they won't provide cover. And remember: insurance pays the cost of replacing something. These paintings are originals. They can't be replaced, so insurance doesn't really help – not if what you want is the painting itself, rather than just a pile of money." He nodded to the security bars. "So now do you have a little more appreciation for the value of 'art'?"

I shrugged. "It's still boring. But since you're going to make lots of money, can I have a new computer?"

"I haven't made the money yet." He raised an eyebrow. "Besides, you just got a new one six months ago."

"Yeah, and in the computer world that's like ten years. It can't do what I need it to. Kieran has one with one of the new GeForce graphics cards and it's amazing."

My father gripped my shoulder. "I think you spend altogether too much time with that boy. Can't you find a friend your own age?"

"He's only two years older than me. And he *is* family."

"There is a big difference between fourteen and sixteen. Quite frankly, he's a bad influence. You know he's been expelled from school twice now."

"Yeah, he told me."

"And did he tell you why?"

"He stood up to a bully."

My father blinked. "Sure. Ask him to share all of the details sometime."

"Well maybe having lost both parents means you should cut him a bit of slack. And stop changing the subject. What about my new computer?"

"Work with what you have. The challenge will do you good."

"This is important," I said. "You might make money selling paintings. I'm going to make *my* money with computers."

"Prove it to me, then we'll talk." He reached out and switched the lights off.

"What are you doing?"

"Teaching you a lesson."

"That you like to work in the dark?"

He laughed. "No, about paying attention to detail. Do you know what profit is?"

"It's money you make."

"It's the difference between the money you have coming in versus the money you have going out. Less money out, means more profit. For example, electricity isn't free, so I've just saved some money. Anything that you have to pay out had better be worth it: stationery, advertising, food and drink, computers." He paused. "Insurance. Whatever it is, work out if you really need it. And if you buy anything, always try to get the best deal."

"The lights were on when we got here."

"So people could see the paintings. Customers can't buy what they can't see."

I blinked in the darkness. "So *now* you don't want to sell any?"

"Fewer people come down this alleyway after 5:30pm. Even if they do, the shop will be shut."

"But maybe they'd see a painting through the window and come back the next day."

My father nodded slowly. "And there's another lesson for you: I don't always know everything."

SIX

Love it or hate it, money is part of life. Hoard it, spend it, give it away, that's up to you. But money always represents a decision. And how you make that decision reveals things about you. Today money was going to enable my business, and being a rational consumer I needed to get the biggest bang for my buck. Which meant I didn't walk into a regular shop and start filling my trolley.

I walked over Richmond Bridge, the sun glinting off the Thames. The Thames can be an ugly, smelly river but there are still moments when it, and London around it, can take your breath away. I slowed only briefly to enjoy the moment: I didn't want to be late for my meeting.

I headed along the towpath south, weaving in and out of cyclists and tourists, past a couple of sketch artists hard at work. Further down, on the middle of three benches, sat a woman in jogging gear and wraparound sunglasses, smoking a cigarette, and apparently listening to music on wireless headphones. I sat nearby and placed my black rucksack on the bench. There was a remarkably similar bag next to her.

"Abigail, this always feels like such a cliché," I said, looking out at the river.

"I was going for 'eighties spy movie'," she replied, crossing her long legs.

"You forgot the leg warmers."

She smiled and stubbed out her cigarette. "How have you been, Jake?"

"Busy."

"I'm glad to hear it. If you're busy, you need to buy stuff: stuff I can sell you."

"And I thought you just liked my conversation."

Her eyes flickered around. "As long as you're buying, I'll talk as much as you wish."

Abigail Norton was my primary supplier of hardware: computers, network equipment, mobile devices, she covered it all. If she couldn't get hold of it, they didn't make it. She could often get hold of items that most people thought didn't exist. She helped me get the best kit possible, which made her a critical part of my business: in many ways, it was our competitive advantage.

When someone gets you the very best it's hard not to trust them. Plus she charged me just enough that I was sure this was just business. If someone is doing a bad deal for the benefit of their customer, that's when you get suspicious.

Abigail slid the bag across and quickly swapped it with mine. "Everything you requested. I took the liberty of upgrading a couple of the specs, at no extra cost."

I glanced in the bag. "Generosity is your middle name."

"I know I have competitors." She tipped her head. "And to show you how much I appreciate your business, I'll give you 5% off your next order. As long as you promise to put it all with me."

I shrugged. "How would you know that I hadn't gone elsewhere?"

"I have my ways." She flashed a smile. "It's good business to keep a close eye on your clients."

"I guess loyalty is a valuable thing." I couldn't help giving a sigh. If only the rest of my day had gone this smoothly.

"You OK? Girl trouble?" She sat forward. "Boy trouble?"

"One of my team decided to leave."

"Artistic differences?"

"Something like that."

"I know some people, if you're looking."

"Everyone knows people, but thanks for the offer. I'm good."

"Your choice." She glanced at her watch. It looked expensive. "Anything else I can help you with?"

I stood up. "Not unless you know anything about paintings."

"Art?" She wrinkled her nose. "It's low on features. Plus the market for spares and upgrades is limited." She pulled out another cigarette and a lighter.

"Someone once told me that art makes the world a better place."

"I suspect that was someone in the art business."

I laughed. "Yes." But to myself I added, *although I'm still not sure why.*

SEVEN

After my meeting with Abigail, I headed back to the station. Glancing at my watch, I saw I was running late so I grabbed a breakfast sandwich and jumped on the 10:32am to Waterloo. With an inward sigh, I realised I was going to have to show my face at the office. My 'day job' office, that is. I called Meg on my mobile.

"Where have you been?" she asked without preamble.

"Meeting Abigail."

"Your stunningly beautiful supplier? You never said you needed anything for work."

"I'm sure I did." Actually, I wasn't sure. Calum's departure had annoyed me and adding the meeting to the team's shared diary might have slipped my mind.

"The point is, Lundy has been asking after you. I said you were out on an install. If he didn't buy it, he didn't let his concern get in the way of his internet shopping and coffee break schedule."

"I'll be there in twenty minutes. Or so."

"Good, because we have real work to get on with. So don't get distracted."

I got off at Clapham Junction. It was much less crowded than in rush hour. The upmarket cafes near the exit were going through their pre-lunch lull and only a couple of tables were occupied. I was about to walk out onto the street when a raised voice caught my attention.

"My bag!" I looked over to see a large, agile man skip between tables and out onto the street. The woman who had raised her voice was staring at me, as if I was the only one who could help. "My bag?" she repeated: less a question, more a suggestion.

Sometimes you can make a considered decision about whether you're going to get involved, weighing up all the pros and cons and making a proper risk assessment. Other times, you just go with your gut.

I started running.

The thief was already thirty metres ahead of me and moving fast. But I ran five miles every day and had a few tricks up my sleeve.

The man slowed then glanced over his shoulder. I didn't stop quickly enough and he saw me. He waved the bag in his hand – almost as if he was taunting me – and took off again. I closed to within twenty metres, but could get no closer. My plan had been to catch him quickly or wear him down, but perhaps I had been hasty. I might run five miles a day, but it was starting to look like this guy ran ten.

We were now skirting the edge of Clapham Common and I could not catch him, nor drive him into any dead end turning. If only I had backup in the area. I pushed harder. And then an opportunity presented itself. He stumbled oddly, tripped and dropped the bag.

It was all I needed. I caught up to him and lunged at the bag, my fingers tightening around the handles. "Don't think this is yours." The thief cursed, scrambling away. I watched his body coil, ready to explode. He wasn't going to give up. He was going to lunge at me. And he was a lot bigger.

But then he turned and ran away. I watched him vanish around the corner. Had I scared him off? Was I that intimidating?

It took me ten minutes to jog back to the station. The woman was sitting there, looking tearful. On seeing me, or more specifically her bag, she burst into a huge smile. "Oh, you are wonderful." She ran up and gave me a hug.

I shrugged and handed her the bag. "It was nothing. Guess I can skip my visit to the gym later."

"Please, let me repay you." She slipped the bag over her shoulder, not looking inside. In retrospect, perhaps I should have thought that was odd.

"There's really no need."

"Nonsense. Let me buy you lunch."

I looked at my watch. "I really have to get to the office. I'm already late and—"

"Your boss will go nuts?"

"Something like that."

"Dinner then. I insist. Doing anything tonight that you can't rearrange?"

"I don't think—"

"Nino's on Northcote Road then. 8 o'clock." She produced a business card: crisp white, with navy embossed lettering that read *Susan R. Statham*.

"Jake," I said, shaking her hand. "I guess I'll see you there."

She squeezed my arm and vanished into the crowd. I stood there for a moment, staring at the card. Was this all coincidence? Or was something else going on? I tucked the business card in my wallet. Perhaps I would find out at dinner.

EIGHT

It was nearly midday by the time I got to the Clapham offices of TechFixed. My boss, Bill Lundy, was just walking out of his office, his coat slung over his arm, looking like he was heading for an early lunch.

"Nice of you to join us, Jake," he said loudly as I walked into the main open-plan area. Meg and Sid were seated amongst the IT crowd, rattling away at their keyboards. Meg widened her eyes slightly but said nothing.

I moved towards my desk. "That install proved difficult. Couldn't leave it unfinished."

Lundy tugged at his neatly trimmed beard. "A lot of your jobs seem to overrun."

"I'm *not* a miracle worker. Shall I give you a run-down of the system faults they were experiencing?"

He blinked twice. "Just have the report on my desk this afternoon."

"Of course," I replied, hoping that would end the conversation. I had a lot to get on with besides faking a report.

Lundy swept his gaze around the room. Everyone looked down. With a huff, and a small shake of his head, he slipped on his coat and walked out. There was a quiet but collective sigh of relief. I sat at my desk and booted up my laptop. Meg waited two minutes then glided over to me.

"I need you to check something on the server."

I was flicking through emails on my company account. All were a complete waste of time. "Hmm?"

"I think one of the drives has failed."

I looked up. "Oh, right." That was one of our signals. We had a lot of failed drives at TechFixed. I followed Meg through the back door, sparing a glance behind me. We had ten other technicians; none even looked up. They were all as bored and unproductive as I felt when I had to be here. I followed Meg down a corridor into the server room, closing the sound-proof door behind us.

"I swear I don't know why we waste our time with all this nonsense," Meg said.

"Don't start with that again, please." We'd discussed this many times. We needed a transparent source of income, otherwise questions would be asked. TechFixed was an excellent cover for operations requiring IT. Bill Lundy was, in many senses, the perfect boss. He appeared to have almost no understanding of what we did, and no interest in any of it. He just let us get on with things, aside from the odd 'grandstanding' moment when he felt inclined to remind everyone who was in charge. Considering how much 'business' we actually performed that had nothing to do with Lundy, putting up with his ego now and again seemed a small price to pay.

"Where the hell did you get to?" Meg asked.

"I stopped to help this woman... Look it doesn't matter—"

She raised a hand. "What you do on your own time is fine by me. Just do it on your *own* time."

I crossed my arms. "So, what progress have you made on the interviews to replace Calum?"

"Three maybes, but one is head and shoulders over the others: Daniel Stockdale. He's good, I guarantee it."

"Send me his profile. If I agree, then let's meet him."

"*If* you agree?"

"If someone's going to join our team, we all have to agree."

"Which actually means, we all have to agree but ultimately it's *your* decision."

There was a knock at the door and Sid walked in. "Is the Council in session? Want to see my report on our new client?" Sid adjusted his glasses and sat down at a terminal with a very large screen. He rattled off a long password, then called up a number of documents. "I thought I'd start with the easy part: analysing the theft. I've queried Meeks on all the primary databases, including the public ones and the private systems we have open access to. From the initial run-through, he seems legit. All his statements check out. He's just a rich guy who wants his painting back."

I looked at the screen. "What type of in-home security did he have?"

"Nothing beyond a standard household burglar alarm."

"Monitored?"

"Yes, but he'd let the contract lapse. He renewed it right after the theft, which you could say is literally closing the stable door after the proverbial horse has bolted."

Meg peered at the screen. "Should we do an on-site?"

I shrugged. It was trading one risk against another. On-site inspections of clients' premises were expensive, could cause delays, and tended to increase our time spent with the client: something I was never keen on. Not to mention that our priority was where the item-to-be-recovered was *now*, not where it used to be. I tapped the desk. "Do a repeat scan, Sid. If you get the same results, let's move forward. And be ready to get a duplicate made: once we've found it, we'll need it for the op."

NINE

I like to check out any new venue before a meeting. Call it paranoia, call it a game, call it sensible precautions or health and safety, I don't mind. Accordingly, I arrived in Clapham an hour early for my dinner with Susan Statham. She was already there.

Nino's was a budget Italian restaurant with faded décor and plastic menus. A smiling waiter escorted me to a booth near the back. Susan kissed me on each cheek then we sat facing each other. She was about my age: somewhere in her mid-twenties. From her sharply cropped hair and clothes she had the look of a city professional, maybe an accountant or a lawyer. But who could tell nowadays?

"Contrary to what you might think," I said, "I wasn't trying to earn a free meal."

"You were very brave." She signalled to one of the waiters. "Not as many heroes as there used to be."

I ran the events of that morning back through my head. "You know, now I think about it, I doubt I was in any real danger."

The waiter arrived with a bottle of Chianti. Susan nodded and he poured two glasses. "Are you sure? He was a big guy. You had no idea what he would do, and yet you still helped me."

"When I was in pursuit, it almost felt like he was pacing himself. Like he wanted to make sure he didn't get too far ahead."

"Why would he do that?"

"Because that was what you told him to do." I sipped from my wine. "A real thief would have tried a lot harder to lose me. He just ran for what felt like a pre-determined length of time, then gave up without a fight. He could have thrown the bag away, over a wall or onto a roof to distract me. Instead, he did nothing."

"Maybe he panicked when you managed to keep up with him?"

I shrugged. "Also, when I brought the bag back to you, you didn't even look in it. You knew he hadn't taken anything."

A smile flickered across her face. "Well done, Jake."

I felt a shiver run through me. "So was this some game?"

"Think of it more as a test. And the best kind, at least from my point of view, because you didn't know you were being tested."

"OK, so I passed your test. Now perhaps you can answer some of *my* questions." I folded my arms. "Let's start with 'Who the hell are you?'"

"I am who I said I am: Susan Statham. And I have a proposition for you: I'm looking for someone to collaborate with."

"To do what?"

"The world is a crappy place. My mission is to change that."

"As in charity work? Good for you."

"Not exactly. My approach is… a little more off the books. I plan on overturning some of the nasty things that make the world suck: burglaries, pick-pocketing, online scams. The stuff that the police don't necessarily have the time or resources to pursue."

"And how are you going to manage that?"

"Computer hacking. Social engineering. Good old-fashioned field-craft. Ten years ago it would have been impossible, but nowadays we have access to enough gear to achieve a great deal. I'm already making a difference, but with a partner I could do so much more."

"So you're a modern day Robin Hood?"

Susan rang her finger around the rim of her glass. "He stole from the rich to give to the poor. Whereas I undo what was bad and return it to the good. But if you like the analogy, then run with it."

"You want to change the world?"

"Not all of it. I mean, sure, that would be great, but every little bit counts. Certainly better than doing nothing, in my opinion."

"Why?"

"Because I can."

"No, really: *why?*"

She laughed. "You mean, what is my origin story? Sorry to disappoint, but it's merely because I have the means and capability to do so. And I feel like doing something more meaningful than sharing photos on social media and partying."

"Good for you." I drained my glass and placed it firmly on the table. "How does any of this involve me?"

She tipped her head to one side. "Jake, I didn't approach you by accident. I'm aware of your work."

"Wow. Jake from IT is famous! Wasn't aware I had fans."

"Not *that* work. Listen, a friend of a friend was caught up in an internet holiday scam. They lost over two grand to this company that took all these bookings, then deliberately went into liquidation before the directors vanished. My friend's friend went to the police and was told that there was nothing they could do about it. Then, out of the blue, the money mysteriously returned to the bank accounts, along with a compensation payment. A hundred or so customers received a refund plus a bonus."

I blinked. "What a happy ending."

"I know." She nodded to me. "As I mentioned, I'm not without skills. When I was digging for information, I especially liked the part I found about where a reporter approached one of the former directors for a quote about the refunds, and she received was a genuine look of confusion and a 'no comment'." Susan smiled. "I assume their network defences were no match for your skills."

"You seem to have it all worked out."

She gave a slight shrug of her shoulders. "Sometimes. What do you say? Join me?"

I looked at her. "Collaborations complicate things. Why do I need you? What skillset do you bring to the table?

"For starters, I'm a specialist in eavesdropping. I bug people."

"I'm not confirming anything, but let's just say I've got that niche covered."

"I'm better than your person."

"And certainly more modest."

She tipped her head to one side. "I could bug you."

"You *are* bugging me."

"Very funny. I mean plant a bug to demonstrate my expertise."

I met her eyes. "Good luck with that."

Susan leaned back and glanced at her fingernails. "Perhaps I already did." She removed a small digital recorder from her purse, placed it on the table and pressed play. Lundy's voice rang out, '*Nice of you to join us, Jake.*' The track skipped, then I heard Meg's voice asking me to check something on the server. Then there was just static.

"You must have gone somewhere shielded. The bug failed after that point."

I let my breath go slowly. The server room was thoroughly protected, but she had come very close to full access to our operation. "If you're trying to win my trust, you have an unusual way of going about it." I reached up to the shoulder of my jacket and found a small, round tab innocently attached near the crook of my armpit. I peeled it off. It was not a particularly advanced piece of tech, but it had done the job. "Clearly I'm getting lax. It won't happen again."

"Don't be so hard on yourself. I'm good at what I do."

I dropped the bug into my glass of water. It fizzed then sank to the bottom. "My answer is no."

"C'mon, Jake. I don't know what other operation you're caught up in – it seems you've gone corporate or something – but once you started charging for what you do, you compromised it."

"I don't know about your personal circumstances, but I need the money. In my experience, no one juggles this sort of risk just for the fun of it. And if you are doing this just to 'save the world', you'd be my worst nightmare as partner. It wouldn't work, you and me." I stood up. "Thanks for the drink, but I think I'll skip the meal."

Susan shook her head. "Maybe this method of approach was a mistake. Even if I did get you here, and I proved my abilities."

"Sorry," I said. "Perhaps in another life. Good luck changing the world."

She sighed. "Why are you passing up an opportunity to do what's right? I already apologized—"

I cut her off, shaking my head. "Things are more complicated than that. I used to think I could do what I wanted, but now? I have to live in the *real* world."

She smiled. "I'll be waiting when you're ready to talk. You have my card."

———

It was cold on the street outside as I pushed my way through a stream of people on the pavement, lost in my thoughts. Was Susan friend or foe? Should I mention her to my team? I was embarrassed that I'd missed the bug. She'd definitely caught me off guard and I vowed it would not happen again.

Perhaps she *was* as good as she said, but I was better. Smiling, I pulled out my phone to check the status of the passive bug I'd planted in her bag earlier that day. At the time I wasn't quite sure why I'd done it, but I'd learned long ago not to ignore my intuition.

I took out her business card and looked at it closely, rubbing my fingertips gently across the surface. I couldn't feel anything embedded within it, but knew full well that advanced tech was often a double-edged sword. Even to an experienced eye it was hard to detect. I prised the layers of card apart but could see no electronics embedded within. Perhaps it would have been a little obvious to try it again. Muttering, I tore it into pieces and tossed it into a nearby bin.

TEN

I SLEPT FITFULLY THAT NIGHT, EVENTUALLY GIVING UP AT 5:30am and going for a long run. It usually helped me think, not to mention stopped me piling on the pounds from the huge quantity of food and snacks I ate in a typical day. I carried enough equipment around with me most of the time that I didn't need any extra weight on top.

I arrived back at home in time to say good morning to the postman: more bills and junk mail. A couple of the neighbours were walking off to the station, ready for their commute. I nodded and half-smiled, but didn't engage further. At 7am on a weekday morning we weren't usually capable of intelligent conversation.

My home was a pleasant semi-detached house in Wimbledon: off-street parking, small garden, even a garage. It was the house my father had bought after my mother died. Now it was mine. I kept the downstairs normal: an IKEA sofa and dining table in the living area, a well-equipped, if slightly worn, kitchen. If I had to ask somebody in, I could show them an ordinary dwelling. The upper floor was different, but I didn't let anybody up there.

At the top of the stairs was a solid oak, steel-reinforced door. Planning permission, or some type of building-regulation approval, might have been required but I never asked. The builders took cash and didn't seem overly concerned with paperwork.

Behind the door was a world of electronics, at the heart of which was my main system, plugged into the net by three different and very fat pipes. There was also a small bedroom, bathroom and a kitchenette. Any space not containing electronics or basic living essentials was given over to books; despite my proclivity for gadgets of every kind, I still preferred reading on actual paper. I had everything I needed in that space: I could stay there for days when I was catching up on a couple of seasons of the latest series from the US… or running a client analysis, as I was about to do.

I sat at my desk, laptop open and three separate ultra HD display panels showing different data and channel feeds. Sid's further analysis of Meeks had uncovered no concerns. With my computer systems, a large cup of very strong coffee, and no planned disruptions, I had everything I needed. I deliberately avoided my inbox, blinking plaintively, and concentrated on the task at hand: finding the painting.

Sid and the others help me with many parts of my operation. But finding things is my department. I have a bespoke system that does much of the work. I wouldn't have my very long list of very happy clients without it.

On one screen I opened up the report from Sid, on another, my own adapted search engine and a Google window on my laptop, because I always figure I might as well see what comes up there.

My process is like solving an equation. I have some knowns, constants if you will, and some variable factors, which I use my system to try to reduce or pin down. It is part science, part art, part luck, but mostly dogged persistence. I can get into the maths, expound on number theory and n-dimensional matrices if I want to try to sound clever. But the underlying principle is simple: with people, there are always connections. When someone has something stolen, something important to them, there are ripples in the fabric of their lives – ones I'm usually more motivated to follow than the police because, let's be realistic, these aren't murder cases and the cops have limited resources.

It's important to look at the key known factors. What was stolen, where from, when and how? How much expertise was required? How 'moveable' was the item? Is there a ready market for its onward sale? Who are the likely customers? Was it stolen to order or on spec? Rarely is the thief the likely 'end user'. In the real world, the eccentric art aficionado who steals paintings for his own collection is a myth.

I started with the artist: Mrs Gerald Meeks, aka Josephine Courteau. I took Sid's initial report and fed it through my system. Josephine Courteau had been an artist most of her life, although she originally qualified as an architect: her work showed a particular focus on buildings. She sketched and painted in oils, and was quite prolific. However, she rarely exhibited and there were few reported sales. There was a lot in her records about her battle with pancreatic cancer - a battle she lost at the age of fifty. A press article showed three hundred people attended her funeral.

As I'd suspected, it didn't seem that money was a prime driver for the theft. While hard to determine precisely – as my father used to say, a work of art is worth exactly what someone is prepared to pay for it – the painting realistically was not worth more than a few thousand. So why bother to steal it?

I researched Meeks next. He was an investment banker, working out of the City, which explained his ability to pay my not inconsiderable fees. There was no suggestion that he in any way supported his wife's artistic endeavours. He was never shown on a guest list at her openings. As Sid had said, there was a security system in their home, but it wasn't being monitored, and the cameras had no recording medium: no tape or hard drive. There was nothing to analyse as no normal street-cameras keep recordings for more than a couple of weeks.

I had both Meeks and his wife's personal email accounts open in seconds. It's amazing what people put in their emails these days without bothering to activate more than the most basic of security. Wading through by hand would have taken days, so I ran some basic intelligent filters and had a useful analysis in seconds. Meeks' account seemed to contain mostly mailing-list offers and junk mail. But when I searched Josephine's… bingo.

Someone by the name of 'Rodney Bickerstaff' had sent two separate emails asking Josephine to sell him the picture, offering £250,000 each time. Based on the fact that she had sold only half a dozen other works, all for less than £5,000, this was an extraordinary sum.

Yet she had said no. Her email read, 'You know I cannot sell you that picture. Thank you for your kind interest.' So was Bickerstaff's offer a joke? Was she embarrassed to accept such a large sum? Did she not need the money, or was it that she couldn't bear to part with a treasured work of art? Her will was available online, but it was standard, passing all her assets to her husband, except for a small sum going to charity.

Next, I checked into Mr Bickerstaff; he wrote historical thrillers under a pen name. Not exactly an international best-seller, but certainly successful and a man of considerable means. So why did he want the painting so much? I searched further. He had a house listed in Highgate. I switched to a street view website and found my first major clue: the painting was of Bickerstaff's house.

While many people are reticent about telling all, even when it might be in their best interests, Meeks appeared not to know about the offer. Was this a simple case of Bickerstaff stealing a painting he had been unable to buy?

I was looking over the screens again when a bell rang on my desk and an LED illuminated: somebody was at my front door. I sighed, stood up and headed downstairs. I tried to show my face around the neighbourhood whenever I actually was at home; better to be the guy seen around doing normal stuff than the guy who nobody ever sees and everybody starts gossiping about.

I messed up my hair, untucked my shirt slightly, and opened the front door to see a young woman in a skirt and jacket, all blonde hair and perfect teeth. Her hair was almost too perfect. She extended a manicured hand. Involuntarily, I shook it.

"Good morning, Sir," she said, beaming at me. "I wonder, could I trouble you for five minutes of your time?" She had an effected upper-class accent and compelling eyes, impossibly blue. I almost stepped back, but caught myself. There was the edge of something familiar about her, but I couldn't place it.

"Sorry. I'm in the middle of some work."

She glanced me up and down, as if taking in the jeans, messy shirt and hair. "It won't take a moment." Her smile seemed to broaden further.

My eyes narrowed. "I don't buy from door-to-door sales reps." I pointed at a sign on my door, which said exactly that.

"Oh, I'm not selling anything. In fact, quite the reverse. My client wants to buy something from you." She pointed behind me. "It might be more appropriate to discuss this inside."

"No, you can tell me here."

She leaned closer to me and lowered her voice. "I represent a major property developer. They're looking to purchase a number of houses suitable for conversion to apartments and are willing to pay well above market value. We're speaking to all the owners in the street."

I sighed. A property agent. "I'm happy living here. This house is not for sale."

Her smile flickered, but only for a second. "That is a pity. Still, can I give you my card?" Magically, she already had one in her hand.

I shrugged. "Sure, whatever." I took it from her, momentarily thinking what thick card stock it was made from. Embossed gold letters proclaimed *Martha S. Tassun, Real Property Investments.*

"A pleasure meeting you Mr..."

"Moro," I said.

"Mr Moro." Something about the way she said it seemed familiar. "Well, I hope you change your mind." She turned and glided out onto the street.

I closed the door and threw the card distractedly onto a shelf in my hallway, on top of numerous other business cards and flyers for dry cleaners, takeaway food and minicab services, along with a picture postcard of a palm-tree lined beach. Then I moved back upstairs and continued my analysis.

Bickerstaff had an active and monitored security system at his main residence: a pretty extensive one, with multiple cameras. I smiled to myself, poured fresh coffee, and got down to business. The encryption on the system was not military grade and my hacking tools were considerably beyond it. Within minutes, I had a live feed from Bickerstaff's camera-control system. I watched the views cycle through and suddenly there it was, hanging on the wall of what appeared to be a gallery.

The stolen painting: *Afternoon Sun on the East Wing*

So now I knew where it was. Next I would recon the house and contact Meeks with an acquisition price.

ELEVEN

As for most operations, I was dressed all in black. It was just after midnight and I stood on a slight hill a hundred metres away from Bickerstaff's house. It was a big place with elegantly manicured lawns and gardens all around, and an eight-foot-high metal fence.

I'd been able to push Meeks to £150k and he'd wired the money that afternoon.

Sid now sat in a black Vauxhall Nova a few streets away. We were using an encrypted two-way radio system: I never touch any type of cellular network on a 'mission' – too easy to hack and to trace. I tapped my earpiece. "You there?"

"Until my flask of Sencha runs out," Sid replied. "Sure you don't want some extra 'punch' for this one?"

"Nah, this will be a piece of cake." Extra 'punch' referred to the additional 'muscle' Calum should have provided to counter unforeseen circumstances, but nothing had suggested that this op would be particularly risky. Besides, not having to pay a Calum replacement meant my profit would increase. In any case, we were prepared. We knew everything there was to know about the house and its security systems. I had multiple exit routes. Sid was close by, and Meg was available if I needed further logistical support. I also had two Mars bars and a couple of non-carbonated energy drinks in my backpack.

"The drone's ready if we need it," Sid said. "Although I haven't quite resolved the noise-reduction issue."

"Let's just get this done. We can talk toys afterwards."

"Tell me when."

"Roger that." I clicked my ear-piece, slipped on some gloves, pulled my headphones into place, and began a gentle jog: just another runner grabbing his thirty minutes of exercise where he could. I was soon alongside the metal fence. A security camera was visible, currently panning ahead of me.

Most building security is not what you see in movies. It's pretty easy to overcome, if you know what you're doing. Still, you have to be thorough: it's all about preparation. First you analyse the target to identify the weak points. Then you exploit them. The trick is ensuring you have more than one way out, and preferably several.

I glanced up and down the street. Nobody around. I tapped my ear. "Now."

"It's done," Sid replied.

The camera light flickered and went out. As we'd found in our initial research, this *was* a monitored system, so Sid was now running a loop of the last fifteen minutes of footage: an old technique that any decent alarm company would quickly detect, but less of a 'red flag' than simply cutting the feed.

I intended to be long gone within fifteen minutes. With a practised motion, I pulled a lightweight black face-mask on. I hopped up to the fence and, with a swing, launched myself onto the top rail. Thankfully there was no barbed wire to deal with. Then I was landing quietly on the grass and running through the grounds to the house. Sid had taken over the cameras here as well. I got as far as the back door then paused. "How's our host?"

"Snoring coming from the master bedroom. Has been for the last hour."

"And you're monitoring the alarm company?" I laughed inwardly for a moment as it struck me I was basically asking, 'Who watches the watchmen?' – turns out we do.

"Of course," Sid replied. "All quiet on the western front."

I reached into a large pocket and removed a device somewhat like a Swiss army knife. The art of old-fashioned lock picking is no longer glamorous. Nor is there an idiot's guide readily available from your favourite internet book-emporium. But I had found someone who would teach me and, like touch-typing, it has been a life skill that's paid dividends a hundred times over. If you have the right tools, then it's all in the wrist. Thirty seconds and I had both locks open. I eased the door open a fraction then froze. "Houston, we have a problem," I whispered, peering carefully at a small metal object inside the frame.

"Where?" Sid replied. "No alarms raised."

"There will be if I move this door a hair further."

"But I've neutralised the monitored system."

"This is a different installation. Older."

"Is it live?"

I reached into another pocket and held up a gauge. "There's power flowing. Have to assume it is functional." I heard staccato tapping from Sid, as he interrogated his laptop.

"Sorry," he said, "I've got nothing here. Want to abort?"

I looked more closely at the metal object. "There's a real chance this attempt will be detected. Then matters will be far more difficult." It's a very different thing stealing something out of the blue and stealing from someone who knows you're coming. "But I think I can manage it."

I reached into another pocket and withdrew my palm-sized static-charge generator, re-primed for this mission. Unlike when I had targeted the traffic warden, I needed to focus the charge, so I pulled a telescopic metal rod, like an aerial, out of one side and held it up to the metal object in the door frame. As it touched, I closed my eyes and pressed the button.

Again there was a pronounced sizzling noise, and the device got very warm. You've probably heard of an EMP – an electromagnetic pulse. A well-known side effect of a nuclear explosion is that it can fry all electronic circuitry in a large area. My device is a bit like that in the same way that a fire cracker is a bit like an H-bomb.

"What just happened?" shouted Sid in my ear. "You there?"

"Uh huh," I replied, holding my gauge out to the metal object. The system was now offline. "Bickerstaff's old system seems to have malfunctioned."

"What a fortunate coincidence," Sid said in a tone that suggested he knew I was being less than open with him.

"Going inside now." I had the floor plan memorised. With no security to worry about, I moved quickly to my objective, thankful there were also no dogs: I'd rather run into a man with a gun than a big, angry dog. Even professionals will hesitate before opening fire on a thief and your average Londoner isn't going to own a weapon. But a dog will go for you every time, no qualms, no pausing. They can be difficult to stop and, to be honest, I would rather not have to work out how. I like dogs.

I arrived at the large drawing room that doubled as Bickerstaff's art gallery. The room was substantial: perhaps fifteen metres square, high ceilinged, with polished wooden floors. It was decorated in period style, with beautifully restored classic furniture, antique rugs, and a dozen oil paintings. I ignored all but one of them.

Afternoon Sun on the East Wing hung innocently on the wall. It was not a large painting: perhaps 40cm wide and 30cm high. Despite the time spent at my father's gallery, I was no art expert, but it seemed a pleasant enough rendition of a house. One could say there was some economy in the brush work – at least if one knew what that meant. The truth was I wouldn't have looked twice at it had I not been targeting the picture.

I unshouldered my backpack and removed a flat, cloth-covered object. The duplicate painting wouldn't fool an expert, but it was a reasonable imitation. We'd used a third party to produce it from the images on record. It had some mock texturing so it didn't simply look like a colour print, and the frame was as close as we could determine from the photos Meeks had provided. Leaving a copy behind means that the 'victim' won't necessarily even notice the loss, at least until some time after the theft, and maybe never, in which case everyone is happy.

There was the sound of a shotgun being chambered close behind me. It is quite a distinctive sound.

"Turn around," said a voice. "Very slowly."

I did so, still holding the fake painting. A grey-haired man, probably in his early seventies, clad in a tartan dressing gown and slippers, stood pointing the shotgun. He seemed to have the safety off. I found myself unable to rule out that he might shoot me. Perhaps a big dog would have been preferable.

"Mr Bickerstaff, I presume. And wide awake at this late hour," I said.

Sid choked in my ear. "The snoring has stopped. Must have been only a minute back."

"Who are you?" Bickerstaff asked. "And what are you doing in my house?" He sounded nervous, but the shotgun was held perfectly level.

Now it might seem to you that this is a very tricky situation. Most people would look at it that way. But this is the type of moment I live for; my wits go into overdrive. And I find a way out.

I carefully shifted my accent, giving it as much south-east London as I could. "Mr Bickerstaff, this is embarrassing. We were told you were away."

"Who told you that? Who else is in on this robbery?"

"Did you not get the letter?" I kept my tone relaxed but sincere. The key to a bluff is absolute conviction.

He frowned. "What letter?"

"From your security company. We're conducting a 'stress-test' of your system. To see if it works."

The old man blinked. "You expect me to believe that nonsense?"

"This must all be pretty alarming. Let me get my manager on the line and he can explain it to you." I leaned forward and placed the fake painting carefully on the ground. "There's just been a mix up."

Bickerstaff waved the gun purposefully. "Stay where you are. Why are you wearing a mask?"

I used gentle, calm tones, like everything was normal and as it should be. "We're re-creating the look and feel of an actual burglary. Then we do a full report to show you what happened. Based on that, we suggest changes to prevent a real break-in." I shrugged and pulled up the face mask. "If I'm honest, we're trying to sell you more services." I pointed to my pocket. "I'm going to slowly pull out my phone and call my boss. Please try not to shoot me."

He looked doubtful but didn't object. I removed the phone and called up a number. "I'm at Mr Bickerstaff's place and there seems to have been a right cock-up." I nodded and held out the phone. "He'd like to speak to you."

Bickerstaff's brow furrowed. "This is preposterous. Give me the phone. Slowly."

I did as bade and watched him pick up the handset. "Who is this?" he asked. I closed my eyes and unclipped a small black object from my belt. It fell to the ground, and exploded.

It was just light and sound, a modified flash-bang grenade, but they are massively disorienting. Your brain screams that something far worse is going on around you. Bickerstaff never stood a chance; he collapsed to the floor. The shotgun fell, hitting the ground, and went off. It made a sizeable hole in the wall behind us both.

"Are you OK?" Sid shouted in my ear.

I stepped quickly forward and picked up the weapon. "Yes. It went off as he dropped it."

The old man was already starting to move, but clearly didn't know where he was. The detonation only disabled somebody for seconds. Those seconds, however, were usually game-changing. I quickly removed the real painting and wrapped it in the cloth that had enclosed the fake. The copy I hung on the wall where the original had been.

"You're not from the security company are you?" Bickerstaff said with a groan, blinking repeatedly. "I should have just shot you."

"I'm glad that you didn't." I slipped the painting into my bag. "I expected you to be asleep."

"Don't take it. Please."

I re-shouldered the bag. "It's not yours. And I've left you a copy: it looks the same."

"I'll know the difference." He paused. "Unlike Meeks, who I'm sure you're working for."

I froze.

The old man laughed. "He didn't tell you?"

"Tell me what?" I was being unprofessional entering into dialogue like this, but something told me I had not seen, and you'll pardon the pun, the whole picture.

"Josephine left me the painting. In her will."

I narrowed my eyes. "I read the will. It's available online."

He seemed momentarily surprised. "Well that just seems wrong. Anyway, the painting was covered in a confidential side letter. Don't take my word for it. Ask Gerald."

TWELVE

In two minutes I was back over the fence and in my car. "Did he try to call the police?" I asked Sid through my earpiece.

"No. Everything is still locked down: landlines and mobile, internet cut off."

"Give me ten minutes then turn it back on." I hesitated. "You OK?"

Sid coughed. "Oh yeah. Sorry about the lack of warning."

My hands gripped the steering wheel. "What happened? It's not at all like you."

"Long week. Maybe I should start back on the coffee."

"Forget about it. We have the item."

Sid hesitated before responding. "What did Bickerstaff mean about the will? Has Meeks lied to us?"

"I don't know. But I will be finding out." I disconnected the call and drove away.

I arrived back home without incident and set *Afternoon Sun on the East Wing* on a table next to my desk.

Then I thought again about what Rodney Bickerstaff had said:

Josephine left me the painting. In her will.

If this were true, it was a terrible revelation. We were supposed to be providing restitution, wronging people who deserved to be wronged, gaining some small measure of justice for innocent victims. After all our preparation could we have been duped?

Sighing, I walked into the kitchen, my eyes flicking over the watercolour that hung on the wall above the table. It always reminded me of a different time, and of a place that I would never visit. I felt like I needed a drink to take the edge off. The only alcohol in the house was in the small storeroom off the kitchen. I pushed open the heavy door, and flicked on the light. It was a tiny space, with bare wooden floorboards. Metal shelving lining two walls was filled with tinned food and other long-life products. There was also a brown cardboard box containing a dozen bottles of Glenlivet single malt. Eleven of them, I knew, were empty. In the weeks following my father's death I had succumbed more than a few times. But the last bottle remained untouched – if I didn't drink that bottle, I knew I wouldn't drink at all.

Tonight was not the night to slip back into old ways. I would manage with something more anodyne. I made myself a cup of tea, then glanced at my emails. There was one from my cousin Kieran, inviting me to his son Liam's birthday lunch. That meant finding a present. It also meant finding his new house because he'd moved again. It seemed that since the loss of his wife, Kieran had moved nearly every year. He had never said, but I suspected it was one way to distance himself from the terrible events of three years ago. There was also a secure message from Meg: a full briefing pack on Daniel Stockdale, Calum's potential replacement. I flicked through the pages, smiling at the quality and tone of Meg's analysis. Calum's departure had been an inconvenience: if Meg left my team, I'd be lost.

Daniel sounded promising and we were a hard outfit to recruit for. We needed people with a tightly-defined skill set and enough moral ambiguity to get involved in a complex business, but at the same time we didn't want a hard-core criminal. I quickly messaged Meg to set up the interview. I yawned involuntarily, then looked at my watch. It was nearly 3am.

On the way to bed I stopped to check the post, just in case Susan had decided to bug me again. It was all bills. Or nearly all. The last item caught my eye: a postcard of a white sandy beach, a number of palm trees and, in the distance, a beach cafe. Idyllic if pretty generic. I flipped it over and wasn't surprised to see my name neatly printed, but the message blank.

It wasn't the first time I'd received a card like this, although it was the second one in a week. I usually got one every few months. I supposed it was some computer system sending them out, but, as with all the previous postcards, there was no return address to follow up with. Muttering, I threw it back on the shelf and padded up the stairs. As I reached my desk I saw the painting again. I had to confront Meeks and put the question to him. To give him an opportunity to confirm or deny. Without thinking further, I rang his number. It diverted straight to voicemail. I waited two minutes then tried again. Same result. Part of my brain was telling me it was 3am, and this was a bad idea, but I was angry and I didn't care.

I was about to try a third time when my phone buzzed. My phone made the same noise for every message, but somehow this time it sounded harsher than usual. A message flashed up on screen, ordering me to an appointment early the next morning. These appointments were always short notice, and always in a new location. And they were always something I managed without my team.

Some things even my most trusted circle could not know about. When I slept that night, It was not peacefully.

THIRTEEN

THE NUMBER OF BAD REASONS TO GO TO A HOSPITAL FAR outweigh the good ones. The worst hospital trip of my life happened just before my sixteenth birthday. It was the Easter holidays prior to my GCSEs and I was supposed to be revising. Instead I'd been up in central London, hanging out with Kieran, who should have been studying for his A-levels. We'd spent much of the day drifting around Portobello Road market, mostly because Kieran wanted to buy a hat. I saw nothing wrong with a baseball cap, but he wanted something that was –'more of a style statement'. He'd ended up with a tan straw boater I really wasn't sure about, but he seemed delighted. We'd been working out which pub might turn a blind eye and serve me when my father sent me the message: *Meet me at the Chelsea and Westminster as soon as you can.*

It was the first time I remembered getting a taxi on my own. I had a twenty pound note tucked in a hidden compartment in my rucksack for such emergencies. When I got there, it took me twenty minutes of wading through crowds, lost in a twisting mass of corridors connecting apparently random buildings, to find the right department. Eventually I reached Oncology. At the time I didn't know what the word meant.

My father was hunched in a battered armchair. He stood up and hugged me. He looked terrible.

"What's going on?" I asked. "Where's Mum? I thought she was just having some more tests."

"That's right." He blinked. "And now we have the results."

"So?" I sounded belligerent.

"She asked me not to tell you. But I'm going to need your support, Jake." He leaned close. "She's *very* sick."

"So she needs to stay in hospital?"

He shook his head. "There's nothing they can do for her. The cancer is too far advanced."

I felt ice crawl through my veins. "I thought she was on a course of treatment for high blood pressure. You both said it was nothing to worry about."

"We were hoping we wouldn't have to tell you. But it didn't work out. They're giving her a month at best."

"You *said* these drugs were going to help her."

"It seems they've made things worse. I've been trying to get answers, but nobody wants to accept responsibility: the drug company has lawyered-up faster than you can say 'profit warning'. None of that really matters – it won't help your mother."

"But there must be something we can do. Speak to another doctor. Try another treatment."

My father shook his head. "They're moving her to palliative care. Some things in life can't be changed, Jake. Some things aren't somebody's fault, they just are. And you can't always have an answer for everything."

"I don't accept that—"

"Then that probably means you don't understand the question." He placed a hand on my shoulder. "I'm not going to tell you how to feel. But right now your mother needs you. And I need you."

I blinked tears from my eyes. "OK, Dad."

He smiled. "One day we will get to the bottom of what happened here. But not now."

FOURTEEN

Most people are terrified as they walk through the gates of secondary school for the first time, but after the first day, most say it was all a fuss about nothing. As it turns out, I was right to be afraid when it was my turn.

Willow Wood Comprehensive was an all-boys former grammar school that still had pretensions to grandeur. I was eleven years old, and wary about that first day. The morning went fine – speaking up at registration, getting allocated a locker, then meeting my new form and surviving our first two lessons. That all went fine. I was packing up my books after double physics, when I got distracted reading a long text message from my mother. When I looked up, I realised the rest of my class had already left for lunch, so I asked an older boy where the cafeteria was. I thought I was being resourceful. He clearly saw an opportunity to have a joke at my expense. He directed me to take a 'shortcut' round the back of the sports hall. I'd never had somebody lie maliciously to me before, so I fell for it.

I rounded the corner of the brick structure and

found five older boys standing there, smoking. One of them held some kind of hip flask. They all looked at me like I was something they'd just scraped off their shoe. Suddenly the rest of the school seemed very distant. I started to back away. One of the smokers moved behind me, cutting off my retreat.

"Who the hell are you?" asked the tallest boy, his face an angry explosion of acne. "Bloody first years. You're not allowed here."

"I… er… I'm sorry. Look, I'll be getting along—"

"Damn right. But before you go, there's a fine to pay."

"Sorry, I don't understand," I said. The problem was, I did understand. Worse, my mother had given me lunch money for the whole week in advance. And now I was about to get robbed.

The boy reached forward, rubbing his thumb and forefinger together. "Give us money."

"I can't…" I shook my head. "It's got to last me all week."

"Sounds good. And it'll be a lesson to you. Better than those given by the teachers." He slapped his fist into the palm of his other hand. "Unless of course you'd prefer the alternative—"

"*Leave him alone.*"

I knew that voice. From behind the tall boy, another figure appeared. My cousin, Kieran. "What are you doing here?" I asked.

He threw me a sly smile, then flipped a coin high in the air before catching it without looking. "My first day too. Only got the place yesterday, when some other pupil moved away. Thought I'd keep it a surprise."

The tall boy turned on him. "Who the hell are you?

His sister?" He smiled at the other smokers, and they laughed obligingly.

"Cute," Kieran replied. "And from your crater-face and bad breath, I'm guessing you're Jordan. I've heard *all* about you."

The tall boy scowled and moved closer to Kieran, who was a head taller than me, but a head shorter than the bully. "You newbies need to learn how things work around here."

Kieran shrugged. "I'm not Year 7. I'm Year 9."

"Am I supposed to be afraid?"

"My point is that you'll have to try a bit harder if you're going to intimidate me. And, to repeat myself, which I hate to do, *leave my cousin alone*."

"Why would I do that?

"I know who you are, but you don't know who I am. Do you know why I'm starting at this school?"

"Why would I care?"

"Because I got expelled from the last one. And the two before that."

The tall boy scoffed. But he looked suddenly uncertain.

Kieran smiled. "I have this habit of bringing knives to school. My Dad was in the army - taught me how to use one when I was five."

"Bullshit," he said, but the other boys took a step back.

"Really?" Kieran asked. "Want to find out?"

The tall boy stared at my cousin for several long moments, then scowled. "Whatever, we've got places to be." He nodded to the other four and they stomped off out of sight.

I watched as the last of them vanished, shaking my

head in bemusement. "Thanks for that. Were you following me?"

"No, I was coming to see that lot. Wanted them to know there's a new guy in town."

"You're funny."

"You think I'm joking? Anyway, let's go get some lunch." He paused. "And, so there's no misunderstanding, you're paying."

"So there's a hidden cost with you?"

"I could have left you to stand up for yourself."

"I was getting to it. Or I could have just paid them."

"If you do that, then tomorrow they'll ask for more. And the next day and the next day."

"Maybe I should get you to teach me about knives. Have you actually got one on you?"

Kieran slapped me hard on the shoulder. "The fact that you have to ask that question makes me smile. Maybe one day you'll learn to work out when I'm lying."

FIFTEEN

Vincent McGuire liked to meet at a random central London café every month. He provided coffee and information: I provided an envelope full of cash.

This morning we were in Islington, in a cramped venue with tables made from railway sleepers. I walked past a woman with wire-framed glasses and short grey hair, a newspaper tucked under her arm, and saw Vince as he looked up from his copy of the *Daily Mail*. "You're late."

I frowned. "It's seven, which makes me exactly on time."

He glanced at his watch: a yellowing old piece of unknown manufacture. "Must be fast again." He shrugged and indicated that I should sit. A waitress seemed to materialise at his shoulder. Vince stabbed a fat finger in my direction and said simply, "Coffee." She produced a filter jug, poured and left. I inhaled the fresh brew and waited.

"How you been, Jake?"
"Good. You?"

Vince grunted, which probably meant he was good as well, but it was best not to seek clarification. This was usually as far as we went with small talk, and today seemed to be no different. He folded up his paper and put his hands around his own drink.

"And how is Max?" I asked.

"That's Mr R to you, young man. If I have to call him that, you certainly do." His eyes flickered around the café. "Sure you weren't followed? That Girl Friday of yours – I wouldn't put it past her to keep an eye on what you're up to."

"I was careful."

He regarded me for several long moments, then sniffed. "Do you have the instalment?"

I slid the holdall I was carrying under the table to him.

In no hurry, he unzipped it, revealing a plain brown envelope. He eased it open to see a stack of twenty pound notes. He riffled them like a professional card player. Fifty thousand pounds. Vince closed the envelope and bag. "Mr R will be pleased."

"That obviously means a lot to me."

Vince's left eyebrow quivered slightly. "Careful, Jake. You don't want me to lose my patience now, do you?"

"I do not." And looking at the size of the figure sitting opposite me, I was being completely truthful.

"Mr R continues to be surprised that you're meeting the payments."

"We made a deal. I intend to honour it." I tipped my head. "You think I'm stupid, don't you, to do this?"

Vince shrugged. "People should take responsibility for their own actions. They shouldn't get bailed out by someone else. I hope our mutual friend appreciates what you're doing."

I looked away.

"Ah. So you still haven't told him."

"That's my choice. And regardless, these meetings are nearly done."

Vince's brow furrowed. "How do you figure that?"

"Because I've been keeping track. As it stands I've paid back 1.75 of the two million."

He blinked repeatedly. "I don't have the figures in front of me."

"I'm sure someone in Mr R's organisation can add up."

Vince moved faster than I was expecting. Suddenly my left hand was encased in his, and he was bending it back, testing the limits of what bone and tendon would allow.

I tried to pull away, but his grip was overpowering. I stifled a cry. A few people in the cafe turned to stare, then sharply looked away.

"Mr R isn't trying to cheat you, Jake. Remember that." He released my hand and picked up his coffee again. "You probably think of me as a gruff old bastard, but I can assure you I represent the *cuddly* end of Mr R's operation."

I looked at Vince. He was considerably over six foot, and more than eighteen stone, much of it muscle. Even in his fifties, his was a physical form you could not ignore. His face and hands bore significant scars that I really didn't want to know the origin of. "If he wanted to be friendly, he could simply waive the debt, given the extenuating circumstances."

"If he showed leniency, he'd come across as soft.

And when you're the head of," he hesitated, "an organisation of a certain nature, you can never come across as soft. As Mr R likes to say, he's in concrete. And if you don't keep your end of the bargain, you will be too." Vince cracked an ugly smile. "It could be worse. There are some really bad people out there. Total scum, with no standards, no rules, no honour. The kind that would steal the wedding ring from your elderly mother." Vince puffed out his cheeks. "Well, I'd best be getting along." He stood, picking up the holdall. "Until next time."

"I want confirmation of the account balance."

He hesitated then nodded. "I'll get back to you."

SIXTEEN

I LEFT THE CAFE AND WALKED SOUTH, PASSING THROUGH Finsbury then Farringdon. All around me the morning traffic continuing to build. I cut west until I reached the relative calm of Lincoln's Inn Fields. As usual, walking helped me to think.

The meetings with Vince had been going on for nearly three years, but the abortive dinner with Susan Statham had touched a nerve about my life. I wanted to be done with clients like Gerald Meeks: a wealthy man who might well have lied to me. I wanted to help people who really *needed* help, whether or not they could pay for it.

If I was going to do that, I needed to be free of my obligation to Maxwell Rouse before further complications crept in. But paying him meant I needed money, which meant deciding what to do about the Meeks job. Did I give him the painting or did I give him his money back?

I pulled out my phone and dialled. This time Meeks answered almost immediately.

"Mr Smith, I didn't expect to hear from you so soon. Is there a problem?"

"I'm calling to let you know I have recovered the painting. It's in perfect condition."

"That's just marvellous. Where did you find it?"

I felt a tingle in my spine. "You know I will not disclose that. We went over this in great detail when we met."

There was a pause. "What if I pay more? What if I double your fee?"

"Why would you…" I hesitated, looking around the park, as if somebody might be watching. I should simply have said 'no', but I could restrain myself no longer. "Mr Meeks, did your wife leave the painting to someone else in her will?"

"Where did you hear that?"

"Is it true?"

"A bit late to worry about that, don't you think?"

"Perhaps I should just put it back where I found it. Maybe that's the right thing to do."

"The right thing?" he hissed. "I'll tell you what's right. That I had the last word. He stole my wife, and now it's too late to get her back. This is the closest to *restitution* that I'm going to get. So I want my painting." He drew breath. "Unless you want me to go to the police."

"That would not be in anyone's interests."

He paused. "I don't get you, Mr Smith. Are you not in this for the money?"

I hesitated. Did it really matter who got the painting in this instance? Something inside said that it did. Otherwise I might as well have given the nod to Calum's suggested approach and saved my team an awful lot of trouble. "I need some time to consider this," I said.

"Don't take too long."

I clicked my phone off but it rang almost immediately. I frowned, then saw it was Sid.

"How quickly can you get to Watford?" he asked, sounding out of breath.

"Hour or so. Why?"

"Daniel is on his way. For the 'interview'."

"Are you setting up a venue?"

"Why do you think I'm out of breath?"

"Send me the location and I'll see you there."

"Will do. Oh yeah, I also have that package put together."

"Package?"

"For you to take to the birthday party."

I blinked. "You're a life saver."

"Maybe," Sid replied. "Or maybe I'm just reliable. Unlike certain other *former* members of our team."

"Then let's hope this Daniel is more like you."

I could almost see the smile on his face as he replied. "Of course. But let's not set the bar too high."

SEVENTEEN

Most businesses don't conduct their interviews in a barn, but Restitution Consulting was not like most businesses; whenever we dealt with someone who wasn't a signed-up team member, it was generally best to operate out of somewhere new and temporary. That didn't mean we had to do things by halves, and Sid had done us proud. There was a conference table plus a couple of smaller tables, several laptops and a large flat screen display. There was also juice and coffee.

Daniel was smaller than I was expecting, and a lot lighter than Calum. His hair was even shorter, basically shaved. He had thin lips and a cautious expression.

"Thanks for coming," I said, as we shook hands.

He looked around at the barn. "Meg told me I shouldn't pass this up."

"She's given you the initial brief?"

Daniel shrugged. "You guys steal stuff that other people have had stolen. And you want some muscle to support that."

I smiled. "Pretty much."

"For an appropriate fee," Meg said. "We do a bit of good, but we're not a charity."

"And how do you actually locate the stolen items?"

Sid started to speak but I quickly cleared my throat. "We have a number of proprietary search systems, but we basically use information that is out there. The secret sauce is in how we collate, analyse and connect it. We're the best at what we do. If there is a connection, we find it." My thoughts strayed to Gerald Meeks. "That said, the real world sometimes turns out a little more slippery than we'd like."

Daniel nodded, and poured himself some juice. "So why do this? You say you're doing a *good* thing, but I doubt the police would see it that way and, if you're going to break the law, aren't there easier ways?"

I tipped my head. "We're providing something the police rarely manage: restitution."

Daniel took a sip of his juice. "Why'd the other guy leave?"

I looked at Meg, but she shook her head. "A disagreement over approach and revenue share. Otherwise he was great and we were sorry to lose him."

"And how *does* the money work?"

"We divide it equally, but with an additional share to fund equipment."

He shrugged. "So what do you want to know about me?"

Sid proceeded to ask questions about Daniel's technical knowledge. It wasn't our prime reason for hiring him, but the use of tech was so woven into how we operated that it was important he be at least 'tech aware'. His answers were fine: good enough for us to build on without undue inconvenience. Meg then led him through a few questions about his background, education, previous work. He spoke French and Spanish. And Klingon. "Find that useful often?" I asked.

"Too much *Star Trek* when I was young," Daniel said with a smile. "My accent isn't great."

"Spoiler alert: he gets my vote," Sid said.

I sighed. "OK, let's turn to the reason we called you."

"My combat training? What do you want to know?"

I laughed and slid back from the table, pointing to a straw-covered area behind us. "It's more a question of 'seeing'."

Daniel was good. Sid kept out of this part, but Daniel bested me easily, and also quite competently dealt with Meg, who is far more accomplished than I, and doesn't hesitate to fight dirty. We tried a few different fighting styles and also simulated weapons. He dealt with us in a controlled manner, containing but not hurting us. Although I'm sure he could have if he'd wanted to. He was a lot stronger and faster than he looked – another plus. Always better to look like you are less of a threat than you are. Ninety percent of fights are lost because one person underestimates the other.

"Where did you learn to fight like that?" Sid asked. "Are you ex-army?"

Daniel shrugged. "That and growing up with two older brothers."

Meg stared at Sid. "I'm vouching for Daniel. That should be more than enough for you."

"Oh sure. Meg says he's OK, so he's OK."

I folded my arms. "Sid, is something wrong?"

He glared at me. "I'm just wondering if we really need another team member. After watching you two fight, surely that's good enough? And then we get larger shares."

"Look," Daniel said, "if this is going to be a problem…"

Meg gripped his shoulder firmly. "It's not going to be a problem. He's fine, Jake. You won't find anyone who fits better." She paused. "And I'm sure he has no more secrets than any of us."

EIGHTEEN

It rained hard the day of my father's funeral. The church was full of distant friends and relatives I hadn't spoken to since my mother died, all conveying condolences with sombre expressions. Kieran, to my surprise, wasn't there, and at the time I hated him for abandoning me. Later, of course, I knew better.

I sat in the front row, as the vicar gave a long tribute to someone it felt like I didn't know, while around me colourless people in colourless clothes filled my world with grey. When the service was done, we walked across the road to the cemetery, filing between row upon countless row of concrete slabs, as water spattered on our umbrellas, six men carrying a coffin that contained almost nothing of my father.

I watched as they lowered the coffin into the ground, surrounded by a crowd of people, but no one who really cared. And all the while the rain fell. If I'd had tears, the rain would have hidden them, but l was still too angry to cry. The explosion had left no body to identify, although DNA analysis of the fragments had proved it was

Charles Moro. That and three eye witnesses who saw him get into the car.

There'd been no explanation as to why my father was where he was. His car had been parked just a short distance away from the offices of one his main clients, the infamous Bernard Prebble. But Prebble's office claimed no meeting had taken place that day, and besides, Charles Moro was supposed to have been meeting me at Heathrow Terminal 5.

Several of my father's clients had made an appearance at the funeral, although I'd met few of them before. Prebble himself had attended, enveloped in a crowd of minders and personal assistants befitting a billionaire. I'd never even seen him in person, but obviously I knew who he was. He'd been all over the news recently over accusations of pension fraud. There were even a few TV cameras stationed up the road from the funeral, although the reporters looked dubious that anything noteworthy was going to happen. Prebble left without speaking to me almost the moment the coffin was in the ground.

Maxwell Rouse stood away from the other mourners, surrounded by large brutes whose suits had come off the wrong peg. I had seen Rouse at the gallery a couple of times; my father said he ran a concrete and aggregates business, and was looking to invest. After the coffin had been put in the ground, Rouse approached me. Black raincoat. Black umbrella. Black sunglasses, despite the gloom. He shook my hand with a grip like folded lead, and I stared into a face crowded by heavy jowls and heavy eyebrows.

"Jake, so sorry for your loss."

I nodded. By then I just wanted to be somewhere

else. I mumbled something and went to turn away, but he was still staring at me, expectant. As were his heavyset attendants.

"My name is Rouse. I did some business with your father." His eyes seemed to be searching for some reaction, but I gave none. "This was a truly terrible thing," he said.

There didn't seem to be much to add.

He cleared his throat. "Do the police have any leads?"

"Not that they've shared with me."

Rouse pulled out a cigar and lit it slowly. "They never do."

Clouds of thick smoke filled the air, and I coughed.

"There's a matter I wanted to discuss with you."

I looked around and realised that the other mourners seemed to be moving away as quickly as was discretely possible. Perhaps because of the rain, perhaps because Rouse and his team looked like people you would try and avoid.

Rouse adjusted his sunglasses, which were spattered with rain drops. "Your father was helping me with a project. Just before he died some money went missing."

I shrugged. "He didn't discuss his business with me."

"It was a very large sum of money. I was wondering if he said anything about it, even indirectly?"

"No, sorry."

"Think hard. Any odd behaviour? Any clue that something was up?"

"My father was just killed by a bomb. I'd like to be left alone."

Rouse nodded to one of his men and stepped away. The huge man moved forward, his expression implacable. He looked down at me like I was a pebble. There was a head shake, almost an apology. And then he punched me.

His huge fist drove into my stomach. I'd never been punched by an adult, and I was not ready. I tried to scream but there was no air left in my lungs. Pain exploded, and I thought I felt a rib crack.

There were lots of witnesses, I told myself, trying not to panic. My attacker was going to jail. Someone must have already called the police. And yet nobody came to my aid, nobody did anything. I should have known then what Maxwell Rouse was.

Rouse stepped forward again. "I appreciate this is a difficult day for you. But you need to understand the gravity of this situation."

I fell to the ground, unable to speak.

Rouse bent and gently patted my shoulder. "You're a smart boy, so your father said. I'm sure you'll be alright." He took out a business card, then tucked it my jacket pocket. "If you do find anything, you just give me a call. Any time, day or night." Then he walked away.

I looked at the grass by the grave, muddy and trampled.

I missed my father. And Kieran had not shown up.

I was utterly alone.

NINETEEN

THE DAY AFTER INTERVIEWING DANIEL I WENT FOR another run, then drove west to the beat of an old U2 album on the stereo. It felt good to be out of London, away from the traffic and the fumes.

Just over an hour later I was entering the village of Ambleford. On my SatNav's instructions, I turned into Meadow Drive. The road was narrow and I had to manoeuvre carefully to avoid a BMW X5 that was parked none too brilliantly. Two men sat in the front seats, reading papers. I gave them the universal look for 'couldn't you have done that better?' but they ignored me

I stopped my battered Ford Focus under the large oak tree at the end of the driveway of Kieran's new house: a detached cottage with a red tile roof. A rather burly man was pushing an old mower around the not inconsiderable lawn, and didn't look very happy to be doing it. I nodded to him but he didn't smile back. I shrugged and turned off the car's engine, then reached onto the back seat and withdrew a card and the large, brightly-wrapped box provided by Sid. Moments later I was standing on the doorstep, ringing the bell. The door opened almost instantaneously.

"Uncle Jake!" screamed Liam.

"Think I'd miss your *seventh* birthday?" I asked, crouching and holding out the present.

Liam beamed and hugged me. "You're the best."

"Leave him alone," Kieran said, appearing behind his son. "A handshake or a punch on the shoulder will do just fine. I don't want him going soft." He adjusted the familiar straw boater perched on his head. "Also, you're late."

"Only because I was on a top secret mission," I replied.

"You know Uncle Jake is a secret agent, Daddy," Liam said with a glare over his shoulder. "His country needs him." He grabbed the parcel and scurried inside.

"Is that right?" Kieran rolled his eyes in a practised manner. "Come in then, *Mr Bond*. Lunch is almost ready."

"I don't believe it!" Liam shouted. He rushed back into the room, brandishing the box he'd quickly unwrapped. "A helicopter drone!"

"A special one," I said. "Not in any shops. You are going to have to do some assembly."

"Sounds like a lot of work," Kieran said. "If he gets stuck you'd better be ready to help him."

"If it's in the interests of national security, I'm always ready to act."

"Sure, whatever you say." Kieran clapped me on the shoulder. "And you are a true hero for driving out all this way."

I smiled. "So, how *almost ready* is lunch?"

The meal was Liam's favourite – a full roast leg of lamb with everything: carrots, broccoli, sprouts, green beans, and roast potatoes. I had two very large helpings.

"That was pretty impressive, Kieran," I said, as I finished the last of my plate. "Actually I'd go as far as 'damn impressive'. When did you learn to cook?"

Liam let out a loud giggle, then looked at the floor.

Kieran sighed. "Yes, thank you, young man. Unfortunately I can't take the credit. It was courtesy of the lady who comes in and cooks on weekdays. I'd usually be at work, and otherwise Liam would just eat chocolate cereal. Normally I'd try and take credit for someone else's work, but… I guess not today."

"I saw you had a gardener too. Didn't realise you could afford a full set of house staff."

Kieran turned to Liam. "Why don't you go and finish building that drone, and let Daddy and Jake have a boring adult chat?"

Liam's eyes lit up and he sprinted from the room.

"Oh," I said. "Sorry, didn't mean to bring up money in front of—"

"It's been a tough couple of years, but we're doing OK. Besides, you don't have to pay much for someone to mow your lawn out here."

"Maybe that was why your gardener didn't look happy."

Kieran's face darkened. "Was he rude to you? Because if he was I'll—"

"No, no." I stood up and walked over to the window. "I passed these two guys sat in the BMW in the lane, and they're still there, over an hour later. Do you have police watching your house?"

Kieran stood up and clapped me on the shoulder. "You're a sharp cookie, Jake. They're actually monitoring the property opposite: I hear they think it might be a dope house."

"What? No way."

He smiled. "Who'd have thought, out here in the country? Anyway, how about a couple of hands of cards?"

I felt myself shiver. "You mean Top Trumps with Liam?"

"No, I mean real cards. Unsurprisingly I don't encourage him to play poker."

"If I beat you, you'll only sulk."

"You're not going to beat me."

"One day it'll happen. But I'm not playing today."

"Pssh, boring. What's the worst that can happen?"

I stared at Kieran for several long moments, wondering how to respond. Wondering if now was the moment we would discuss all the things we should have talked about long ago. As each time before, I decided 'not today'. "Sorry. I have to get back into London. Got a lot on."

"What's the time?" He glanced at his wrist and I saw a heavy, gold-plated watch.

I peered closer. "Is that a Rolex?"

Kieran smiled. "Got it from a guy down the pub: twenty five quid. Want me to get you one?"

I laughed and shook my head. "It looks pretty impressive. But I prefer a few more functions on mine."

"A smart watch? Who wants to charge their watch every day? And I have to at least try and look successful if I'm going to sell somebody a Maserati. Anyway," he said, "I know we're celebrating Liam's birthday, but we should take a moment to remember your Dad." He walked over to the drinks cabinet and poured two glasses of scotch from a decanter. "I haven't forgotten it's almost the third anniversary."

I took one of the glasses from him and nodded.

"I know he didn't like me very much, but he just thought he was protecting you. And in my opinion he was a pretty solid guy. Wherever he is now, I wish him all the best."

I looked upwards. "So do I." I took a sip. "And, of course, to Carol as well. I know how much you and Liam miss her."

"Life has to go on." Kieran blinked and nodded. "Thank you. Now are you sure I can't tempt you with some dessert before you leave? It's apple crumble and custard…"

TWENTY

I EVENTUALLY GOT AWAY FROM KIERAN'S MID-afternoon, after getting co-opted into 'flight-certifying' Liam's new drone. I also found time to hide some 'leeches' around the house: not blood-sucking parasites, but rather low-powered electronic monitoring devices of my own design. These weren't to spy on Kieran, but part of my regimen of trying to keep him safe. I would have left a set of hidden cameras as well, but they required far more frequent maintenance. In the end I settled on one, a low-power model tucked in a bush with an angled view of his front door.

The following morning I arrived early at TechFixed, carrying an extremely large coffee and an egg muffin. Starting early usually brought the benefit of arriving before Lundy – he usually waltzed in late, claiming he'd been at a breakfast meeting. Today, to my surprise, he was already there, leafing through post at the reception desk.

"Making up time after your late start the other day?" he asked, adjusting his small framed glasses.

"I didn't start late - I was out on a call, remember?"

"As long as you're making me money." He walked back into his office and closed the door.

I stared for a moment. I occasionally got the feeling that I was underestimating Lundy and his disinterested facade was all an act. Could someone really be that stupid? And yet, I knew I should be grateful to him. He had offered me this job when I was young and inexperienced: I'm not sure why he took a chance on me. Was it brilliant insight, or simply that he got lucky? While I had outgrown the job, it still served a useful purpose.

I turned and walked to my desk.

Meg was the only other person in the office, typing rapidly while staring at a spreadsheet. She looked up and tapped her nose before immediately heading to the server room. I took a bite of muffin and followed her, ignoring the 'no food' sign on the door. "I meant to ask: do you need me to arrange delivery of the painting to Gerald Meeks?"

I swallowed. "No, I can manage that, thanks."

"Good. I presume there was nothing in that claim the painting was left to Bickerstaff in the wife's will?"

"No evidence that I uncovered."

"Excellent. Do you want some more good news?" she asked, looking slightly disturbed by the way I was demolishing my breakfast. "We had two new enquiries overnight that check out."

With a business like ours, you don't tend to advertise or run a public website. Both would flag us to competitors, law enforcement and the criminal fraternity. We have a couple of 'vanilla' webpages that previous clients know about. New prospects who are well-connected or resourceful post generalised messages using them, to flag their interest. From there we establish an anonymous encrypted connection through Tor. Eighty percent of enquiries fail at that point.

"You've run them already?" I asked.

"I'm efficient."

"And they both check out? That's fantastic." And it truly was: our pipeline of new projects was looking somewhat empty at the moment. "What are the highlights?"

"One's a businessman operating in London: his name is Edgar Johnson. He wants to meet yesterday."

"Tomorrow will have to do. Brief Sid."

"Already done. The other enquiry is from a journalist called Jacques Flaubert. Guess where he wants to meet?"

"Relieve the suspense."

"Paris."

"That's a bit random. Who does he work for?"

"A website called Paris Aujourd'hui. I looked it up and it's part of Bernard Prebble's media group."

I blinked. "If this Flaubert's a journalist, can he afford us?"

"He's paid the twenty thousand deposit, so he's not a time-waster."

I didn't usually accept work outside London, let alone outside the UK. But if the client was this highly motivated, and willing to pay, then – given the present circumstances – it could be worth pursuing. "When is he proposing to meet?"

"Within the next three days."

"I don't like going in blind. Then again, any excuse

to drop in on Paris. Set it up. I presume you'll come too?"

"Presuming there's a dinner in it for me. And that you're paying."

"Sure. Know anywhere good?"

She smiled. "Lots of places. Don't worry, I'll pick the most expensive."

I rolled my eyes. "Given that we're going to be busy, I think we'd better hire Daniel and get him up to speed."

Meg smiled. "Yes, I think we better had."

TWENTY-ONE

SOMETIMES A CLIENT WANTS TO MEET AT THEIR OWN offices; they prefer the reassurance of operating on their own turf and nothing will persuade them otherwise. It's a lot more work for us to prepare, and so many things are outside of our control – we have to make the call that the prospect is worth the risk.

Edgar Johnson was one such client. Meg and I met him at his penthouse London office: all smoked glass and marble, with whisper-quiet lifts and alert security guards. I was glad this wasn't our target. One of the guards waved us into an express lift to take us to the top of the building. The floor's reception room, which smelled strongly of fresh paint, looked out across London, the Thames immediately below us. Meg and I were shown into a conference room, also freshly painted. We were both dressed in sharp grey suits, although Meg somehow managed to make hers look twice as expensive.

As before, I'd given my name as John Smith. Meg had adopted the name Marla. Edgar Johnson was probably in his fifties. He had the relaxed, power-dressed look of someone with real money. His accent had strong hints of South Africa, with a bit of a twist – it almost sounded affected. Once coffee was served, he closed the door and adopted a more serious air.

"This," Johnson said, "is a matter of some delicacy. The item I want to recover is a necklace: diamond and platinum, a one of a kind piece. It was a present for my," he leaned forward and spoke more softly, "girlfriend."

I saw Meg's expression harden: according to our research Johnson was married.

"I can't simply report this and claim on my insurance. I don't want all the paperwork and police forms. Something will leak. I can't have my wife finding out. She'd destroy me."

Meg gave me a sideways glare.

I tapped my fingers on the table. "We appreciate the sensitivity, but it should not prevent us recovering the item."

"I'm glad to hear it. Sofia is distraught. Here are some pictures." Johnson slid a dossier across the table. Meg snatched it and flicked through several pages showing the necklace from every possible angle. There was also a receipt. Meg sucked in her breath: it showed a price tag of two and half million pounds.

Johnson shrugged. "Personally I liked another, more expensive piece, but this is the one she wanted. And the designer has sworn never to make another, under any circumstances."

"Where was it taken from?" I asked.

"My apartment in Kensington."

"You have security? Cameras and alarms?"

"Latest generation tech. But they bribed the guard

and somehow messed with the systems. All I have are some very blurry images. They're in there, at the back."

I closed the dossier. "For now this is enough. I should stress that whatever happens, we won't be able to tell you where we find the item."

He laughed. "I just want it back. So how does it work from here?"

"We'll do our research. If we locate the necklace, we'll assess its recoverability. If it can be recovered, we'll communicate a price."

Johnson shook his head. "I need this to be your top greater priority: I will pay you half a million for the privilege. I'm sure that's more than twice what you would typically charge."

I tried not to react. I think I pulled it off. Meg bit her nails distractedly.

"Simply prove that you have it and I will pay before you have to hand it over. Just so you know that there is no risk."

"That's very trusting," I said.

"I suppose. But if you met Sofia you'd know why I need your help. She's not going to give me a moment's peace until she gets it back."

"Let me discuss it with my team—"

"You give me a yes, here and now, or the deal's off. I'm not paying to wait around. If you won't do it, I'll find someone who will."

"Mr Johnson," Meg said, "there are no guarantees that we'll be able to—"

"Young lady, this is not a negotiation."

I raised a hand. "You give us until tomorrow to do some preliminary research before we decide, or your answer is 'no'. Take it or leave it."

Johnson stared at me, then smiled. "Fair enough, Mr Smith. Let's talk tomorrow."

Meg and I rode the lift back to the lobby. "I don't like him," she said. "I don't like him, or trust him."

"You never like or trust our clients."

"OK, but him particularly."

"Because he has a mistress?"

"This is a man who lies to his wife on a regular basis. Why would he not lie to us?"

"You could say his willingness to disclose that he has a mistress is a remarkable indication of candour with us at least." The lift doors opened and we glided through the lobby in silence. Emerging into the sunshine, I lowered my head and whispered, "It's ironic, really. Calum leaves us and we promptly land our biggest-ever payday. Not only that, but it's exactly the amount he was looking for from the last job."

"I thought you said never to believe in coincidence?"

"I did. But that is not the reason we're going to turn down this job, despite needing the money. There's something about him that's off."

"You're basing a half-million-pound decision on your… gut? That doesn't sound like you at all."

"Something about Johnson seemed familiar. His mannerisms. He seemed to be having altogether too good a time talking to us. And he was first too pushy, then too weak in his negotiations."

"Sure. And what about his nose? All misshapen. Never trust a rich man with a crooked nose, that's what I say." She rolled her eyes. "If you're simply going to turn him down, why didn't you tell him up there in his office? Why string things out?"

"Because I thought it would be polite to discuss it with you and Sid first."

"You're all heart." She blew a kiss at me. "But what did you mean by 'needing the money'? Is there something going on I don't know about?"

I coughed. "I mean, we always need money, right? And it is a *lot* of money. Call Sid and Daniel. Let's meet at the office and start running searches. If we have any doubts, we don't go ahead."

"Fair enough." She folded her arms. "Did you bug him?"

"I couldn't get close enough. He never offered to shake hands, and it seemed like that was intentional." I paused, then smiled. "But I did bug his office. I'll wait a few hours then turn it on."

TWENTY-TWO

When we got to TechFixed, Sid had already signed Daniel in as a temp: joining Restitution Consulting meant playing along with the TechFixed cover story. Lundy waved but didn't come out of his office, so we got our new team member set up at a desk. Ten minutes later there was another drive failure. Five minutes after that, Meg, Sid, Daniel and I were in the server room. Sid had printed off copies of the electronic dossier provided by Johnson and passed it around.

"Wow," Daniel said, as he read the receipt. "Two point five million? Is that for real?"

"That'll be one of the first things we check," I replied.

"It would be the most expensive item we've ever recovered," Sid said. "How much do you think he'll pay for it?"

"Normally we determine that after research, but he has specified a number already. *500K*. The important thing is that we don't get distracted by the number: we still need to make the right decision about whether the risk's worth it."

"That's a hundred grand each!" Sid continued. "I can tell you now, it gets my vote."

"Yes, yes," Meg said, "that's a lot of raw carrot juice. But why don't we actually do our analysis."

First we hacked into the security-camera feed from Johnson's apartment. It was, indeed, partially corrupted; we could see two figures enter the property, but none of our many digital-enhancement techniques made any difference. On the footage, the two burglars made a clean entry, drilling the lock and forcing the door. Then they professionally searched each room. Very quickly they found the necklace at the back of a clothes drawer.

"Hardly the most inventive hiding place," Daniel said.

"She probably assumed the apartment was safe," I replied. "Pretty careless."

We expanded the search to include the CCTV in the common areas of the building and the street outside, but again we met the same obscuration of the footage, so we moved on.

It took some time to break into Johnson's various email accounts. There were emails on his private account between him and Sofia that confirmed the dates of the purchase and the theft. Then we hacked Sofia's account, which was just webmail without dual-factor authentication, meaning it took about thirty seconds to get in. Everything dovetailed, but nothing provided a clue. Finally, we checked Johnson's wife's accounts: absolutely nothing of relevance. If she knew what her husband was up to then she hadn't put it in an email.

Meg frowned. "Is it me or do these email conversations look a little stilted?"

Sid scrolled through several on screen. "Not everyone has your literary standards."

Daniel coughed. "I've got the jewellery store up." We gathered around his screen. The necklace was fully documented and described in their inventory; the sale was recorded on the correct date. We even found camera footage of Edgar Johnson and a young lady in a very tight dress looking closely at the necklace.

Meg sighed. "He could be her grandfather."

"It's not our place to judge our clients—" I began.

"Well perhaps it should be. Is this someone we want to help?"

"In a minute we'll vote," I replied. "And you can make up your own mind, however you wish."

"Really?" Sid said. "I thought we were supposed to make decisions based on the rigorous use of data and predictive analytics. Not personal prejudice."

"Says the eco-warrior vegetarian," Meg muttered.

"I'm a vegan. And that's beside the point—"

"Enough with the bickering," I interrupted. "At least until we've completed the analysis."

"Hang on a minute," Sid said. "Look at this. I've managed to track our thieves a block further to a corner where they got into a white van."

"Fantastic," Daniel said, "one of only a hundred thousand white vans in London."

The vehicle drove away. For two seconds the number plate was clearly visible.

"But one of *one* with that registration." I clapped Sid on the shoulder. "Nice work."

"Rookie mistake, considering the other effort they went to," Daniel said.

I gestured for Sid to track the vehicle. Hooked into a virtual CCTV network, we were able to follow the van ten minutes across London. It came to a halt outside an upscale apartment block and a man climbed out, wrapped in a long coat, with a cap over his face. The van drove off. The man in the cap turned and went inside the apartment.

"Can we ID him?"

Sid rattled away at the keyboard. "It's night, and we can hardly see any of his face. It might even be a woman."

Meg shook her head. "With that frame, those proportions? I doubt it. The movements are all wrong."

"Look at this," Daniel said. He had pulled up an attendance list at the jewellery store – it was the kind of place you only got into by appointment. One listed the penthouse of the apartment block as the home address.

"What can we get on that apartment?" I asked.

Sid smiled. "CCTV in the hallway." More keyboard bashing, then a grainy feed came up. "No encryption, which is odd these days." On screen the man in the cap had just walked into the apartment and closed the front door behind him. He reached into the carrier bag he was holding and withdrew something wrapped in cloth. Carefully he opened it, removing a sparkling necklace. The image was poor, but it could not hide the man's smile.

"Seems almost too easy," Daniel said.

"And that's because," Sid replied, "we're *that good*."

"Fine," I said. "So let's vote. Is this a job you want to do?"

"Before we deal with that, I have a question."

"Go on."

"Why," Sid asked, "haven't we been paid for the Meeks painting recovery?"

I rubbed my temples. "Because I haven't returned the painting to him yet."

Meg frowned. "You said there was no issue."

"I want to make a few more checks first."

"What checks?" Sid asked. "Should we presume that money isn't coming in?"

"If the painting wasn't stolen, we shouldn't pass it to Meeks."

Sid folded his arms. "Fine. Then as regards Edgar Johnson, I'm in. Unless you have a solid, fact-based reason why we should not do it."

"Meg?" I asked.

She narrowed her eyes. "You go first."

"If you want. And I say 'no'. I don't trust Johnson."

Sid slapped the table. "So what? This is a hunch? Are we a bunch of psychics now? I thought I was the new age hippy of the group."

"Everyone gets a vote," I replied. "I've placed mine."

Meg looked at Daniel. "We do it," she said.

Daniel raised his hand slowly. "I guess I'm going with the money."

"Fine," I said with a sigh. "Then – subject to Edgar Johnson passing a rapid due diligence check, and he'd better come out cleaner than clean – it seems we have our decision."

TWENTY-THREE

WE RAN EVERY TEST WE COULD THINK OF, AND JOHNSON checked out. I even activated the bug I left in his office. It caught him planning a charity event, then having a phone conversation with his granddaughter. So it seemed I was wrong. And the Great Reverse Diamond Heist was on. With the impending trip to Paris in the diary, we decided to tackle it immediately. By 9pm we were ready to roll.

Apartment missions bring a whole extra set of issues: preparation needs to be taken to an entirely new level. You have to deal with the security systems in the apartment itself, but you also have to worry about the common areas and any access-control measures they have. And let's not forget the other occupants of the building, who often seem to turn up at the most inconvenient moment, either as helpful or nosey neighbours, or simply as awkward passers-by.

This particular apartment belonged to a company. The chain of ownership led back to a Cayman Islands trust, and there was no lease officially documented. With regard to the resident, we had footage of a bearded man regularly entering and leaving, always on his own. We didn't know who he was or what he did. But we didn't really need to know any of that to relieve him of an item of jewellery he had acquired in dubious circumstances.

Daniel and I emerged from our car, parked two blocks away, and began a slow jog, chatting to each other like training buddies. We padded along the pavement in worn trainers and tracksuits, caps low over our eyes, and were soon in front of the building. Nonchalantly I pulled a key-card from my pocket and waved it at the panel to the left of the front doors. There was a soft tone and they swung inwards. "Thank you, Sid," I whispered.

"You're welcome," floated his voice through my earpiece.

Inside, we went straight for the right-hand lift. It would need a special key to access the penthouse level, but we weren't going that high. At least not straight away. I pushed the level-eight button and the lift glided upwards. We emerged three floors below our target, and strode down the corridor to an access cupboard.

Daniel looked around then produced a couple of very odd-looking keys. He selected one and wiggled it purposefully inside the lock; there was a click and the door opened. We stepped into the cupboard and closed the door behind us. Our intelligence had told us that the resident was currently at home. He didn't seem to go out much, and we didn't have time to wait and build a profile of when he might: if we couldn't wait for him to leave, we'd make him do so.

Pulling the fire alarm is an old trick, but it can still be incredibly effective. Of course with large, professionally-managed blocks we have to do something a little more sophisticated than just smashing some glass. Otherwise the actual fire brigade will arrive within ten minutes and big guys with axes will start asking us awkward questions.

Daniel shrugged off a small backpack and removed a laptop computer, which he flipped open and booted up. "You didn't explain why we didn't do this from outside," he said in a low voice.

"Three reasons," I replied, pulling a set of cables from my own backpack. "*One:* these systems are quite hard to hack into, and if we do then we'll leave evidence that might be traceable. It's cleaner just to access the hardware directly. *Two*: we can time things perfectly so that we are in here, hidden, while the residents play their part." I ran my finger down a control panel. "Sid, I have three patch panels here. Which one am I looking for?"

"Any regular ethernet socket," came Sid's voice in my earpiece.

I plugged the lead in as directed then did the same with the laptop. "And the *third* reason: to make sure people are convinced it is not a false alarm, we'll pipe a little smoke in." I removed a canister from another compartment in my backpack and, reaching up, slotted it into a recess in the air-conditioning duct. "Sid, when you're ready."

"Cover your ears," he replied.

Inside the cupboard, the alarm was quite muted, a blue flashing light providing visual confirmation. Outside it would be deafening.

"We'll give them five minutes," I said, "then move out."

Daniel nodded. "Is it usually this straightforward?"

"This job has moved forward surprisingly quickly, but we're good at what we do." The minutes passed quickly. Meg reported in from her vantage point in a vacant apartment in a building opposite. "Our host is out."

"Excellent. Let's—"

"He's got several people with him. Big guys. In suits. The kind of big guys who don't normally wear suits or, if they do, they certainly don't look comfortable in them."

"Thugs," I replied. I'd seen guys like that before.

"Probably," Meg said. "Just who is this guy?"

I was starting to wonder. "Are they armed?"

"Hard to tell, but they look big enough that it might not matter."

"Should we abort?" Sid asked.

"Negative," I replied. "We won't get another chance. We'll just have to be quick. If the situation changes, let me know immediately."

"The alarm system thinks it has dialled the fire brigade. You can move now."

Daniel and I left the cupboard and moved quickly through the wisps of smoke hanging in the air to the stairway. Nobody was in sight. We sprinted up three flights and through what would normally have been a key-card-locked door. The fire alarm had conveniently deactivated it. The eleventh floor landing had plenty of our fake smoke and a single door. "Cameras still out?" I asked.

"Of course," Sid said.

We approached the door. It was open.

"Too easy," Daniel said, smiling.

"Yes," I said. "Status outside?"

"All still there, though they appear to be wondering why the fire brigade haven't shown yet."

I turned to Daniel. "Let's make this quick."

It took us only three minutes to find the necklace in a floor box with a padlock that was no match for Daniel's abilities. That was good. Everything else was bad.

We also found a bag with two hundred thousand pounds in cash and a considerable volume of what I had little doubt were bags of cocaine. On one of the tables was a copy of the Moscow Times. In *Russian*.

Daniel placed the necklace carefully in a padded case and then in his backpack. "What about the money and the drugs?"

"We don't touch them. These are not people we want to mess with any more than we are already."

"What is that?" asked Sid's voice in a confused tone. "That's the third time I've got interference on the line. If I didn't know better, I'd say someone was trying to eavesdrop. And what was that about drugs?"

"Never mind. We're getting out of here."

"You'd better hurry," Meg said. "They've got fed up waiting and are on their way back up."

We ran out of the flat. "Lift or stairs?"

Meg cursed. "They're using both. I think they've realised something is amiss."

I tapped my earpiece. "Sid?"

"There's a service elevator through the 'no entry' door to your right. It comes out in the basement."

We were at it in seconds but hit a problem. "It needs a key. That didn't show up in our recon."

"And it's not a lock I can pick," Daniel said. "Electronic."

"Working on an override now," Sid replied, his voice not sounding calm.

"Hurry," I suggested. We could see the display indicating the lift was on level three and climbing. Then I heard footsteps from the stairwell. Running steps. "Really hurry!"

The doors slid back and we leapt inside, stabbing at the basement button. With painful slowness the doors drew closed just as two large figures burst onto the landing. The lift began to descend.

"Meg," I said, keeping my voice low, "can you retrieve us?"

"I'm on it."

The lift arrived in the basement car park. We emerged warily, scanning for trouble, but there was nobody in sight. We sprinted to the exit and there was Meg in the car, looking somewhat pale. We jumped in and, like a true professional, she drove off at a controlled pace. "Is it usually like that?" Daniel asked, his face fixed.

"We usually aim for something a little less edge of the seat," I replied.

Meg turned and glared at me. "What was in that apartment?"

I swallowed. "Drugs. Lots of drugs."

TWENTY-FOUR

I will never forget getting that phone call from Kieran, two days after my father's funeral. He hadn't shown up, and he hadn't contacted me. I'd tried to get hold of him and he'd not replied. I was starting to wonder if something was wrong. Then he made that phone call – the sole call that he was allowed to make. An hour later I was walking into the interview room at the police station.

My cousin – strangely, for him, hatless – just stared blankly at the wall.

"Kieran, I'm so incredibly sorry. I can't even imagine what… Are they sure it's Carol?"

"I identified her." He stopped and blinked. "If you were expecting me to look more distraught… I've rather cried myself out. I'm just exhausted."

"But… I don't understand. What happened?"

"I came home from work and found her. Just lying in the bathtub."

"She drowned?"

"That's what they're trying to work out."

I froze. "What does *that* mean?"

"They're considering the possibility of foul play. As a consequence of which, they've been questioning me non-stop for more than forty-eight hours."

"What? Why?"

"Because if it turns out she was murdered, statistics tell them that the husband's usually worth a look. Because they don't have another suspect yet, and for PR's sake they've got to work someone over. It's just to eliminate me from their enquiries, at least that's how they're pitching it. A matter of routine."

"What possible reason would *anyone* have to kill her?" I shook my head. "This is all just so messed up. My father, now Carol? I don't understand the world."

"Thank you for coming to see me when you've got your own… grief."

"Don't be daft, of course I came." I ran my hands through my hair. "Where's Liam?"

A smile flickered over Kieran's face. "He's being brave. He was staying at a friend's place, and they brought him here to see me. Social services have him right now, while they… process me."

"The DI who signed me in asked my whereabouts on the day."

"And you told them you were at your father's funeral. I bet that shut them up."

"Kind of," I replied. "It was a bit odd. They didn't look like regular police."

"What do you mean?"

"Something was off. Too precise, too educated. Suits too perfect."

"That's very observant of you."

"Is there something going on here that you're not

telling me? Some reason why someone would want your wife dead?"

Kieran shook his head.

"So what are you going to do? Once they realise you're innocent, and they apologise."

"I just want to be there for Liam. He's the only thing that matters. And I'm going to need your support."

I reached forward and gripped his shoulder. "Whatever you need, whatever I can do, just let me know."

"Thank you. That means a great deal. And I haven't forgotten what you've just gone through. We need to stick together. We're family."

TWENTY-FIVE

WHAT IS MONEY? MOST PEOPLE WILL SAY THAT IT'S notes and coins. An economist will tell you that it's a store of value, and a means of exchanging it. They'll also say it should be scarce, durable, transferable and divisible… but by then people have usually lost interest. My mother used to say it was the root of all evil, and I won't argue that she had a point. My father said a lot about it, but mostly that it made the world go round. Just not in a direction that everybody liked.

We discussed it in detail once, a year after my mother's death. I was just back from college and heading for my father's study, maintaining the inviolable Moro family tradition that if you made a cup of tea for yourself, you had to make one for everyone else within those four walls. It was also a useful pretext. I knocked on the door and walked in without waiting for a reply. An old Kenny Roger's record – *Coward of the County* – was playing on the antique turntable. My father was sitting in his leather swivel chair, his reading glasses on as he studied a grey folder labelled BP. He seemed startled at my appearance and hastily closed the folder shut, putting it up on the shelf above the desk. "Trying to startle me?" he asked.

I turned the music down, then placed the mug before him. "Thought you might be in need of this." I nodded at the BP folder. "What are you doing? Researching oil companies?"

"Not exactly. Actually there's something you can help me with." He pulled another folder off the shelf, one that bore the letters BC in thick black pen. "Do you know what a Bitcoin is?"

"Sure. Why do you want to know that?"

"Because one of my clients wants to pay me using them."

"I thought your clients were rich."

"They are. And they get that way by being clever with their money. At least that's what this one told me. It all sounds a bit… dodgy."

"You think your client is a crook?" I shrugged. "There's nothing illegal about Bitcoin. It's just a digital form of currency. There are hundreds of different variants in use now: Ripple, Quark, eBonds, Nxt."

"And you store these Bitcoins on a computer? What's to stop someone copying them?"

"It's inherent in the block-chain technology on which they're built. You can use powerful computers to farm them… but as for duplicating Bitcoin you already have? No, that doesn't work."

He nodded. "So, you think it should be OK?"

"Their value fluctuates a lot. If you don't mind the uncertainty, sure."

"So why does anyone use them?"

"Anonymity. Keeping your money out of the control of the government and banking system."

He took a sip of his tea. "This is stewed. Which means you were distracted while you made it. What's on your mind?"

I blinked. My father was good at keeping his own secrets, but he seemed even better at seeing through mine. "I want to drop out of college. I'm not enjoying it."

"I see. You do realise that qualifications set you up for life?"

"Maybe when you grew up. The world's different now. Particularly in anything to do with computing. You need to learn on the job, not in the lecture hall."

"Maybe. Or maybe Kieran has been putting ideas in your head again? Just because he dropped out, doesn't mean you have to. And I still don't understand why anyone would drop out of Oxford to take a sales position in an insurance company."

"He gets to travel a lot."

"There's something odd about that job of his. Look, Jake, this is a big decision. Just think about it properly, please. Ultimately, it's your choice. I'll support you, whatever you decide."

"Thanks." I hesitated. "So you're not going to try and get me in to the family business?"

"No, Jake, I am not. I only got into this because we needed to pay for your mother's treatment. I thought it was the right thing, but I sunk us in debt only to make things far worse—"

"You have to let it go, Dad. It wasn't anyone's fault."

"That's what the drug company says."

"But you don't believe them?"

"I just want restitution." He put the folder marked BC back on the shelf, next to the BP folder he'd been looking at. "But if I can't get that, then I'll settle for someone paying for what happened."

"In Bitcoin?"

"Something like that." And he smiled. It was a smile I still missed.

TWENTY-SIX

By a somewhat tortuous route, we ended up back at my house in Wimbledon just before 11pm. We crowded into my living room and I laid the necklace in the middle of the table. Nothing truly sparkles like a diamond. I stared at each of the team in turn. "Anyone got anything to say?"

"You can spare us the 'I told you so' routine," Meg said, folding her arms. "We made the decision based on the information we had. The question is 'why was it bad information?'"

Daniel rubbed a hand over his shaved head. "To state the obvious, how did we not discover we were robbing a drug dealer?"

Meg extended a manicured finger nail towards Sid. "Yeah, *how* did we not?"

"Why is it my fault?" he replied. "I'm as confused as you are."

"You were the one so keen to do it. Maybe you were just lax in your checking—"

"Sid is a pro. And our systems have never let us

down like this before so something odd was going on," I interrupted.

"You said," muttered Meg, "that we would not be getting involved with organised crime. You *promised*."

"Do I need to remind you that I was the one saying we shouldn't do this job?"

"I'm sorry," Sid said, pulling at his ponytail, "but this simply doesn't make sense. We should run the analysis again: figure out how this happened."

We did. And the results were completely different. We had robbed the believed head of a major drugs syndicate: a Russian 'businessman' called Andre Coralov. If I wanted further confirmation as to his credentials, it appeared he'd had dealings with Maxwell Rouse. Obviously I didn't flag the meaning of the last part to my team.

"Jake, this is appalling," Meg said. "Daniel's only just joined and this crap happens, for goodness sake."

I counted to five. Then five more. "I agree. And we will be getting to the bottom of it."

"If they trace who did this, what do we do?" Meg blinked. "Jake, we don't go up against this type of outfit."

"We could go to the police," Daniel said.

Meg turned on him. "Oh yeah, great idea. Should we hand ourselves in too?"

"We could provide the information anonymously."

"And get the police looking for us as well? Brilliant."

"I was just thinking—"

"Well don't," Meg said. "Right now we may have just annoyed this gang. We don't actually want to declare war."

It was all too much. I banged my hand on the table.

"How could the results be fake? Someone would have to hack the entire internet."

Silence echoed around the table. After several long moments, Sid spoke. "No, they wouldn't. They'd only have to hack all our computers."

"Pretty implausible. You know how good our systems are. And how unusual. You'd have to have detailed inside knowledge."

Sid coughed. "What about Calum?"

I shook my head.

"He did walk out," Meg said.

"There's a huge gulf between walking out and selling out. Besides, does anyone think he would have had the technical know-how to do this?"

"Maybe not," Sid said. "But we need to check the systems anyway."

I stood up. "There must be another explanation." I walked over to the fireplace and kicked at the grate. I was slow to trust anyone, but Calum had been one of us. I glanced at the pile of junk mail on the mantelpiece then saw the stack of business cards for taxi companies, take away restaurants and estate agents. Gold embossed lettering glinted in the lamplight. I picked up Martha S. Tassun's business card and turned to the others. "And I think I've found it."

———

It was one of the most sophisticated bugs we'd ever seen – a passive sensor hidden in the middle of the card: thinner than paper and smaller than a pin head. It took more than an hour of focused analysis to identify it.

I'm pretty sure we would never had found it had we not been specifically searching.

"You're a real pro," Meg said, with more than a touch of sarcasm.

I frowned. "Do you scan everyone who comes to your door? Every leaflet? Every fast-food delivery carton?"

Meg ignored my question and raised her eyebrows. "Pretty, was she? Distracted, were you?"

"At least we have the cause."

Sid looked unconvinced. "I'm not sure."

I glared at him. "You think we have another bug on the premises?"

Sid was looking at the bug under a microscope I had brought down from my office. "There has to be. This is a passive device. There'd need to be an active relay nearby."

It only took us five minutes to find it, taped against the outside wall near my front door. It was the size of a matchbox. I tore it off in anger and ripped out the batteries.

Sid took it from me. "Range of probably 300 metres. They could monitor from anywhere nearby."

"Perhaps the girl who gave you the card works for Calum?" Daniel said.

Before anyone could answer, Sid spoke. "What's this?" He had opened up the box. Inside was a single ink character: a letter S. "What does that mean?"

Meg and Daniel shrugged, but I didn't. I had been careless not to defend against such an obvious threat. I sighed. "It means it wasn't Calum. Or Johnson. You can call Johnson and let him know we have his necklace. I'm going to take care of the person who planted the bug."

Sid frowned. "You know who it was? Do you know how to find them?"

"I need to take care of this myself. I'll make the problem go away."

Meg folded her arms. "You'd better."

I nodded, reflecting again on the name on the business card: Martha S. Tassun. Or if you're adept at anagrams, *Susan R. Statham*.

TWENTY-SEVEN

With the many other distractions, I had forgotten to follow up on Susan Statham; clearly I should have given her a greater priority. The whole performance with the mugger, the dinner, her profession of a higher purpose had all been designed to distract me from something altogether more sinister. To what end I was not sure.

But I would be finding out.

The passive tracker I had planted on Susan had done its work. Every two hours it had quietly sent out a ping to the nearest wifi or cellular network. Then it had shut itself down until the next ping. Aside from that brief moment when it sent the tiniest packet of information possible, the device was almost undetectable. Of course it only gave me a location, no other information. But it was time to up the ante.

Presuming Susan was even half competent with her IT set up, it would be very difficult to hack her, which meant I had to do what she had done to me: get an access point inside her firewall. And *that* meant paying her a visit. Given that she might realise her bug had been discovered at any moment, I needed to move fast. You never wanted your target to know you were coming.

Her apartment was situated next to the canal near Brentford Lock. It was a third floor duplex: all glass and no curtains. It was gone midnight and I had been watching for half an hour, seeing no sign of movement, including when a rather irritated pizza-delivery guy had knocked loudly for several minutes in a vain attempt to deliver a large Hawaiian I had ordered. I glanced at my phone, waiting on one final test to establish whether the apartment was truly empty. Any moment now…

Susan's tracker sent a ping from central London. I shouldered my backpack and pulled my cap low over my face: it was time to move.

Five minutes later I was standing by Susan's front door, staring at a very complicated lock. I had a full set of picks with me, but this would clearly take some time, and with every minute that passed came the chance that a neighbour might appear and ask what I was doing.

My foot stubbed against the edge of the doormat. I stared at it a moment – could the solution really be that easy? I crouched and lifted up the mat. There was nothing on the ground. I let it drop down. The rubber material slapped back onto the floor, along with the tiniest metal click. I froze then lifted the mat back up. Taped to the underside was a key. With a wry smile I eased it from the tape. Some people just asked to be burgled.

The key fit perfectly. I let myself in and closed the door.

Inside, all the lights were off, but a fair amount of illumination came through the expansive windows from the moon and the streetlights. The apartment was mostly one huge open area, with a balcony staircase up to the bedroom. I listened carefully for any sound that someone might be in the apartment. There was none. Releasing the breath I hadn't realised I was holding, I looked around. To one side was a large desk on which sat a desktop computer. I moved forward and opened up my backpack, removing a USB key logger and pen drive pre-loaded with decryption tools. I'd get what data I could while I was here, then I'd rig up a bespoke data-collection device that would transmit further data once Susan was using the machine again. She would no doubt find the leeches I'd plant before I left, but not right away – and by then they would have done their work and I'd know more about who she was and what she was doing.

I slid the computer forwards and reached for the button to open the case, preparing to get to work.

Every light in the apartment came on at once. I stifled a gasp as I tried to adjust to the brightness. Had I triggered some automatic defence? Were the lights on a timer? Then, from above, I heard a woman's voice.

"You certainly took your time."

TWENTY-EIGHT

I looked up and saw Susan Statham smiling at me, her sharply-cropped dark hair perfectly styled.

"C'mon, don't look so surprised," she said.

I felt the floor shift under my feet, although I was fairly sure that was not actually happening. "You left the key out on purpose didn't you?" I said. "It was too easy."

"I'm amazed that didn't make you hesitate. Or do you have such a low opinion of me?"

I swung my gaze around the apartment. I could see nobody else. "I thought—"

"—that I was in town? Yes, I had your tracker couriered there an hour ago. That's the risk with intel: if it's bad, it can count against you."

"You found it? But how—"

"I told you I know bugs. Like most things I said, I was telling the truth."

"OK. But how did you know to send it off exactly an hour ago?"

"Because I've been tracking *you*. C'mon, Jake, catch up."

"But I found your device."

She rolled her eyes and started walking down the stairs towards me. "You found *one* of them."

"Yeah, well that's why I'm here. This has got to stop. And you need to explain what on earth you're doing."

"We could have had this conversation at the Italian restaurant, but you didn't want to stay." She reached the bottom of the stairs. "Fancy a cup of tea?"

"For goodness sake, this isn't a game. I want the truth."

"Jake, I've already told you the truth." She walked past me into the kitchen area. Picking up a kettle, she appeared to judge it was full enough of water, then set it down and switched it on. "So many things in life appear to make no sense when you don't understand them properly."

"Who are you?"

She tipped her head. "My name is Susan Statham. I'm twenty-six years old. I went to a private school in Windsor, then to Oxford. From there I worked at a leading design agency in central London. Until I got bored."

"A real story of struggle."

"You could say I had a reasonably privileged upbringing. My dad left my mother ten years ago, taking all of our money with him, and I've no idea where he is, nor do I care. But it made me realise what's important in life."

"And your quest to put the world right? Why not start with tracking down your father?"

"That would put my mother through it all again." She shook her head. "I know you lost both your parents. That must suck."

"I'm sure you know a lot more than that. But I still don't know anything about you."

"Then put me through your process. Verify me." She nodded towards the desk. "You can use my computer. Run whatever tests you like."

"You knew I was coming. I expect that's a computer set up precisely for this purpose."

She shook her head and opened a jar with tea bags in it. "You're really not making this easy. Look, I will happily answer any question you have."

"Why?"

"Because if we can't be honest with each other then we can never work together."

"You're still after that? I just broke into your home."

She threw two tea bags into mugs and poured boiling water on top. "I am. I'm usually a really good judge of people: I thought I'd have at least piqued your interest by now."

I shook my head. "You've proved you can do some stuff, but what you did put us in danger. Messing with our system analysis meant we walked in on the Russians completely blind."

She blinked and turned away from the tea cups. "What Russians? I didn't do anything like that!"

"You said you'd be honest."

"I am! What would I have to gain? At least come up with something that makes sense."

"I've been hacked and you've been, by your own admission, hacking me…"

"If I wanted to get away with it, why would I have met you? Would I have left a business card which was an anagram of my name?"

I frowned. "So it was one of your team members who came over and left the card?"

"Was my performance that good?" She gave a mock bow.

"You? There was something familiar but I didn't—"

"I'm good with accents. Look, we all see what we expect to see. Even someone like you can't be switched on the whole time. When you meet your clients you're all revved up and super alert. Other times you're merely human." She turned back to the mugs. "Milk? Sugar?"

"No, thanks. I think I'll be leaving. I clearly can't trust my eyes or ears, biological or digital." I saw disappointment in her face and, despite everything, I was sure it was genuine.

She gave a tired shrug. "You do what you think is best. But clearly somebody else has been hacking you. Someone with an actual motive. Perhaps you should ask what that motive might be. What do you have that somebody else would want? It must be something very valuable."

"I have nothing like that."

"Perhaps. But maybe someone *thinks* you do."

"I think it's best if we stay out of each other's lives. If you're what you say you are, you don't want to be near me. And I mean that genuinely."

Susan rubbed her temples. "I'm sorry this didn't work out. And also for contributing to your 'Russian situation' in any way." She turned and opened a cupboard, pulling out a small, grey cardboard box. "By way of an apology, perhaps you might find these useful."

I took the box, feeling the weight of objects inside. "What are they?"

"Bugs like the one I placed on you. You could use them to track your team members."

"Why would I do that?"

"Somebody else has hacked you, Jake: you have to consider whether it was an inside job. Do you trust your people?"

"Yes."

"All of them? If they've got nothing to hide then why resist?"

"I promised them I would not bug them."

"What about safety? Do it so you can all know where you are if something goes wrong."

"It's not going to fly."

"Well, I'm going to place one of them on me and provide you with the tracking app. Then, if you change your mind, you can find me." She reached forward and squeezed my shoulder. "For whatever reason."

TWENTY-NINE

I don't remember much of the week after my father's funeral. It all passed in something of a blur. I drank a lot. I slept a lot. I achieved very little. What I do remember is the morning a week later when there was a loud and repeated knocking at my front door. I struggled down the stairs in my dressing gown, unshaven and unkempt. After several attempts, I got all the bolts undone and pulled the door open. Kieran stood there, wearing the stupid straw boater that he never seemed to take off.

"You look like shit," he said, tossing a coin in his right hand, then catching it with a snap. "Expect you feel that way too."

He'd texted me the day before to explain that the police were no longer questioning him so he was free to come and help me go through my father's stuff and get the house straight and tidy. I'd said no. He'd kept offering. Now here he was.

"You didn't need to come today," I said. "You must feel worse than I do. This can wait."

"We both have to start moving forward. And it gives me something to focus on."

I glanced behind him. He was alone. "Where's Liam?"

"Staying at another friend's. I've got the whole day if you want me."

I stepped back and gestured inside. "I'll make coffee."

"What about something to eat?"

"There's some tins of beans in the larder. Not much in the fridge – at least nothing much that's not past its use-by date."

He gave a loud sigh. "Get dressed. I'll buy you breakfast."

"I don't feel like going out."

He slapped me on the shoulder. "You've got to eat."

Ten minutes later we were tucking into full cooked breakfasts at a nearby cafe, washed down by what the New Zealand owner referred to as 'gum boot tea'. Neither of us spoke, as if we could pretend the world was normal once again.

Later, back in my house, I stopped in the middle of the narrow hall, refusing to let Kieran past. "So, what exactly happened? With the police?"

"The autopsy was inconclusive."

"What does that mean?"

"It means they think it wasn't an accident. But they can't prove it."

"But why would they–?"

He shook his head. "I really don't want to go into it."

"And they've dropped you as a… suspect?"

"Obviously. They can't even prove there was a crime.

I heard the detectives suggesting that meant only one thing. That it was a professional job."

"What? Your wife? Why?"

"We may never know. What about your father? Have there been any developments?"

"They've identified that the bomb was an adapted military design." I blinked and turned away. "But they've not made much more progress."

"Is there a link with Bernard Prebble?"

"Other than it went off outside his offices, they've not said." I hesitated. "He was a client, but then my father did business with a lot of people with a lot of money."

"Maybe he pissed off the wrong person."

"Maybe." I swallowed. "Could the two murders be connected?"

Kieran raised an eyebrow. "What would the connection be? Me? You?"

I sighed. "Yeah, I guess that seems unlikely."

"I mean, maybe I sold insurance to the wrong guy and this is payback but..." He tipped his head and gave an awkward smile.

I tried to laugh, but it felt forced. "Doesn't seem like the kind of business to create enemies. I just want to know what happened."

"Shall we stop making pointless guesses and actually sort your house out?"

"You're not going to stop pushing me around, are you?"

"Sometimes *Uncle Kieran* knows what's best for you."

We started in my father's home office. Kieran was like a force of nature. He pulled open drawers and cupboards, turning out all the contents with little restraint. We categorised everything into discard, sell or keep piles. I cleared all the folders from the office shelving, noting idly that those marked BP and BC - the ones I'd previously seen my father looking at - were no longer there. There were a lot of folders with receipts and invoices relating to the art dealing business.

"What about the gallery?" Kieran asked. "Do we need to go there as well?"

"He kept all his papers here, so there won't be much to go through. I believe the unsold paintings have been returned to their owners: they didn't hang around in claiming them. And the lease will expire at the end of the month, so basically nothing to do there."

He nodded and started riffling through one of the folders.

"Looking for something in particular?" I asked.

"Maybe there's an unpaid invoice. I'm sure you could use the money." He sighed and threw the folder into the discard pile, giving me a half smile. "Nothing."

"It's almost like you're enjoying this."

"When you pull off a band-aid, you do it with a flourish."

Eventually we finished in the office and moved to the master bedroom. In a few minutes we'd pulled out all the clothes and placed them in bags for charity.

"Did your father leave a will?" Kieran asked.

"Just a simple one. He left me everything, which beyond this house wasn't much."

"Sometimes people leave a 'to be opened in the event of my death' message. Something that could help explain what happened."

"No. There was nothing like that."

We continued through the house. In the spare

bedroom, Kieran pointed at two desks arrayed with computer equipment. "What did he have all these for?"

"These are mine."

"Geez, what a mess."

"They're old, but they work."

"You should set up a proper computing space. More secure. You're a genius, after all. Or at least that's what I always tell my friends."

"You do?"

"Almost as clever as me, I usually say."

"Thanks."

Finally we moved to the kitchen. Kieran started tapping away at the walls.

"What's up?" I asked. "Looking for secret passages?"

"Funny. Actually I was wondering if this was a solid wall. I know a guy. He'd give you a great price. Open the whole place up for you. Go on holiday for a month, come home and it'll be like you have a new house."

"I'm fine with how it is."

"Really? I thought you'd want to make a change." He opened the door to the storeroom. "What's that smell?"

"Cleaning products?" I shrugged, following him into the tiny room. "Maybe one of those tins is leaking."

Kieran stared at the shelves. "Soup, beans and custard. Seems unlikely." He lifted a box off the top shelf and placed it on the ground. Then he pulled out a large bowie knife and cut the tape closing it.

"Whoa," I said, looking at the twelve-inch blade in alarm. "Where'd you get that?"

He glanced at the knife almost distractedly. "Present from my father. It looks more serious than it is. I just use it as a box cutter." He lifted open the cardboard flaps. "More soup."

I pushed past him. "There's only one item of interest in here." I lifted up a cardboard cube printed with solid green lettering. FINEST SINGLE MALT.

"Now we're talking." He looked inside. "Hey, there're only two bottles left."

"A week ago there were several more. I'll share one of them with you today, if you like. The other I'm not drinking until I've found out what happened to my father."

He nodded. "Fair enough: he deserves another toast. He was a good man."

That was the end of our clear out. We drained the penultimate bottle, talking late into the night. While Kieran was all about moving on, about starting afresh, I knew that part of me could never do that. Not until I knew what had happened.

One day I swore that I would drink that last bottle – when I'd earned it.

THIRTY

After returning from Susan Statham's apartment, I slept fitfully. At 6am I gave up and called both Meg and Sid, conferencing us all.

"So, what happened last night?" Meg asked. "You said you were going to take care of things."

"Unfortunately I was mistaken. The devices we found at my house were unconnected. Which means we have to keep looking for the breach. Meg, can you complete the prep for our Paris trip?"

"You still want to go ahead with that?" she replied.

"We need to stay in business, but we should take additional precautions. We'll travel separately to make us harder to monitor. And make all the bookings from a completely separate computer system – pick an internet cafe at random or something."

"I'll reserve tickets for mid-afternoon on different airlines—"

"Actually, book me on the Eurostar."

"Fine. And separate hotels a few blocks apart?"

"Perfect. Sid, meet me at the office as soon as you can."

"Want me to bring anything?"

"I want you to bring everything."

Sid and I were first in at TechFixed. We got quickly to work in the server room and, within an hour, had all our systems disassembled and their components neatly arrayed on the meeting table.

We found three monitoring devices: crude but effective. Sid tugged at his ponytail in irritation, frowning at one of the small boxes that had been jacked into a motherboard. "This is a real amateur job. I'm almost insulted."

I shrugged. "There are no points for style in hacking."

"Well there should be."

"More importantly, who did it? And how long have these devices been there?"

"No more than two weeks because I did a system tear-down then."

"Two weeks is a long time," I said. "Could this have been Calum?"

"I don't buy it. He wasn't the type for a plan like this. Besides, he wouldn't have the capability." Sid looked around the room. "What is Lundy going to say when he sees all this?"

"He's not going to say anything because by 9am we will have it all put back together."

Sid puffed out his cheeks. "Sure. Even if it would take a normal human six hours."

"You're good with the impossible. That's why I keep throwing it at you." I paused. "Speaking of which, have you been able to progress that GPS project?"

Sid picked up one of the motherboards and frowned at it before slotting the processor back into place. "I have it working."

"That's great news."

"Unfortunately it's only going to work once. I can't prevent automatic alarms being raised. And, once they are, the system administrators will uncover the flaw. After that it either won't work or our usage will lead them straight to us. Probably both."

"You can't mask our identity?"

"There's no way of knowing it would work. Besides, they'll still shut it down. Call them eccentric, but the mobile network operators would rather the public can't access the location data of their users. They take that privacy stuff pretty seriously these days."

"Then I guess we'd best not use it unless we have no other choice."

"That would be wise. Now, are you going to let me get on with fixing things, or are you going to keep on asking questions about stuff that can wait?"

I laughed. "Will this solve the issue?"

"Without the devices we've removed, they have no way to monitor us, so yes."

"Good. Because I have a train to catch."

"Ah, yes. Paris! You sure you don't need a bag carrier?"

"Meg has already locked in her position on this trip," I said. "I need you here. You can check all the bags for bugs before we leave, if it's any consolation. And sweep everywhere else again."

"Always the one left behind," sighed Sid. "Bring me back an organic wholemeal croissant or something."

THIRTY-ONE

It was busier than usual at St Pancras International Station. I queued to collect my ticket, then queued again to get through check-in. I even started to worry that I might be held up enough to miss my train. However, the crowds proved to be a bonus: when I reached the check-in point, I was told that economy was overloaded and I was being upgraded. I challenge anyone to say that wouldn't put a smile on their face.

Forty minutes later the Eurostar eased out of St Pancras. I was right at the front of the train, in a four-seat booth with a table in the middle. I placed my luggage in the rack above, noting that the carriage was more than half-empty. Diagonally opposite from me, a middle-aged, severe-looking woman with wire-framed glasses and short grey hair sat reading a paper. There were a couple of businessmen in suits further down, someone who looked like a student and a wealthy-looking woman at the far end, glaring at me snootily. She probably thought I was in the wrong compartment.

I flicked open my laptop and started scanning

documents. I'm always careful reading anything in public, but I'd redacted all the really sensitive information and my laptop has a special privacy screen that dramatically narrows its viewable angles.

Time slipped past and, before I knew it, a sudden change in the wind noise told me that we'd entered the Tunnel. I looked up and saw intermittent lights flashing by. Then I noticed that both the wealthy-looking woman and the student had left the carriage. The two businessmen chose that moment to stand and walk towards me. Their suit jackets hid considerable muscular bulk. The severe-looking woman stared directly at me. I didn't like that look.

My instincts kicked in. I didn't know why this was happening, but I was being hemmed in. I moved, bounding the only way I could – towards the front of the train. I had few options: I was about to run out of train with only the engine itself in front. Then I stopped. Two similarly-dressed men were walking towards me. They must have been stationed in the engine carriage.

A woman's voice floated in the air. "Why don't you have a seat, Jake? You're not going anywhere."

My head jerked back and forth. She knew my name. Then I realised I recognised her. She had been in the coffee shop when I had first met with Gerald Meeks to discuss the recovery of the painting. And she had been there when I last met with Vince. Who on earth was she? I glared, then walked back to my seat. The first two men moved aside to allow me access, then stood blocking any further attempt to run. "I presume the seat upgrade was your idea?" I said. "No such thing as a free lunch, is there?"

"Indeed." Her voice was crisp and clipped.

Something about her looked familiar. "My name is Ellie Winslow."

I looked at the two men. "Exactly who are you, Ellie Winslow?" I brushed my fingers over my watch.

She reached into her jacket pocket and withdrew a leather wallet, which she flipped open on the table between us. I picked it up and examined it carefully. *Officer Ellie Jane Winslow, Security Service* – MI5 to most people. It looked genuine.

"How impressive," I said. "And what could you possibly want with me?"

"To engage your services."

"You need some IT support? Don't you have people in-house for that with higher security clearance?"

Winslow smiled. "Your other business-line. We want you to find something for us, Mr *Smith*."

My heart skipped. "I'm sorry, what?"

She took her ID back and pocketed it. "I expect that your first reaction will be that it's best not to say anything. You're probably wondering just how much I know about you. The answer is that I know a great deal. You are Jake Edward Moro, son of Charles and Celine Moro. You are an only child. Your mother died in 2010, of cancer. Your father was murdered in 2014. You've always been interested in computers, electronics: gadgets, if you will. You now work for an IT company that helps small businesses set up networked computing systems. But you also have an 'off the books' business. You find things for people: usually things that have been stolen. You call yourselves *Restitution*."

"You have a vivid imagination."

"I'm not known for it. And we've been watching you for some time."

"Why not just call me in for a meeting at your offices? Why all this…" I gestured around at the train carriage, and the men in suits, "…performance?"

"First, you wouldn't have come – borne out by your reluctance to talk to me now. Second, it should be no surprise that all our facilities are watched almost constantly. It wouldn't be ideal for us, or for you, to have your role in assisting us publicised. We prefer to keep matters discrete – as much for your benefit as ours."

"And what, exactly, do you want me to do?"

"This location isn't sufficiently secure to go into the details." Winslow slid a plain white business card over to me. "If you have any questions you can reach me on this number. Otherwise we'll be in touch within the next seven days."

"What makes you think I want to work with MI5?"

"We're confident we can persuade you." She stood and the two seated men rose in unison, joining their other two colleagues. I watched them leave the carriage, the men eyeing me closely, Winslow not looking back.

I did not bother to try and follow. I had nothing set up.

The train made an unscheduled stop shortly after emerging from the tunnel. I saw three figures climb out, one of them waved at my carriage as the train moved off. Stopping a Eurostar train: that was quite a trick. I'd have to check, but it seemed likely that Ellie Winslow was exactly who she said she was.

THIRTY-TWO

The yellow taxi dropped me two blocks from the Paris hotel Meg had booked me into: I never get drivers to drop me at the door of where I am staying. It adds another break in the chain if somebody is trying to follow me; it's good tradecraft, or so Meg once told me. Necessary or not, it made me feel professional and, given events on the Eurostar, a little more secure.

The hotel itself was well-located, clean and otherwise unremarkable. My room, north-facing on the 5th floor, was, like most budget Paris hotel rooms, hardly larger than the bed. There was a small desk and I hungrily set up my mobile office. Whenever I travel, I take a bag of standard 'survival kit' that I can't do without it. Some of it is hi-tech, some just basic common sense. I always pack multi-way plugs and extension leads, plus a couple of bright reading lights. I also bring powerful wifi scanners and a small satellite antenna, along with a pack of jasmine teabags for when I've simply had too much coffee.

For a data connection I rig up my mini-satellite dish,

for which I need a north-facing room. Within minutes I was up and running with secure super-high-bandwidth internet. In minutes I had what I needed. Agent Winslow appeared to be legitimate. Of course she was not actually listed as an MI5 agent but as a civil servant who worked in Whitehall. I could trace her education through public school, then Oxford. A deeper search would confirm the specifics of her MI5 role, but I could not be certain my current connection was sufficiently untraceable for that. Better to wait until I was back at one of my home facilities.

Next I played the recording of our conversation on the train. It still did not add up. Could I really offer MI5 anything that their own in-house people couldn't? Obviously I rated my own abilities, but I wasn't convinced. Were they actually investigating me? That was a distinct possibility. While my activities almost always had moral justice on their side, the reality was that the cold, hard eye of the law might view things differently. Scratch that: *would* view things differently.

I shook my head and turned my attention to the reason I was in Paris: my prospective client, Mr Jean Flaubert. We were scheduled to have coffee tomorrow morning at 8:30am. I looked at my watch and saw it was after midnight – time to try to get some rest. But I had to make a phone call first.

"Evening," replied Meg immediately. "Wondered when you might get around to calling in. You should have got there an hour ago. I've been at my hotel for nearly three."

"Yeah, well, you always were more efficient." I gave a small smile.

"Conferencing Sid in now."

"Hey, Boss," he said. "How's the steak tartare?"

"I prefer my meat with more heat through it," I replied. "Any news?"

"Yes, there is," Sid replied. "And it's of the good variety: Johnson has paid up."

I raised my eyebrows. "All £500k? Good news."

"Of course, the flip side is that we may have just agreed to sell a £3m necklace for £500k."

"It's not our place to question the job. It's done now."

Meg gave a sigh. "I still don't like it."

"Get it done, Sid."

"Understood," he replied. "That all?"

"Anything else you have to tell us?" Meg asked. "Anything at all?"

I thought of Winslow, then closed my eyes. "Nothing."

"Fine," she replied. "See you tomorrow."

"Looking forward to it."

THIRTY-THREE

I got up at 6:30am and went for a 5k run, mist rising off the streets as the city began to wake up. Running helped me think, and gave my body a jolt sufficient to cut one cup of coffee from my daily intake. I did a criss-cross loop, passing over Pont Neuf, skipping past Sainte Chapelle and the flying buttresses of Notre Dame, then heading back to the hotel. By 8am I was showered and making my way through the early morning crowds at a more leisurely pace. As I walked I sent a text message to the client, confirming the meeting location.

The traffic moved around me in a pattern that was alien: an angry buzz punctuated by horns and the occasional shout. I'd only been to Paris a few times, and I was reminded that this city breathed at its own pace, moved to its own rhythm. I was at a disadvantage here, and I knew I would do well to remember that.

Five minutes later I found the cafe near to Place de la Concorde and chose a patio table. All the seats were arrayed to look out at the street, in typical Parisian style.

I ordered a short, strong coffee and laid the grey dossier on the table: my background brief on Jean Flaubert, the journalist. Finally I turned on my earpiece and inserted it. "Good morning."

"Nice of you to turn up," Meg said, her voice echoing quietly in my ear.

"This is the agreed time." I spoke through gritted teeth, although it probably wasn't necessary. A few years ago sitting talking to yourself would have flagged you for attention. These days people assumed you were speaking on some type of phone headset. The world changed so quickly.

"What's up, Jake? You always arrive at least an hour early to check out the venue."

"I… needed a longer run this morning."

"Whatever. I'm happy just sitting up on this roof all day. You take your time."

"Roof?" I looked around. "Where exactly are you?"

"Seriously? Do you want to give me away? I have enough problems already: the signal keeps dropping in and out."

I stared at the crowded pavement in front of me. "Probably just the number of people: I'm sure the airwaves are saturated."

"Too late to worry now. Our client is due any minute. I'm not seeing anything on my cameras. You?"

I flicked my eyes around. "You'd think with the amount of money at stake he'd be prompt."

"Is this really the best place for a meet?"

I paused. "I wanted somewhere I wasn't going to get hemmed in."

"But it's also an environment we can't control. I don't like it."

"You supported coming to Paris. Have you changed your mind?"

"It's my job to be suspicious."

I swung my head back around and froze. There was a man standing in front of me.

"Monsieur Smith?" he asked in an accent that almost sounded *too* French.

I stared at his face. He was a match to the photo, but I still needed him to prove himself. "Who wants to know?"

He extended a hand. "Jean Flaubert. Thank you for meeting me today."

I gripped his hand briefly, then indicated the seat next to me. "Please."

He nodded and ordered a coffee, with more disdain than I was expecting. "Did you have a pleasant flight?"

"Actually I took the train." I paused. Flaubert was not looking around nervously. He was just looking intently at me. It was disconcerting.

"Ah yes. City centre to city centre, not beholden to the weather. But you do have to travel with the great unwashed." His coffee arrived, so quickly I thought they had made a mistake. It was as if they'd been expecting him. That was more than disconcerting. It was wrong. "Would you excuse me a moment? I need to use the toilet."

He blinked. "Of course. Through there."

I smiled and ducked inside the cafe. With a nod I threw a twenty euro note onto the counter, smiling at the unsmiling cashier and pointing with my thumb to the table outside. He snapped up the note, still not smiling. I shrugged and pushed open a fire door that was already slightly ajar. Then I was out on the street. I started running.

Meg's voice crackled in my ear. "What on earth is going on?"

"Something is wrong. He knew this place far too well. I only told him about it an hour ago. He wasn't nervous. This is a set up. I'm getting back to my hotel. The job is a bust. Assume you're being listened to. Burn your comms."

"What if you get into trouble?"

"I can take care of myself. I'll see you back home." I pulled out my earpiece, stamped on it, then ran on.

THIRTY-FOUR

I FOLLOWED A PRE-PLANNED ROUTE BACK TO MY HOTEL: A tortuous looping path more than three times the necessary distance. I used three Metro lines, two buses, and one taxi. The whole time I saw nobody following me. Was I being overcautious? Had I misjudged the situation and thrown away a perfectly good job? Was I just being extra jumpy after what had happened on the train? That was something to reflect on another day.

I reached my hotel, walked quickly past reception, then bounded up the stairs. Less than a minute later I was unlocking my door, breathing hard. There were two men in my room. They had the grim, flat expressions of people who were dangerous for money. I'd thought MI5 following me was bad news, but these people were not MI5, they were something else: fighting them would not be an option. At least if winning was a goal.

I smiled and leapt backwards, pulling the door closed. Oddly the two men did not rush to follow me. As I turned to run, I saw why. Two similar figures were standing in the corridor either side of me. I wasn't clear where they had come from. They each folded their arms without speaking and stood waiting.

I looked around, assessing my options. They weren't many. I could only go left or right, or back into my room. From down the hall I heard more voices. Who could afford so many goons? I was in a lot of trouble.

The man to my left suddenly groaned in pain and collapsed to his knees. Behind him stood a familiar figure, holding a baton. *Meg*.

I had never seen her look so dangerous.

She raised something in her other hand. At first I thought it was a gun, but then I saw it was made of black plastic. The other man started to back away.

"A taser?" said a voice from nearby. "Really? Jake, can you make this any harder?"

I stared. Jean Flaubert had appeared from another room. But now he was speaking with a decidedly British accent – one that I recognised.

"What the hell is going on?" I asked, moving to stand next to Meg. "Why are you here? I told you to go home."

"I was pretty sure you were going to get into some trouble." She waved the baton. "And I was right."

Flaubert shook his head. "If you'd just stayed at the cafe, we could have talked there. You were never in any danger. It's not how I work."

"Then why the heavies?" I asked.

Flaubert reached up and pulled off a wig then a layer of rubber: false nose and cheeks. I looked at him, stunned. The man who stood before me could easily afford the large number of security personnel. Although the last time I had last seen him in the flesh was at my father's funeral, I probably saw him on the news several times a week.

Flaubert was Bernard Prebble.

———

WE TOOK OVER A ROOM NEXT TO THE HOTEL BAR. Prebble's men sat outside, waving any curious hotel guests away. Meg sat out there too. She had been furious at the suggestion, but Prebble had been unmoved; eventually, she acquiesced.

"Shall we start again, Jake?" He indicated a seat and I cautiously lowered myself into it. He adjusted a very expensive suit and straightened a very expensive tie – somehow he'd managed to change in the minutes since we'd met outside my room. "My apologies for the deception in bringing you here. In case you're wondering, Jean Flaubert is a real person – one of my employees here in Paris actually. The background you will have checked out is entirely genuine. Mr Flaubert has the fortunate distinction of being approximately my height and weight, so I can disguise myself as him if I want to move around more freely. It's not easy being me, Jake." Prebble held his hands in the air. "Running a media group is a complicated business. I know the press likes to paint me as a villain. I'm sure your father did too, after our negotiations."

"He never discussed his dealings with you."

"Then that was very discrete of him, particularly after I screwed him on the commission he was trying to earn. But I'm sure he would have agreed that I'm really just a normal guy. I started with nothing and made my own fortune. Alas, now that I'm rich it's hard to be seen as likeable."

I stared across at the man in front of me, replete from too many opulent lunches and almost gleaming in clothes clearly handcrafted for him. "Why am I here?"

"Because I need your help."

"Why would you need *my* help?"

"For the same reasons anyone else might come to you. I love my family and I'd do anything to protect them."

"That doesn't really sound like my thing—"

"I need you to help me find my daughter."

I blinked. I'd read plenty about Prebble: there were stories in the press most days. His private life was pretty well known. "I thought you just had two sons."

"With my wife, yes. But I also had an affair." He placed a folder on the table and withdrew a five by seven photo showing a dark-haired, olive-skinned girl of about twenty. "My daughter, Ariadne. I want you to find her."

I glanced at the image, then slid the photo back towards him. "I'm sorry but there's been a mistake. I don't find people: I find *things* that have been stolen."

"What's the difference?"

"With missing people things get… complicated; it always involves law enforcement, and it rarely ends well."

"She is the most precious thing to me. And she *has* been stolen. She vanished four weeks ago. The authorities say it was not a kidnap because of the note." He sighed. "She left a handwritten message saying she was running away with her boyfriend. But I know my daughter. She did not go willingly."

I sipped from my coffee cup. "Have you considered making a public appeal for witnesses?"

Prebble placed his hand on the table. "I cannot do that without disclosing my connection to her. It would change her life. She'd never have any privacy; she'd never get any peace. She might never forgive me and then I'd lose her a different way. I will pay you whatever you ask. Just find her."

I sighed. "Mr Prebble, with all the wealth and resources at your disposal, there will be other people better suited to this task."

"I spent a lot of time with your father, before his death. When he was brokering that deal for me, he spoke about you quite a bit – in glowing terms." He straightened the knot on his tie. "Since then I've made it my business to keep an eye on you."

"You've been following me?

"That's not how I'd characterise it, and you certainly haven't made things easy. I had to go through three detective agencies before I found one that could keep up with you."

"Then hire them."

He shook his head. "You're who I need. You're smart and resourceful; you find a way to get things done. That's what I need right now to find my daughter."

"I gather you didn't agree with her choice of boyfriend?"

"I never trusted him, but what daughter listens to her father about her love life?"

"Does anyone else know about this?"

"Besides my closest aides, no one. I need it to stay that way."

I puffed out my cheeks. This was exactly why I did

not get involved in missing people matters. It was always more complicated than it appeared. I was sure I'd hardly scratched the surface. "I'm sorry, but I cannot take this on. Despite what you believe, she might not even *want* to be found."

"One million pounds."

"What?" I swallowed. "It's tempting, but I'm really not the right person—"

"Two million."

"That's ridiculous. Look—"

"Five million. Payable the moment you find her." He paused. "If that won't motivate you, nothing will."

I thought fast and hard. I could pay off Rouse. I could start over. I could pursue the path that Susan Statham had suggested. "I'll need an upfront payment of—"

"I didn't get rich by paying for things before they're done. Find my daughter, then you'll get your money." He adjusted his tie again. "I can assure you that I'm good for it."

"Send me everything you have and I'll look through it, but I'm not making any promises."

Prebble smiled. "Do this thing for me and, quite apart from your fee, I will remain indebted to you. One day I might be able to help you when you need it."

THIRTY-FIVE

Despite everything, or perhaps because of it, Meg still wanted to do dinner. She'd gone back to her hotel to change, leaving me with instructions to the restaurant, including the most important one: *don't be late*.

The restaurant was hidden between a *boulangerie* and a small *tabac*. It didn't even have a sign, which either meant it was run-down, or exclusive and expensive.

Of course it was the latter. Meg had recommended it with the phrase 'Don't get cheap on me now'. As I leafed through the menu, I started to wonder if I might need to collect on finding Prebble's daughter before I could afford the bill.

"Thought you'd start without me?" said a voice from behind my right ear. I still don't know how Meg could move so quietly; as usual, I hadn't heard a thing. I turned around to comment on this and blinked. She wore a slender black dress, elegant heels, and a silver pendant. Her red hair seemed to flash in the candlelight.

"I… er… wouldn't dream of it." I suddenly felt rather rumpled in the suit I'd been wearing all day.

"Oh, please, Jake," she said. "Don't pretend you're going soft on me." She slipped into the booth and grabbed the menu. Her fingers flicked the pages over then she pushed it aside. "I'm not ordering from this anyway. *Henri* is going to put something together for us."

"Been here before?"

"In a former life." She gave a gesture with her hand and a waiter glided over to us. A rapid conversation in French ensued, then he nodded and whirled away. He didn't spare me a glance.

"You made an impression. Or have you been here recently?"

"The former. If that's what I want to do, that's what I do. As for the latter, stop fishing, Jake. It's not part of our agreement." She took a sip from her glass of wine.

I glanced at her fingers around the wine glass. "And how much is this meal going to cost?"

She raised an eyebrow. "The important thing for you to know is that it's going to be worth every cent. Anyway, since Sid dropped the necklace off this morning, we should be celebrating. Although, after we've eaten, I may kill you for not insisting that I sit in with you and Prebble."

"After what you did to his guy, we're lucky he didn't have you arrested."

"You're kidding, right? I was saving your arse."

"True. And to be clear, I appreciate you coming after me. Even if it was exactly what I told you not to do." I reached out my hand to touch hers. She deftly flipped my palm over and started twisting my little finger several degrees beyond where it wanted to go. I stifled a yelp, gritting my teeth. "Do you *want* to hear about the meeting?"

She increased the pressure on my finger. "After you apologise."

I paused, forcing an expression of contrition on to my face. "I'm sorry, Meg. It was a mistake."

She nodded, and let go. "So what did our friendly neighbourhood billionaire want?"

"He has a recovery job for us."

"Bernard Prebble wanted your help? How would anyone manage to steal something from him?"

"It wasn't something: it was some*one*. He wants us to find his daughter."

She hesitated. "We don't do that."

"That's exactly what I told him. Then he said he'd pay us five million to overlook that fact." I paused. "It wasn't his first offer: I had to haggle."

She stared at her glass of wine, then knocked it back in a single motion. "Why?"

"He wants someone who thinks differently. He wants someone discrete."

Meg raised an eyebrow. "Does he know that the *someone* in question can't even keep his own secrets?"

I sucked in my lower lip.

She shook her head. "Anyway, why so much? If he's prepared to pay five million, then there's a catch. Is she in trouble? Is this a kidnap?"

"That's not clear. She left him a note, but he thinks it was forged. There's been no ransom demand. I think he just wants to know where she is and, to him, five million isn't a great deal of money."

She poured more wine into her glass. "Maybe we should be asking why he hasn't offered more."

I took a sip from my own glass, noting in passing that Meg certainly knew how to choose a Bordeaux.

"Perhaps we should just view this as a lucrative business opportunity. I'm sure Sid will relish the challenge."

"When someone offers you five million to do something that you're not an expert at, they probably have a goal other than the one you think they have. This is a man who supposedly defrauded his company's pension scheme, then tried to blame it on someone else."

"Nothing was ever proved."

"His complete lack of cooperation with the police didn't help."

I frowned. "So you're saying we should decline?"

"I'm saying we should be very, very careful." She closed her eyes. "Anything else you want to tell me about?"

The directness of her question caught me by surprise. Should I share my meeting with Ellie Winslow? I didn't want to unsettle my team even further. "Isn't the Prebble meeting enough?"

"I know Prebble was a client of your father."

I froze. "How would you know that?"

"Because I met Charles once. At a function with Prebble."

"You've… never said."

"There wasn't much to tell. I shook his hand. Didn't really have a conversation. I was there with a client of mine. I used to work as a private bodyguard. I presumed you'd worked that out."

I shrugged. "I've respected your privacy. Didn't realise you were doing the opposite."

"Don't exaggerate. Anyway, after all the jobs we've done, you still tell me nothing. Like why you surround yourself with a bunch of people you know very little about, and all to recover property stolen from people who mean nothing to you. *Why* do you do what you do?"

"That's my business."

"Until that business affects my business." Her lip curled. "My point is that *you* need to open up to us more or we can't help you. Otherwise we'll start to wonder if we can trust you. Look what happened with Calum."

"We're better off without him."

"I don't disagree, but my point is still valid."

I leaned towards her. "I trust you with my life. I just have trouble opening up to people. Even those closest to me."

She blinked. "So I'm one of those closest to you? Even though you know almost nothing about me."

"After all the jobs we've done, I think your actions have revealed the real you."

She stared at me then took a sip of her wine. "OK. Then why am I working with you?"

I folded my arms. "Because you enjoy it. Because you're good at it. I think the money helps you not have to do something else."

"Fine." She interlaced her fingers. "And since we're playing therapists, you seem like someone who isn't doing what he wants to do."

I shrugged. "Bernard Prebble is not my ideal client. I know we try to pitch it that we are righting a wrong, but maybe that should be our sole focus – just to do 'good'. Why limit it to people who can pay?"

"Because we're not a charity."

"Yeah, I guess. And if we went all altruistic, you probably wouldn't hang around."

She laughed. "Probably not. You can count on me to think of myself."

"And that is why I trust you."

"I believe you." Meg looked back into my eyes. "Be careful how you dole that out."

"Trust?"

"I'm just saying there's a quid pro quo. It's a great idea, to want to give your trust. But sometimes you will be disappointed."

"Talking from experience?"

"Trusting the wrong people can be your undoing."

"Ironically my father used to say that, too." I shook my head. "Everything keeps coming back to Calum - trusting him was our big mistake."

She took a drink of her wine. "I'm still not sure I can credit him with causing all our problems. The drug dealers, Prebble… There's a bigger picture than a disgruntled team-mate."

I sighed. "All this because I want to make things right."

Meg ran a hand through her red hair. "Don't we all?" She looked, looking over her shoulder and signalling to the waiter. "Speaking of which, I'm starving. Let's eat."

THIRTY-SIX

My journey back to London was uneventful. This time I was not accosted by intelligence agencies or errant billionaires. It was almost disappointing.

I called ahead to the office and briefed Sid about getting everyone together. Meg had flown in earlier and was already with him at TechFixed. Daniel was due in shortly. He wasn't at all happy about having to spend some of his time doing data entry for the accounts department, but we'd persuaded him it was a necessary part of his cover. Besides, if we were to talk freely we needed somewhere secure, which meant we had to use the TechFixed server room. Sid had swept it half a dozen times in the last twenty-four hours and swore it was clean.

On the final leg of my journey – the train from Waterloo – I got a message from Kieran. He wanted to meet for a coffee while he was in London for work. I stared at the message. Kieran did not usually ask to catch up. Especially not on short notice. I wondered what was wrong. I really didn't need any new problems right now.

When I walked into the TechFixed office at 11:45am, I saw that Lundy had already gone out for lunch, so, with a quick hand signal, we all moved to the back of the premises.

"We have a new project," I said, after Meg closed the server-room door.

"After the diamond job, I thought we might be taking things cautiously," Sid said, adjusting his wire-framed glasses. "Are we really sure we're no longer being hacked?"

I narrowed my eyes. "Didn't you look through all the systems? We found the cause. And we'll make damn sure it doesn't happen again."

"So what's the new job?" Daniel asked.

I quickly summarised my meeting with Prebble. When I finished, there was silence. I forced a smile onto my face. "This is a real opportunity."

"I'm always wary when anyone feels compelled to say that," Sid said, fiddling with his ponytail. "Are you trying to convince yourself or us?"

"I thought you were all for making the big bucks?" I said.

"I heard Prebble's a crook," Daniel said.

I shrugged. "Face to face he seemed a lot more pleasant than the press paints him."

"Some people describe Prebble as a criminal who went respectable," Meg said. "Others say he's only one of those two things. And not the second one."

"He seemed like a father looking for his daughter. He seemed genuine."

Meg snorted. "If you say so."

I cleared my throat. "I'm sure it goes without saying that this is somewhat more sensitive than our usual work – the diamond necklace situation aside. Prebble has money to throw around messing us up if we fail."

"So, yeah," Daniel said, "as I was saying, is this really a good idea?"

I frowned. "That's a very good point. If we're going to do this, we all need to be on board."

"You can't argue with the upside," Meg said.

"I'm not so sure," Sid replied. "This feels different. Plus the money isn't real unless we actually find her. And our systems aren't tuned to finding people."

"Then we adapt them," I said. "For this money it will be worth it."

"Will it?" Daniel shrugged. "You said your team likes to avoid complications. Surely finding people will involve complications? It isn't the same as recovering an item."

Sid folded his arms. "You probably wish Calum were here to add his thoughts."

"I'm not quite at that point," I said. "I hadn't expected you both to be quite so cautious though."

"Really? After the Russian encounter? Normally you'd have turned this thing down on the spot," Sid said. "You seem to be making some questionable decisions lately. This goes against our purpose and we've just had a big score. What's the urgency?"

I closed my eyes. "You can never plan when the next job comes in. We should consider each opportunity fairly. Let's mull it over for the day before making a decision. In the meantime, we'll pay everyone for the diamond job." I pointed to Sid's laptop. "Call up the accounts: let's do the transfers." There were smiles around the table.

Meg leaned close and whispered, "Nice work, boss. Wear them down gradually. Then show them the money."

"They earned it," I said. "We all did—"

"Er, Jake," Sid said.

When Sid said 'er' it was rarely good. I walked round to look at his laptop. "What?"

"The money has gone."

I blinked. "What money has gone?" Sid almost swallowed his words. "The five hundred grand from Edgar Johnson."

Meg swore and moved next to me. Daniel's face went white.

"What are you talking about?" I said. "How can it be gone?"

Sid screwed his hands into fists. I'd never seen him look so agitated. "I don't know. What I *do* know is that it appeared in our account yesterday." He sounded like he might be sick. "If it hadn't, I wouldn't have told Meg to arrange the drop-off of the necklace."

"Call the bank," I said. "It's probably their error."

"Yes," said Sid, sounding unconvinced.

But five minutes later we knew that there had been no mistake. The bank's systems had no record of any such transfer. It had been a ghost.

"How did this happen?" I asked.

"I have no idea," Sid replied. "But it looks like we've been hacked again."

"I thought we removed the bad chips!"

"Apparently that didn't stop it. And now we've lost the money and the necklace." He looked like he might cry. "I don't know what else to do."

"I do." I pulled out my phone and dialled a number

that I had added only recently. It was answered almost immediately. I tapped the speakerphone function and a thin voice filled the room.

"Edgar Johnson speaking."

I cleared my throat. "Mr Johnson, it's John Smith."

"Thank you so much for the excellent work recovering my item. Is everything OK? I thought our business was at an end. At least until I have another problem for you to fix."

"Actually there's been a complication with our payment."

"Oh?"

"It seems to have… bounced back."

There was a pause. "How embarrassing. I'll look straight into that. Actually, tell you what," continued Johnson, "why don't you come to my office tomorrow morning first thing and we'll get everything straightened out?"

Sid raised his eyebrows in a hopeful expression.

"Sure," I replied. "That would be great."

"See you at 8am. I'll provide the coffee."

The phone cut off and I stared at it.

Meg shook her head. "This isn't adding up. Can you use that bug you left behind to listen in on what he's doing now?"

I shook my head. "Battery will be flat by now. Look, he *said* he'll straighten it out."

"Let's hope so."

THIRTY-SEVEN

Despite everything going on, I still needed to meet with Kieran. If I couldn't make time for him, then who could I make time for? I arranged to call in at his work at 4pm.

The car showroom was one of three on Park Lane. Through the immense plate-glass windows Porsches, Ferraris and Aston Martins gleamed under the intense lights. Everything was arranged to show each vehicle to optimum effect. I shook my head as I looked at them: an unreachable luxury for the huge majority staring in. Of course there were still enough people with the money to buy one – the kind of people my father had been trying to attract to his art gallery.

I stepped through the automatic glass doors and Kieran, alert as always, immediately saw me. He approached, immaculate in a sharply-pressed suit and a sleek navy tie. Only his name tag ruined the executive image. At least he wasn't wearing his stupid hat.

"Ready for that coffee?" I asked.

"I really appreciate you coming in." He looked around. "But I can't leave the sales floor right now. My manager is in drill-sergeant mode." Kieran leaned forward, lowering his voice. "But numbers are up, so maybe he's onto something."

I shrugged. "Money is important." I straightened. "Why don't I act like a customer, then you'll have to talk to me." I walked over to the nearest car, a black Ferrari 458 Spider, according to the info plaque. "How much is this one?"

"If you have to ask, Jake, you can't—"

"How much?"

"For 650 BHP, a 5.8 litre V12 engine, active suspension and a Blaupunkt 16 speaker stereo system? For an unparalleled driving experience that will make you forget—"

I cleared my throat. "That was every number but the price."

"We never just give it out."

"Make an exception."

He glanced around. "Fine. It's listed at £195k, plus VAT. And if you order today, there's a fourteen-month waiting list."

I whistled. "What about hiring it?"

Kieran laughed. "Try AVIS down the road."

"So if you wanted one sooner, you'd have to steal it?"

"Good luck with that. They have a proprietary tracking system, with data nodes hidden at three different places within every vehicle. Unless you get very lucky or know exactly what you're doing, it would take you several hours to find them, by which point you'd be under arrest. You might be able to steal it, but you wouldn't get to keep it."

"Almost seems unfair."

"Ferrari don't like their cars being stolen. It's bad for the image."

"Nothing's unhackable," I said.

"Well, I wouldn't know. I mean, do I look like a criminal?" Kieran lowered his voice. "Not that we don't get a few in here, I'm sure. They're the ones with the money to blow these days."

"So, what did you want to talk about?"

He beckoned me over to a gleaming table, pulling a brochure book from a shelf, keeping up the pretence. His gaze lowered to the table. "This is a bit embarrassing actually."

I stared at him. Kieran wasn't normally embarrassed by anything. "Go on."

"I got into a poker game with some friends of friends. One thing led to another and, well…"

"How much did you lose?"

"A few thousand." He blinked, like the words were stuck in his throat. "Quite a few thousand. More than I have to hand. They don't seem to be the kind of people who you can stall for very long."

I ran a hand through my hair. "So what are you asking? Do you want to borrow money?"

Kieran puffed out his cheeks. "No. Of course not. At least not from you. I wouldn't put you in that position. Unless you have a spare hundred grand kicking around."

"A hundred grand?" I gasped.

"That was just a figure of speech." He sighed. "Look, I wondered if you knew anyone who would be prepared to lend it on a short-term basis."

"You think I know someone rich? You're the one

who works in luxury-car sales. Kieran, how did you let this happen?"

"I guess I don't like to lose. I kind of got caught in the moment."

"Who are these people? The ones you owe money to."

He flicked a glance at his boss across the room then leant forward to open the brochure in front of me, pretending to point to some fact or figure. "Just have a think. If some idea strikes home, maybe we can give it a shot."

I stood up. "Sure, Kieran. I'll think about it, but I'm not sure it's going to do much good."

He rose and gripped my shoulder. "You're the best."

"If only we could say that of your card playing. Although I remember you being unbeatable when we were younger."

He tilted his head to one side. "I was."

"I guess you just weren't ready for the big leagues."

"Oh it was just bad luck." He grinned awkwardly.

I forced a smiled, removing a slim cardboard box from my pocket and sliding it across the table. "A special 'secret agent' phone I had made up for Liam. Tell him it's so we can contact each other in the interests of national security: it's connected to my top-secret satellite wrist-phone."

"You and your imagination. I'll make sure he gets it."

I walked out of the showroom and headed south towards Hyde Park Corner.

I now had two new big problems. First, the money Kieran had lost.

And second, the fact that – while Kieran thought I didn't know - this was not the first time he had landed himself in this type of trouble.

THIRTY-EIGHT

My life changed forever the day my father died. But that was the kind of change that I had no choice in. There was also a day that my life changed in a different way, even if it wasn't apparent in the moment.

It was a couple of months after my father's funeral. I had arrived at Kieran's house in Twickenham mid-morning. We both had the day off work and Liam was at pre-school, so we were going to have a lazy lunch. As I walked up to the front door it opened and a large figure in a hoodie pushed straight past me. He kept his face low, hands in his pockets, yet there was something familiar about him. I watched him walk quickly up the street and out of sight. I turned and knocked on the half-open door. "Kieran? You all right?"

There was silence for a moment, then a weak reply. "Gimme a minute."

Something in his tone made me march into the kitchen. I found him leaning over the sink, blood dripping from his nose. "What the hell?" I asked.

"I did tell you to wait. Thought you might be squeamish. What are you doing here?"

"We're having lunch?"

"Oh, yeah. Slipped my mind."

"What happened to you? Who was that guy?"

"What guy?" He dabbed at his nose with a wad of kitchen towel. His whole face was swollen.

"The huge man wearing a hoodie."

"Door-to-door sales. Cleaning products or something."

"You let him into the house while you were bleeding all over?"

"It didn't happen until after. Look, he left and then I… tripped over one of Liam's toys and fell onto the coffee table." He winced.

"That looks nasty." I peered closer. "You should get some ice on it, you might even need stitches. Are you sure you got that from hitting a table?"

"I'll be fine in a minute. Then we can head out."

I stared at him. Then I pulled my phone from my pocket and pretended to read the screen. "I'm sorry, something's come up. Let's do this another day."

"Oh? That's a shame…"

I was already out of the house, moving fast. Kieran was hiding something – something that had got him hurt. If I could catch up with the man in the hoodie, maybe I could get some answers.

I reached Twickenham High Street and looked around. There were many, many people and no sign of my target. Perhaps I was too late. I started looking in cafes and pubs, just in case he had ducked into one of them.

Nothing.

I cursed and kicked at a metal lamp post. It jarred as I did so and, above me, something rattled. My eyes were drawn upwards and I saw a CCTV camera positioned to capture the street.

All I needed to do was work out how to access it.

Although my skills were anything but well-honed at that point, it wasn't my first foray into building devices that could tap into other electronic systems. It took me three days to crack the CCTV camera's security, working from a cafe across the road. Looking back, three days seems painfully slow. But, at the time, I was new to the whole game.

The footage was better quality than I was expecting. I watched the man in the hoodie walk up the High Street, standing outside a pub for two minutes then climb into a stretched black Mercedes. And as he did, he pulled the hood back, revealing his face. Heavy jowls, grim expression. I felt the air cool. It was the man who had punched me in the stomach at my father's funeral: one of Maxwell Rouse's henchmen.

I reached into my pocket and pulled out my wallet. Then I extracted a business card I had not thought I would be needing.

The black Mercedes picked me up from a car park on a disused trading estate. I climbed in the back, noting the seats were arranged so four people could face each other in comfort – although I was pretty sure I wasn't going to be feeling comfortable for very long. I was pointed emphatically to one of the rear-facing seats, next to the huge man who'd beaten Kieran. Opposite was Maxwell Rouse, resplendent in a dark three-piece suit. Away from the atmosphere of a funeral, he was somehow even more menacing.

"Jake," he said, furrowing his heavy eyebrows. "I was hoping to hear from you sooner."

"I never found anything about any money my dad owed you, so I had nothing to tell you."

"I'm sensing from your tone that that hasn't changed. So why call now?"

"Your man here paid a visit to my cousin, Kieran. Broke his nose. I want to know why."

Rouse looked at his henchman. "Vince? Did you do this?"

Vince shrugged. "I think it was an accident involving a door."

I forced myself to stay calm. "I want you to stop hurting him."

"That is touching. But if Vince visited him, then he owes us a sum of money."

"How much?"

Rouse glanced at Vince and smiled. "Why don't you ask your cousin?"

"He won't even admit there's a problem."

"Because he's not stupid. He knows how this works. You should stay out of it."

"How *much*?"

A smile crossed Rouse's face. "Two million, plus some change."

"How the hell did he manage that?"

"Poker. In a single night. Your cousin is nowhere near as good as he likes to think he is."

I swallowed. "You just let him run up a debt like that? What made you think he could pay?"

"We didn't make him do anything."

"You're barbaric. He has a kid, for goodness sake." I stared out of the window of the car.

"Be glad it's not your problem."

"I'm making it my problem."

Next to me I sensed Vince shifting.

Rouse frowned. "Oh? Is that some kind of threat?"

I swallowed. "That wasn't what I meant. I was asking, what if I pay?"

"Two million pounds. What are you going to do? Rob a bank?"

"Isn't that *my* business?"

"Let's just assume for a minute that you can find the money. And that I agree. When could I expect payment?"

"Give me six months."

"I love how you think this is a negotiation." Rouse smiled. "You can have one. Take it or leave it."

"And if I leave it, you break Kieran's legs but you don't get any money. Which would you prefer?"

Rouse inclined his head. "Go on."

"Give me three months to make a first payment. 50k. I'll pay you faster if I can."

Rouse sighed. "Like I said, you get one month. And I'll expect 50k every month after that. Vince here is going to become your new best friend. He'll call you to arrange collection. And if you're late, Vince will give you more than a bloody nose."

THIRTY-NINE

Meg and I arrived at Edgar Johnson's concrete and glass office building at 7:58am. Sid and Daniel were in the van, parked a hundred yards away: well within range for Sid's box of tricks. We would not go into this blind or stupid. If things did not go as planned, we would make Johnson reconsider whatever he was up to.

"Good to go?" I asked Meg.

She nodded. "Let's go get our money."

We walked up to the main entrance, then stopped abruptly. The automatic sliding doors had not opened. Frowning, I tried the manual door to the left. It seemed to be locked.

"What is going on?" Meg peered through the doors. "I can't see anybody inside."

"Fire drill?" I offered, not really believing it.

"There'd be people outside." She looked around. "And there's no-one."

From the right a uniformed security guard, with a beard and a heavy cap, walked over to us. "Can I help you?" he asked in a gravelly voice.

I forced a smile. "We have a meeting here with Edgar Johnson. His office is on the top floor."

The man looked confused. "This building is vacant."

"Since when?"

"More than a year. Last tenant went bust. If you want to view the premises, you'll need to speak to the agent."

"Is this some kind of a joke?" Meg said, almost spitting. "Mr Johnson's idea of a game?"

"I'm sorry, I don't know who that is." He adjusted his belt. "Now if you could move along—"

"Nobody tells me to—"

I gently gripped Meg's arm and guided her away. "Leave it. There's no point shouting at the guard."

She glared at me but did not reply. As we walked, I glanced over my shoulder at the building, starting to feel distinctly uncomfortable. This was something I would do: take over a vacant office building and set it up as a temporary office space. If you did it right you were untraceable.

We had researched Johnson thoroughly. We had run checks on computers completely separate from our own. There was no possibility our research was wrong. So why would Johnson need to fake his office premises? Unless the person I had met with was not Edgar Johnson.

"What just happened?" Sid asked through my earpiece.

"I don't know. The office building is vacant. Johnson only made it look like he was operating there."

"What? How did he do that?"

"I'm not sure. But the bigger question is why he did it."

As we reached our van, I saw another larger van had parked behind it. The side door slid open and a man in a suit stepped out. Both Meg and I froze, dumbstruck.

Edgar Johnson raised his hand in a half wave. "Morning, Jake, Meg."

"What the…" I began, then stopped. Johnson had used our real names.

"We really need to get you up to speed," he said, pulling at his face. The beard, nose and eyebrows peeled away. The change was subtle and I realised now why something had seemed familiar.

Edgar Johnson was really Gerald Meeks.

"What is going on here?" I asked.

Meeks removed a patch on his throat – a voice-box, just like I used in my disguises to alter my voice. "You've been played, Jake. But when you swim with the sharks, sometimes you meet one bigger than you."

Meg took a step forward, balling her fists. "And yet you came here alone. Perhaps that was unwise."

"Not entirely alone." He raised his hand and beckoned.

The security guard strolled up to us. Before I could speak, he was pulling off his cap, then his beard. *Calum*.

Meg lunged forward, faster than I could follow. But Calum calmly stepped aside, grabbed her arm and twisted it behind her, slamming her against the side of the van.

"I missed you too!" he said into her ear.

"Let her go," I shouted, "or I'll… call the police."

Meeks and Calum just laughed.

"Is this all because I didn't give you the painting?" I asked Meeks. "I'm not sure you even want it."

"You're right. I just wanted my wife's lover not to

have it. This isn't all about the painting. This is about something I cooked up after Calum contacted me, so why don't we all sit down and have a proper conversation? I did say I'd provide the coffee." He nodded to our van. "Your other friends can come too. Rest assured, it's all going to make sense soon."

FORTY

We all walked two streets over to a basement cafe that bore no signage and, perhaps unsurprisingly, had no-one in it. The lady behind the counter filled a large cafetiere, placed it on the table in front of us along with six mugs, then vanished out back. Calum locked the front door then stood next to it, his arms folded.

"So," Meeks said, "here we all are. My new best friends."

"You wish," Meg muttered. "Because you can go shove—"

"It might be smart to hear me out before you start with the threats."

I placed my hands flat on the table. "Say what you have to say."

"Perhaps I should start with a little context. Calum here approached me after I initially contacted you. He said you were a capable guy with some talented people. But that you weren't exploiting your combined talents fully. And that, in my eyes, was an opportunity. So I asked Calum for more information, did my own research, and it became clear he was right."

"You met with Calum before us?" I asked. "So when we met – that was all a set-up?"

"It was a test of sorts. I wanted to see if you properly valued what you do. Since you didn't, that gave me an opportunity to insert myself into the process to add value. And margin."

"You don't understand. Our business is about putting things right."

"You can kid yourself, Jake. You can call yourself a vigilante, a modern-day Robin Hood, or whatever. But the truth is that you have a particular set of skills and you should be charging appropriately for them."

Meg scowled. "Even if we were to do things differently, we wouldn't work with you."

"If a client wants to know where the item was recovered, what do we care?" Calum said. "If a client can afford a huge payment, who are we to argue? And yet you wouldn't accept when Meeks doubled the offer for his wife's painting."

"What?" Sid cried. "You didn't even discuss it with us."

"If," I said with a scowl, "we do that, we will attract the attention of organised crime. Both because of the money we're charging, and because they could use us to provide intelligence on high-value targets."

"That's a problem for the future, *if* it ever happens."

"It will."

"Not if you're careful," Meeks said. "Of course you'd have to be much more careful than you have been. Calum and I rather took your operation apart."

"Because Calum had access to everything," I said.

"Life isn't fair. What's your point?"

"Did you even want the painting back?"

"Only to stop Bickerstaff having it."

Meg slapped her hand on the desk. "Johnson checked out."

I shook my head. "But he's not Johnson, so our intel didn't uncover the right data."

"Also my experience in banking means I'm good at faking financial records and payments. You're an amateur moving into the big leagues, and you need help."

"I'd never work with you." I looked at the others. "None of us would."

"I'm not giving you a choice."

"Where is our money for the necklace job?" Sid asked.

"Really?" Meeks asked. "You're serious?"

I took a slow breath.

Meeks smiled. "Thank you again for recovering *all* my missing property."

"I hope your *girlfriend* was pleased," Meg said icily. "If she's even real."

"Did you like my performance? Oscar-worthy, I thought."

I stood up. "The necklace was never yours, was it?"

Meeks smiled.

I ground my teeth together. "You mean we just stole it then? You know that's not what we do. Do you know who we took it from? One of us could have been killed."

"You undersell yourself. It was a well-managed, well-executed operation."

"It was not what we signed up for."

"Jake," Calum said, "I'm sure you're upset. I would be too, knowing that somebody else was three steps ahead of me."

"You caught us by surprise. It won't happen again."

Meeks leaned back in his seat. "Jake, I don't want there to be any misunderstandings. You're part of my team now." He pointed at Meg, Sid and Daniel. "All of you. You'll take on the jobs I ask of you."

Meg's eyes flashed. "*Not* going to happen."

"If you don't," Meeks spread his hands, "it's really a question of who I go to first. The police? The drug dealers?"

I stared at Meg. Her expression suggested she might go for Meeks' throat, even though Calum could probably take us both down one-handed. I closed my eyes. "Before we discuss anything else, you owe us our share of the 500k!"

A smile crossed Meeks' face. "Think of it as the price of admission."

"I… *we* need that money."

"Oh I know, Jake. It's amazing the things we've discovered since we've been monitoring you. Although I'm sure you don't want us discussing them in front of your team."

"What's he talking about?" asked Meg.

"He's saying whatever he needs to, to freak us out."

"Tell you what," said Meeks. "Why don't I give you all a chance to mull this over? Say forty-eight hours?"

"And then what?"

"Then we'll talk about the next job and how we can all make some money." He paused. "Alternatively, I can see to it that you are locked up. Or worse."

"Don't try anything smart," said Calum. "We're three steps ahead, remember?"

I looked at him. That was going to change. It wasn't the first time. I'd had to do something radical to solve a problem.

FORTY-ONE

Three weeks after I'd made the deal with Rouse to pay Kieran's debt, I was running out of options as to how I was going to get even the first fifty thousand. I had stupidly thought that I might be able to restart my father's gallery and make some quick cash. But the landlord had no interest in granting me a new lease and as for my father's old clients, they didn't know me, and other dealers had already pried away their business. Finding new clients was impossible: there was no reason anyone would deal with some kid who had no particular knowledge or interest in art. I couldn't even sustain a bluff. If I was going to earn money, it would need to be doing something I was good at.

Of course I had scoured the house again to see if my father had hidden any money. But Kieran and I had already been thorough and there was nothing else to be found. Even if I cashed in all my savings, it wouldn't cover the first instalment. I could try to sell the house, but that would take time and it would barely cover a quarter of what Kieran owed. It wouldn't solve anything. I had to come up with something better.

The one bright spot was that I had been offered a job. Shortly after I'd finished calling all my father's former customers, I got what I thought was a call back, but it was someone I'd never heard of: Bill Lundy. He said I'd been recommended by a friend to work for his IT services company as a technician. The money wasn't bad, though it was nothing like enough to pay Rouse. I thanked him and said I'd think about it.

Then I got another phone call. And it *was* from one of my father's old clients. He said he was too busy to worry about new paintings: he'd just had one stolen. The painting was insured, but that wasn't the point. It was an original. He wanted it back. He asked me if I might be able to track it down.

"Why would you think I could do that?" I asked.

"Your father was known as a man with connections into the… underworld. Perhaps you know people too."

"I'm sorry, but I'm not the—"

"Obviously I wouldn't expect you to comment over the phone. But if I were to get the painting back, I'd be willing to cover your expenses." He paused. "Would one hundred thousand cover it?"

"That would certainly—"

"So you'll do it?"

I swallowed. "I'll see what I can do."

I put the phone down. My immediate thought was that Rouse, as a crime boss, might know where it was. But I couldn't very well go to Rouse. If he did know anything, he was hardly likely to help.

I thought back to how I had used the CCTV cameras to identify Vince leaving Kieran's apartment.

Cameras like that were everywhere. Data of every conceivable kind was stored, ready to be searched. I knew computers. I knew systems. Perhaps I could bring my skills together in a way that would bring results. And while I was at it, in a small way I'd be striking back at criminals like Rouse: undoing what they'd done. Most importantly, if I could do it right once, I could do it again.

That very first mission was nearly a disaster. But it laid the groundwork for what was to follow. I made a lot of mistakes, but I also got lucky. I got the painting. My ecstatic client paid up without hesitation. And I was able to make the first payment to Rouse.

"Your cousin doesn't deserve you," Vince said, as I handed over the money.

"He's been there for me in the past," I said. "I'm just returning the favour."

He riffled the notes in his huge hands and nodded approvingly. "You're fighting someone else's battles, Jake. You should be careful where that leads."

At the time I didn't realise quite how prescient those words would prove to be.

FORTY-TWO

I DROVE WITHOUT KNOWING WHERE I WAS GOING UNTIL I found myself pulling up in one of the car parks in the vast reaches of Richmond Park. The morning mist had burned away, but the ground was still damp from recent rain; the smell of earth and leaves rising around us.

It was a place I often came to get clarity. Which was why I had brought Meg, Sid and Daniel here. In the middle of the week there was almost nobody around: other than a group of disinterested deer, we were alone. We left the van and crunched along a gravel path, a vast expanse of grassland on either side. A few minutes later, we reached a small group of trees, one of which had fallen years before in a particularly fierce storm. I turned and sat on the crumbling remnants of the trunk, trying to find the right words. They did not come. Instead I picked up a dead branch and tried to snap it. "Who wants to go first?"

We all just stared at each other for several long moments. Finally Meg spoke. "We've been royally screwed, wouldn't you say?"

I shook my head. "Calum was with us for over two years. Did any of us think he was smart enough to dupe us the whole time?"

"That's just it," Meg replied. "It wasn't the whole time. Things changed. But we should have spotted something was amiss. There must have been clues." She snatched the branch from my hands. "You're too trusting, too willing to see the good in people."

I glared at her. "So, what? I should be a complete cynic? Perhaps I shouldn't trust any of you either?"

Her jaw hardened. "What do you mean?"

Sid coughed. "Look, let's keep some perspective. Maybe things aren't so bad. It's not like they're stopping us working."

Meg spun towards him. "Did you not hear what was said in there? Do you not understand what has changed?"

"What I understand is that we can either cut him in on our jobs or we can go to jail. I think that summarises things."

I folded my arms. "We're not working for another criminal."

"*Another* criminal?" Meg asked. "What do you mean?"

I blinked. "Nothing. We're just not doing it. We don't know where it will lead."

"Perhaps to more money?" Sid suggested.

"What's with you?" I asked. "Are you part of his team now?" I turned to Daniel. "And you're not exactly offering any opinions. What do you think?"

He scratched his shaved head, his eyes flickering to Meg. "I'm more of a do-er. Just tell me what to do that doesn't involve prison."

"Great, really helpful. My point is, it's not going to help getting angry, any more than it will help to go along with what he wants. We have to fight back."

Meg narrowed her eyes. "Meeks is rich: he has resources. And he's got the march on us. He's probably still bugging our systems. With Calum's help too, who knows what he knows? And are we sure that we don't have any other problems?"

I hesitated. Should I mention my encounter with Winslow? I trusted my team, and I didn't like having secrets from them, but right now wasn't the time for further bad news. "I agree we're behind, but we can still catch up. We need to go back over our systems. We need to stop every leak. After all, our situation has improved in one key respect. Meeks has shown his hand. We know what he's doing now."

"Big deal. We don't have the funds to do anything."

"That's exactly why we need to get cash into the business, so I've come to a decision."

Sid reached forward and slapped me on the arm. "It's the right decision, Jake."

"What?" Meg asked.

"We're going to replace all our IT: I'll get in touch with my supplier right now. We're going to get clean. And then I'm going to call Bernard Prebble. Because we're going to find his daughter."

Meg's face flickered into a smile. "Now you're talking."

FORTY-THREE

I have a habit of doing things that aren't in my own interests, if they're the right thing to do.

For example, five years ago I came home from college in the middle of a particularly trying day to make myself a sandwich, rather than putting up with the crowd in the cafeteria. It was a few years after my mother died, so the house should have been empty at lunchtime. Instead, as I walked into the kitchen, my father emerged from the small adjoining box room. It was originally supposed to be a bedroom, but it was far too small and only had a single, tiny window. My father had it decked out with cheap shelving and used it to store random old junk – as I still do now. Back when he was alive, I wasn't exactly banned from going in, but he always kept it locked.

He looked up sharply. There were flecks of something dark on his hands and the smell of solvent in the air. "Why are you home?" He fumbled with the key, then turned it forcefully in the lock of the box-room door.

"Shouldn't you be at the gallery?"

"Closed early." He paused. "And I had to go and speak to your tutor."

"About what? I didn't know there was a problem. And shouldn't I have been informed?"

"I thought it was strange, but it turned out he had something he wanted to discuss in private. You were trying to hack their computer system, weren't you, using that new computer you talked me into buying?"

"Where would you get that idea?"

He reached into his jacket pocket and produced a palm-sized black metal object. "They found it installed near the Computer Science Faculty." He tapped it with a finger. "Care to comment? I'm not tech unaware. It's some type of remote analysis device, isn't it?"

I sighed. "It samples electromagnetic radiation in its proximity. If it detects data activity, it records it. When you retrieve the device you can access the data." I paused. "I call it a leech."

"And what were you hoping it would *leech*?"

"The end of year exam papers. Look, this device should have been very, very hard to detect. How did they find it?"

"Complete chance: a new cleaner being over-enthusiastic. You really should have hidden it better."

"How did they know it was me?"

"Your tutor thought you were the only one who was capable of building such a device. I suppose that's a form of compliment."

"The hardware isn't really so complex." I let my mouth twist into a slight smile. "The real sophistication is in the programming."

"Sure, make a joke of it." He glared at me. "What

were you thinking? You're the one who least needs to steal exam papers. You're top of the class."

"It was more about the challenge: to see if it could be done. Besides, the exam's a joke. This is a *real* test of computing."

"Didn't your mother and I raise you to know that stealing is wrong?"

"It's not exactly stealing. The exams are still exactly where the lecturer put them—"

"You *stole*. And what I don't understand is that it's not even an exam you're taking. It's the finals paper for the group two years ahead of you…" He folded his arms. "You did this for Kieran, didn't you?"

"What difference does it make?"

"Did he ask you to do it?"

"Of course not. Nobody knows I can do this. At least they didn't until now. I just heard him talking about how things were going so badly with his coursework, how he was failing… I wanted to help."

My father reached out and gripped my shoulder. "Jake, you can't take risks like this."

"He's my best friend."

"Maybe he needs a cold, hard dose of reality."

"I think having lost both parents so young gave him enough of that. Why don't you trust him?"

My father sighed. "Look, it's not him. It's people in general. I tried trusting them, and it didn't work out."

"You trust me, don't you?"

"Asks the boy who just committed electronic fraud."

"It's not a one-way street. Kieran has my back too. He sorted out those older boys who were picking on me."

"Did he now? Even so, I still don't want you

continually putting yourself out for people. You'll get taken advantage of."

"That is so cynical. Anyway, what's going to happen with school? Am I being expelled?"

"Did you actually steal the exam?"

"Not yet."

"Which means no crime has been committed. I made that point quite forcefully to your tutor. The one person you can trust is me, Jake. I will *never* abandon you. Remember that." A smile crossed his face. "Besides I don't think your tutor actually wants to have to write a new exam paper, so he'll have to let it go."

I let out a long sigh. "So we're good then?"

"In a manner of speaking."

I nodded and reached out for the device, but he was quicker, snatching it up.

"No, you don't. I'm going to destroy this. And you're going to promise me not to do anything like this again. It's a slippery slope. You don't want to know where it leads." He shook his head. "You can't do things like this for no reason."

I hesitated. "So, if there was a really good reason, it would be OK?"

"If you use something like this, someone'll build a defence to stop it, so you'd better use it for something worthwhile. And this is clearly not that thing." He seemed about to say something when his phone chimed for a text. He muttered as he read the message.

"Is everything OK?"

"Work stuff. The people I have to deal with are a bunch of crooks."

"Rich crooks?"

"Without doubt. If you were going to use your device to take something, you should take it from them."

"Because stealing from crooks is OK?"

"That's debatable. But definitely not if they catch you."

I laughed. "And what are they going to do? Go to the police?"

He did not smile. "No, Jake. They won't go the police. They'll just hurt you. Anyway, one of my clients is stopping by to talk about a deal, so it's best if you aren't around. Go and study, or do something else you won't get arrested for."

FORTY-FOUR

The rain slammed hard on the corrugated roof of the disused warehouse. I watched as the small grey van drove cautiously under the roller door and pulled up next to my car. Abigail climbed out, wrinkling her nose.

"Nice place," she said.

"Not my first choice, but it's certainly discrete. Did you get everything?"

She raised an eyebrow. "No time for pleasantries?"

"I'm a little pushed today."

Abigail shrugged and walked to the back of her van, opening the doors to reveal a cluster of computer boxes. "Everything on the list, despite the short notice. Your largest ever order. I may get myself a case or two of something cold and bubbly to celebrate."

"About that." I scratched my nose. "On this occasion can I ask you to defer payment?"

It was already quiet in the warehouse, but it seemed to have suddenly got quieter still. Abigail frowned. "Of course, Jake. If you don't mind me deferring delivery."

"I'm asking for a little faith. I've got a big payday coming."

"Of course you have. And the moment that money comes in, give me a call." She started to close the van doors.

"Abi, please. Have I ever let you down?"

She hesitated. "No, and that's because of my very clear policy of cash on delivery."

I eyed the collection of boxes. "It's going to be a very big payday."

"Jake, you're a good guy. I like you. But this is business. Do you think I just make all this stuff myself? I have suppliers of my own and they also need paying." She shook her head. "If I'm to put myself out, what's in it for me?"

"Ten percent on top and I'll pay you in the next month."

She tipped her head to one side. "You said *very* big. I think that's worth forty, don't you? In my experience, big paydays tend to carry some risk." She shrugged. "You can always see if one of my competitors will cut you a better deal, let alone deliver as quickly as you need."

I rubbed my temples with my index fingers. "Twenty-five percent, otherwise you can just carry that stock until someone else comes along." I tipped my head. "There can't be that many clients out there with my particular requirements."

She gave a quiet snort, then picked up the first box and held it out. "To be clear, you'd better pay up in a month."

"I won't let you down." I took the boxes and started loading them into my car. There was enough room, but it was going to be tight.

"I trust you, Jake. I just don't trust the other people you are dealing with."

I DROVE AWAY FROM THE WAREHOUSE, THINKING ABOUT Abigail's final words. I was being forced to deal with a number of people I didn't trust. I called Sid. "I have the new batch. We'll continue with my place and hit the office tomorrow."

"Meg's here with me. We finished the tear-down ten minutes ago."

"So you've already had a break."

"You're a funny guy, Jake. Bring coffee."

"Not jasmine tea then?"

"I'm past the point of pretend stimulants." He paused. "Meg's asking for bourbon."

"I bet she is." I closed the call with a smile. It felt good to be on the front foot.

My phone rang. I looked down at the number and felt a shiver as I tapped the button to accept the call. "Hello, Vince," I said.

His voice was typically unsympathetic. "We need to meet. Tomorrow lunchtime. I'll send you the location. You had a question. We have an answer for you."

FORTY-FIVE

We worked through the night installing the new systems, which meant I had to let Sid and Meg upstairs. Sometimes you just have to trust people. Meg glanced around when she first walked in, but she didn't seem that bothered about the place. Given that it was the hub of my technical activity, the very centre of our business, I'd expected she'd be more interested. Sid was the complete opposite: a fount of enthusiastic curiosity. His energy helped get me through a very long night. About 2am we stopped for pizza, fresh from the freezer.

"How did your supplier get all this kit so quickly?" Sid asked, re-tying his pony tail. "It's like she knew what you'd be asking for."

"Abi knows her business," I said. "And how much did it all cost?" asked Meg.

"I said I'd take care of it. Let's just get back online."

We eventually got the systems running sometime after 4am and celebrated with a round of bourbon, then we collapsed on my couches and grabbed three hours sleep. I got up at 6:30am to make everyone breakfast, then dashed down the road and returned with a round of super-sized lattes. As I reached the house, I interrupted the postman delivering several bills and another of the anonymous postcards. I threw them on the hall mantelpiece and shared out the hot drinks.

By 7:30am we were heading to TechFixed, where we would have to do the same all over again. We declared a major system fault, took everything offline and got to work in the server room. When we had our private server reinstated, we called Lundy to tell him the fault was resolved and he seemed suitably impressed.

"I'll start reinstalling from the backup," Sid said. "I've thoroughly analysed the files for anything nefarious, and I've manually checked everything as well to rule out any kind of key-logger device or physical intrusion. We should be functional by this evening."

I looked at my watch. "I have to go out," I said, grabbing my backpack. "Back in an hour."

"You have to be kidding?" Meg asked. "What's more important than this?" She put her hands on her hips.

"Personal matter. Sorry."

"It's not good enough, Jake."

Sid raised a hand. "He just gets in my way, pretending he knows what he's doing."

"Thanks, Sid."

"Anytime. Anyway, the sooner you leave, the sooner you're back, right?"

IT WAS STARTING TO RAIN OUTSIDE. I'D FORGOTTEN TO bring an umbrella, so, as I walked to the main road, I started looking around for a taxi. With good timing, one parked just up the street switched on its light. I strode over, called "Camden" through the open window and climbed in. Before I could close the door, two other people followed me: a heavyset man with an expression like granite, and a woman with grey hair and wire-framed glasses – Ellie Winslow.

"Jake, how have you been?" she asked with a smile, taking the seat opposite and clicking her seatbelt into place.

I glanced up at the driver, expecting him to say something, but he just pulled into the traffic. "Ellie, do you not grasp how normal people arrange meetings?" I asked. "First you surround me on a train, now you abduct me."

"Nobody's abducting anyone." She held out her hand. "Your phone, please."

I gave it to her. "What exactly do you think I was going to do with it?"

"You're the electronics wizard," she said. "And the other one."

I puffed out my cheeks then pulled out my secondary phone. "I'm getting these back, right?"

"We have no intention of degrading your capabilities." She placed them in a zipped pouch and put it on the floor, then nodded to the heavyset man. He pulled out an electronic wand and tracked it up and down my legs, arms and torso. It made a few pops and squeals, but they both seemed satisfied.

"Are you following me 24/7?" I asked.

Winslow pursed her lips. "If only we had that much resource."

"I'm not even sure you are who you say you are."

The taxi was now heading along the south bank of

the Thames near Waterloo. Winslow glanced across the river. "Perhaps you'd like to come for a meeting at Thames House? Now, why don't I show you what we want you to do?" She picked up a slim attaché case and unzipped it, removing a tablet computer. She typed in a long code and applied her thumb to a fingerprint reader then turned it to show me the screen. It displayed a close-up of a painting. "We need you to locate and recover this."

I studied the image, then swallowed. I was no art expert, but the colours and style looked pretty distinctive to me. I took a deep breath.

"Picasso's *Le pigeon aux petits pois*, painted in 1911," she said.

I started to feel the world twisting around me. "Is this a joke?"

"It was last insured for forty million pounds. So, no, it's very serious."

I turned and stared out the window. We were crossing the Thames at Westminster Bridge. I turned back to face Winslow. "Was it stolen?"

"Does that make a difference?"

"It makes all the difference."

"Of course it was stolen. On more than one occasion, actually. Most recently from a private collector three years ago."

I sighed. A cold case: the worst kind. "Why do you care about a painting being stolen? Especially from a private collector, not a public museum?"

"Your only concern is the 'what', not the 'why'."

"OK. But surely you have other resources capable of doing this?"

"You're the best person for this job."

"And how much money are you putting behind that faith?"

"You're going to help us because it's the right thing to do. Let's call it our 'good citizen programme'."

"It doesn't sound compelling."

"If you don't cooperate, we'll have to conclude you are a bad citizen, and I'm sure I don't need to say what happens to those. Jake, you put yourself in this situation. Nobody made you start this business you run." She shrugged. "There's one other reason for you to cooperate: I can provide you with something you've been looking for."

"And what is that?"

"Information about your father's murder."

The taxi pulled to a halt at a set of traffic lights. My heart seemed to halt as well. "I don't understand. The police investigation came up with nothing."

"My information wasn't part of the investigation." Winslow delicately scratched her nose. "Your father used to work for us. On a consultancy basis."

"Why haven't I heard this before?"

"Because it was classified."

"And yet you're willing to tell me now?"

"A combination of the passing of time, and a quid pro quo for your assistance."

"Maybe I don't want to know."

Winslow folded her arms. "We both know that's not true."

FORTY-SIX

I GOT THE TAXI TO DROP ME AT THE EDGE OF CAMDEN, well away from the restaurant. Pocketing my two mobile phones, I walked in circles for fifteen minutes. I deployed all my tradecraft, and a couple of times thought I saw the same slim brunette following me, but I could have been imagining it. After fifteen minutes of jumping at shadows, I gave up and headed for the rendezvous. Either I'd lost them or I was never going to lose them. Vince was at a table at the back. He looked tired and tense.

"You're late," he said. There was a plate of linguini before him, but he didn't seem to have touched it.

"Traffic," I said. "My apologies."

He nodded at the seat opposite. "Want something to eat?"

I sat down. "Just coffee."

He signalled to the waitress, who walked over with one apparently pre-prepared. I took it, noting it was cold.

Vince waited until she had left the table then

stabbed at his pasta. "You wanted confirmation of the account balance."

"I want more than that. I want an explanation."

Vince blinked. "You're forgetting who you're talking to. We don't owe you explanations. That's not how this works. Paying us was a decision you made on your own. There were never any promises on our part."

"I hear Kieran has racked up new debts. Gambling again. I'm guessing with you."

"What if he has? He lost money fair and square. That's just life. People make their own choices."

"How am I supposed to pay that back on top of everything else?"

"Who said that you have to? It's his debt."

I tightened my fists. "And if he can't pay it, you'll do what?"

"What we have to do." Vince frowned. "Things not going well? Everything OK with our current payment arrangement?"

"You shouldn't have let this happen."

"We never made any promise to stop him. Perhaps you should have discussed it directly. Shared the benefit of your exemplary self-control."

I ground my teeth together. "What is this about? I thought I'd been keeping up my end of the bargain."

Vince folded his arms. "I suggest you focus on how to make the next payment."

"I'm going to need more time. I've had a couple of setbacks recently. It happens."

"Your problem, not ours. Or rather," he paused, smiling, "Kieran's, if it comes to that."

I banged my fist on the table. "You remind Max that I'm good for the money. He just needs to be patient. Or

I can go to the police with this nonsense. And we can see what they make of it all."

Vince sighed. Looking around, I saw that the restaurant seemed to have emptied. There were no other customers, and the staff had all vanished. At the door stood two very large men in suits. They were looking out at the street.

"You can tell him yourself," Vince said, as he stood and stepped away from the table. At the front of the restaurant the two large men pulled down the blinds, screening the windows. Then they looking to the back of the restaurant and snapped to attention.

I turned and saw a figure appear from the door to the kitchen. Dressed in a suit nearly as expensive as the one that Prebble had worn, with more grey in his hair and a few more pounds on his frame, I still recognised him instantly.

"Hello, Jake," said Maxwell Rouse.

FORTY-SEVEN

Rouse took the chair where Vince had been sitting. Two huge bodyguards stationed themselves either side of us. Vince stood on the far side of the room, watching. Rouse pushed aside the plate of linguini with disdain, then picked up a bottle of mineral water and opened it with a sharp twist. "I thought it was time we had a little chat, Jake." He poured himself a glass of water. "We're both busy men and I'd hate for us to miss this opportunity to see eye to eye."

I swallowed. "Good of you to make time for me."

He looked at me, nodding slightly. "I like that you say that. Good manners. So what did you want to discuss?"

I stared at him. It was impossible that Vince had not briefed him on my request. And he must be aware of the new situation with Kieran. "I wanted to know how much Kieran still owes, and your guy over there wasn't able to answer. But I've just discovered the situation has become worse. You've let Kieran run up significant new debts."

"Your friend is a grown man, capable of making his own decisions.

"He's a parent raising his son alone because his wife was murdered. Have you no compassion?"

"Of course. For my wife and kids. Occasionally for my dog. Beyond that it's all business." He gave an exaggerated shrug. "Sometimes bad things happen to people: it's just the way of the world. You can't keep on cutting them slack forever." He glanced at Vince then back to me. "I know we don't meet very often – mostly because of my substantial security requirements – and it may not feel like we are working together. But we are." He took a slow sip of his water. "I appreciate that you're taking on the responsibility of someone else's mistakes. I wish there were more people like you. It would make my job a lot more straightforward. I take no pleasure in enforcing a debt. I just want to make a living." He took a sip from his glass. "You've been doing a great job, Jake. Better than anyone could ever have expected. Your father would be proud."

"Given who I'm helping, I doubt that. Especially now it looks as if the situation is only going to get worse. That there's not going to be any end to this." I coughed. "How do I even know Kieran lost the money fairly? Maybe you duped him. I'm starting to wonder whether I should ever have trusted you."

"We never asked you to. And you can always just step away and let… *nature* take its course."

I stared at Rouse. I wanted to leap up on the table and smash his face in. I'd get to him before his bodyguards or Vince. It would feel good for a brief moment. Then it would hurt. A lot. And it wouldn't help things. But then Rouse's words echoed in my head, and realisation hit me. And I knew why I was having so many problems recently. It wasn't about Kieran.

It was about me.

"I've been doing too well," I said. "I've been earning too reliably, and now you don't want to let me go. I'm never going to be free of this, am I? I'm effectively working for you, which was never what this was about. It's about helping my cousin, even if he doesn't seem to be able to help himself."

"Well, at least he has you. So are you going to carry on? Or shall I ask Vince to revert to enforcement mode? I'm good either way."

"It seems I'll keep going."

"A wise choice. But I tell you what, if I can do anything for you – if anything is getting in your way or causing you problems, be it one of your team, a supplier," he paused, "or the police – just let me know and I'll make it go away."

I froze. Had he been following me? Did he know about Winslow or was he just fishing? "I'll be sure to do that."

"Good." Rouse picked up the menu, flicked through it, then threw it back on the table. "We don't get ahead by standing still. And I really don't want to see you standing still – you're too valuable."

"I'm flattered."

Rouse's fingers tightened on his glass. "I overheard you just now, talking to Vince about going to the police. I suggest you never say such words again. Not even as a joke." He leaned forward. "Don't even think them. Am I clear? Because I know where you live. I know where your team lives." He leaned closer. "And of course I know where your cousin and his son live."

My breath caught in my throat. "If you so much as look at my nephew—"

He smiled and patted me on the arm. "It's all about motivation, Jake. I just want you to do the right thing. And if you do, then you'll be taken care of."

"What?"

Rouse stood. "I'm glad we had this chat. I hope we understand each other properly now."

―――

I LEFT THE RESTAURANT, HANDS IN POCKETS, SO LOST IN thought I didn't notice the figure bearing down on me until it was too late. There was a flash of a dark wool overcoat, the swish of shoulder length dark hair, then long limbs were propelling me down a side street. I tried to call out, but a hand was clamped over my throat.

There was the waft of a fragrance that seemed familiar, and I realised with a start that my assailant was a woman. Whoever it was had technique far surpassing my own and seemed to anticipate my every move to break loose. I was pushed into a doorway and pinned against the frame. A voice hissed in my ear, "Who the hell did you just meet with?"

"I don't know what you're talking about." I struggled but the woman pinned my arms and jammed her knee in the back of mine.

"I said no more secrets. You made a promise."

There was an exasperated sigh then the same long limbs spun me sharply. I found myself staring into a familiar face. Meg reached up and pulled the dark wig from her head, shaking out her long red locks.

"So," she said, "shall we try that again?"

FORTY-EIGHT

I stared into Meg's eyes. I'd never seen her so angry. "You followed me?" I growled.

"Damn right I followed you. And what do I find you doing?"

"It was just lunch. With a possible new client."

"That guy had a small army protecting him. Any reason why you wouldn't mention the meeting, especially given everything that's happened recently?"

"I said it was a personal matter."

"So not a new client? You seem confused."

"It's best if I don't tell you. You'll just have to trust me on that."

"Jake, have you been paying attention to what is going on? Now is not the time for secrets."

I pushed her hands away, although I got the feeling that if she hadn't wanted me to, I wouldn't have been able to. "Then go work for someone else."

"I don't want to, you idiot." She took a step back and glanced both ways down the alleyway. Nobody was in sight. "Who was that?"

"You really are better off out of it, Meg."

"Let me be the judge of that. Now shut up and start talking."

"*The* Maxwell Rouse?" she asked, in hushed tones. "You have to be kidding."

"I wish."

"Your first principle is that we don't become criminals. And here we all are, working for *him*."

"It's not that simple. I've deliberately kept you all out of it. The connection came because my father had dealings with him. Rouse came along to the funeral." I paused. "How do you know who he is? He's not exactly a public figure."

Meg sighed. "I became aware of his work in that former life I haven't told you much about. I was working on protection duty for a client and our paths crossed. His reputation preceded him."

"Regardless, it's my problem to manage."

"No, Jake. It's my problem too. And Sid's, and Daniel's."

I folded my arms. "I have it under control."

Her eyes narrowed. "Maybe you did, but things have changed, haven't they? I can see from your expression." She put her hands on my shoulders, more gently this time. "The only thing to know, the only thing to remember, is that you can't trust him. He'll tell you whatever he thinks you need to hear. Who knows what he's lied about already? Maybe about your father's involvement with him. Maybe *Rouse* killed your father."

"Why would he do that?"

"Just because you don't see the reason doesn't mean it isn't there. Who knows what other schemes Rouse might be working? Your father's life might have been inconsequential." She hesitated. "Sorry, I didn't mean that quite how it sounded."

I shook my head. "Forget it. I've had a few years to adjust."

"Yeah," she said, standing closer, the shoulder squeeze turning into a hug. "But it wasn't enough, was it?"

"Not really."

She suddenly seemed to realise what she was doing and stepped sharply back, bringing her arms to her side. "So, what's the problem? Do you owe him money?"

"Not exactly. I've assumed a liability for… a friend."

"Your friend owes him money? Is that the kind of friend you need?" She snapped her fingers. "Your cousin Kieran?"

I swallowed. "I didn't say—"

"Oh shut up. You have no friends apart from us and him."

I ran a hand through my hair. "Sometimes I hate you."

"Join the queue. So how did Kieran get into this mess?"

"I've never spoken about it with him."

"Then how… Rouse told you." Meg's eyes widened. "And you just believed him? You complete idiot—"

"It's not like that. I saw Kieran getting worked over by a thug and decided to find out who the thug worked for. I chose to get involved."

"How much money is it?"

"Two million. It's why I started the consultancy."

She laughed. "Rouse 'created' you? That's priceless. So what has changed?"

"That's the problem I was here to discuss. Kieran lost more money gambling. I thought I could make Rouse see sense, but it's clear he thinks he owns me, especially as I now have no money to pay him after the Meeks stuff."

"Which is why you're taking the Prebble job."

"Yeah. Although it's a real long shot."

"And if you don't pay?"

"Kieran's in trouble. And I'm sure I will be too. And before you ask, I'd just create trouble for everyone, you guys in particular, if I tried to go to the police. I have to solve this myself."

"How wonderfully dramatic of you," she said with a laugh. "Anything else you want to tell me while we're at it?"

I rubbed my eyes with my palms. "Yeah – the reason I'm not that worried about Rouse: I'm more worried about something else. In the spirit of full disclosure there is one other issue you should know about. But let's not talk any more here. For this discussion, I think we'll both need a drink."

———

Venues picked at random on short notice are the best kind if you want to avoid being monitored. The bar was only notionally open, but the barman seemed happy to take my money. I carried the tray with six glasses on it back to the booth where Meg had established herself.

She raised an eyebrow. "Tequila? It's not even midday."

"Just drink it."

She picked up one glass as I did the same then we clinked and downed them. With a wheeze she asked, "So what the heck is this about?"

"I had a meeting on the Eurostar. I didn't arrange it. They knew I'd be there and had a full team coral me. Given that we were under the Channel at the time, I didn't have a lot of places to go."

"Smart, on their part. But who would have that kind of resource?"

"Her name was Ellie Winslow. She's MI5."

Meg blinked. "Now I understand the tequila."

"I've checked her out as best as I can. I'm pretty confident she's the real deal." I stared hard at Meg. If anything she seemed less surprised than when I'd given Rouse's name. Maybe she was just getting numb to it. In which case, I knew how she felt. "No comment?"

"I'm still reflecting. What did she want?"

"To engage my services. She didn't say for what at first. But then she got back in touch. She kind of ambushed me on my way to meet Rouse."

"I've been with you the whole time, except when you were riding in that taxi."

"She met me *in* the taxi. If you were following me, why didn't you see anything?"

"I was staying well back."

"She said she knew my father: said he was working for them as a consultant."

Meg blinked and picked up the next glass of tequila. She knocked it back without waiting for me. "This is proving to be quite a day."

"I don't disagree."

"If what she said is true, maybe Rouse found out and had him whacked."

"If that were the case, why the ongoing interest in me?"

"Maybe your father had something he wanted. What was your father doing for MI5?"

"Classified, apparently."

"How convenient. So what did she want from you?"

"For us to find a painting," I replied. "If we do, she says she'll tell me more about my father… maybe even give me some idea who killed him."

"And if we don't, she'll shop us to the police?"

"Are you sure you weren't in earshot?"

"I've seen her sort in action before: it's part of the standard playbook. So what's the job?"

I sighed. "She wants us to recover a stolen Picasso."

Meg stuffed her hands in her pockets. "And what's she going to pay us?"

"She's offering us 'stay out of jail' tokens. Look, you can't tell the others about any of this."

"You want to lie to them?"

"I want to protect them. Their best defence against Rouse is not to know anything about him."

"I don't agree. You have to be honest, Jake."

"My father said not to trust anyone."

"And where did that get him? If you can't trust us, how can we trust you?"

FORTY-NINE

There are very few places in London busier than Piccadilly Circus, whatever the time of day. Right now those crowds were an opportunity for camouflage.

Sid and Daniel had reacted with confusion when I said where we were to meet, but I didn't want to tell them too much over the phone. We needed to go somewhere where it was impossible we would be overheard. Somewhere random, somewhere busy.

We walked around and around Piccadilly Circus as I talked. It took me nearly an hour to tell them everyone, by which time we'd drifted, winding our way to the very heart of Soho, where I steered us into a cafe-bar that seemed to have a mix of Greek and Italian influences. We shuffled into a booth near the back, and clustered around a red and white formica table. A rattling ceiling fan gyrated worryingly above us.

"So, that's about the size of it," I said after four beers arrived, and we'd declined to order food to the clear irritation of the owner.

Sid folded his arms. "That's quite a lot to take in, Jake. More than quite a lot."

"I don't disagree." I turned to look at Daniel. He just shrugged.

"What I'd like to know," Sid said, "is why you told Meg first."

"Because," growled Meg, "I was the one actually paying attention. Because I was the one who forced it out of him. So… you're welcome."

"Fine." Sid looked at me. "But why didn't you tell any of us earlier?"

"I didn't think it affected you. And, to be clear, it still doesn't. At least not directly."

"What affects you," Meg said, "affects us."

"Look, I made a mistake. If you all want to leave me to it, I won't try to stop you."

Meg leaned forward. "If we wanted to leave, what makes you think you could stop us? But then what makes you think we'd want to leave?"

"It's my mess—"

"I'm not going anywhere," Sid said. "I need the… I mean, I wouldn't leave you in the lurch." He lowered his voice. "Of course, the bigger question is could we leave even if we wanted to?"

I stared at Daniel again. "I know you're new here, but surely you have an opinion."

He scratched his shaved head and glanced at Meg. "It's… not really my style to get rattled. I trust Meg, and she says she trusts you."

"Yes," Meg said, "and the Jake I trust would not take this lying down. He would have a plan."

"Thank you all for your support," I said quietly. "I guess the next step is to discuss my plan."

"You have one?" Sid asked.

I forced a smile. "First, we prioritise."

We talked the rest of the afternoon away in the cafe-bar. Meg called Lundy to tell him we'd been called out on an emergency job. That would require some serious back-filling later to create the paperwork, but we'd worry about it then.

That evening we set to work. We had two priorities. First, find Prebble's daughter and collect our payment. Second, find a stolen Picasso. If Winslow didn't want to pay for our services, surely the previous owner, or the insurer, would be interested in paying for its recovery. Possession of a £40m painting would give us options.

Meeks and Calum we would ignore for now. Calum was OK, but he wasn't brilliant. As for Meeks, we'd find a way to outwit him. He'd had the advantage before. That was about to change.

Unfortunately, after two hours the search for the painting was going nowhere. According to the information provided by Winslow, and verified by us, it had last been listed on the books of a well-known collector, Reginald Monday, who lived in an exclusive penthouse apartment in Mayfair, with considerable security measures. However, the system had been taken offline the night of the theft and there was no CCTV footage from inside or out. Monday had raised some eyebrows at the time by refusing to claim on his insurance; an interview afterwards noted that he said he didn't want the money, he just wanted the painting returned. I needed to speak with him, but Winslow's instructions forbade it: he was a suspect in the theft and she did not want us tipping him off. Instead, we ran our pattern-matching algorithms, putting our refreshed computer systems to the test. The painting proved too well-known for this to be much use: the theft alone had produced hundreds of images in the press, all indistinguishable to our software. Worse, it had acted as a catalyst for people to buy reproduction prints. So when we looked for the painting, we found it *everywhere*.

Sid threw up his hands. "Our systems are working better than ever, but if any of these were the real painting, we wouldn't be able to distinguish it. We don't have anything like the resolution needed to tell if any of the hits coming up are even actual oil paintings."

"OK, where does that leave us?" Meg asked.

"In trouble," I replied. "We need Winslow to back off. It would help if we could find some leverage on her. We're not looking hard enough. How about Prebble?"

"Nothing much," Sid said. "The daughter's a socialite, so she's all over the net. There's a metric ton of rubbish, but none of it more recent than two months ago. Of course, there have been sightings of her in all sorts of places, but she's too ubiquitous for us to trace her reliably."

"I thought nobody knew she was Prebble's daughter?"

"They don't. She's famous in her own right. Social media and crap like that."

"What about her boyfriend?" I asked.

"Yeah that part didn't seem to align," Sid said. "There were gossip columns naming several men, but none of them seemed to have reached boyfriend status."

"That's odd," I said, "given that Prebble seemed to think the 'boyfriend' was linked to her disappearance."

"We need more personal details," Meg said. "Stuff that isn't in the public domain. You should go meet with Prebble and see if he makes good on his claim of wanting to help. I'll prep a list of questions."

I frowned. "He went to the trouble of meeting me in a private room in Paris. He's hardly going to want me walking up to his front door with a clipboard."

"I'm sure we can sort something discrete."

FIFTY

Prebble answered the private number he had given me in seconds. Within an hour I was travelling in an SUV with blacked-out windows, descending into an underground car park beneath his central London office. An express lift took me straight to the penthouse.

Prebble, wearing yet another expensive suit and tie, greeted me as the doors slid open. He led me into a large room with a desk, and windows on three sides. We looked to be somewhere near Bond Street.

"No concerns about long lenses?" I asked. "Or parabolic mikes?"

He gave a snort. "I have mirrored glass, and noise cancelling vibration on the panes. We're secure."

"And you sweep for bugs?"

"Daily, but nobody gets in here. You can say what you want and it will go no further. I don't make recordings either."

I stared out at the traffic going past below. "I find that surprising."

"I was told that if I have cameras and other

monitoring devices it's too easy for someone else to take them over."

"Very true." I turned back to the room. Something was nagging at my attention, but I couldn't work out what it was.

Prebble took a seat at his desk, set against the wall with no window. Three pictures hung behind him. "Have you found her?" he asked.

I smiled and sat opposite him. "I'm here to get more details: anything and everything you can give me. Credit cards, bank statements, phone records, travel itineraries, friends and contacts. Anywhere she might have been, stayed, visited. Anyone she might have gone with. I need filters to apply in my search, additional connections to weigh."

"Can't you get all that stuff yourself?"

"It'll be a hell of a lot faster if you give it to me direct."

Prebble stretched his hands behind his neck and leaned backwards. "I'll get one of my people to pull it together. Was that it?"

I swallowed. "I thought you might be more hesitant to provide it and I would need to impress the importance upon you." I was once again getting the feeling that something really obvious was staring me in the face.

"It goes without saying that you need to treat all the information I provide with the utmost sensitivity."

"Of course. And…" I froze. My eyes had focused on the middle painting of the three hanging on the wall behind Prebble. My eyes started to glaze over. I had spent some considerable time staring at digital versions in the course of the last twenty-four hours. And now here it was.

I was looking at the real *Le pigeon aux petits pois*.

Prebble saw me staring. "Art buff?" he asked.

"Not really." I took a slow breath but couldn't help myself asking. "Is that a…"

"A Picasso?" Prebble smiled. "Funny story, about that," he said. "I thought I'd got myself an absolute bargain. I paid £30 million, which was about £10 million less than its valuation. I had an independent expert verify it and he said that recent successes at auction suggested it was likely worth £75m."

"Why would the owner sell for less than it was worth?"

Prebble adjusted his suit. "Things are only worth what people are prepared to pay."

I looked at the painting. I couldn't help myself: I had to ask. "I remember reading about a Picasso being stolen, maybe three years ago."

His expression darkened. "I'm sure you did. It was all over the news."

"Not this painting, obviously."

"No, Jake, it *was* this painting." He tipped his head to one side. "Do you think *I* stole it?" He slapped me on the arm. "It's OK. It was actually the dealer having seller's remorse. He kicked up such a fuss, tried to accuse me of theft. But I bought it fair and square. He never claimed on his insurance, as that would have been fraud."

"At least you had the last laugh."

"Yeah. Unfortunately I didn't laugh that long. Two weeks later the price dropped: seems like the valuation was based on erroneous data and this isn't one of the better Picassos after all. It's worth only £20m."

I blinked. "You were *conned*?"

"Something I've never admitted to anyone. Take it as a show of trust that I'm sharing it with you."

"Why do you still have it on your wall?"

Prebble shrugged. "I like the picture. Whatever someone else tells me it's worth, it's still the same as it was yesterday. And if I ever want to sell it, maybe the market will have moved."

"Remarkably pragmatic of you."

"I'm actually a straightforward guy. Not the monster the press likes to paint me as."

I shrugged, staring at the painting one last time. "If you love your daughter like you say you do, you can't be a monster. And I will do my very best to find her for you, I promise."

FIFTY-ONE

Prebble's SUV dropped me round the corner from TechFixed's offices. As the vehicle drove away, I permitted myself a smile. The billionaire had, unexpectedly, not relieved me of my watch: I'd recorded the whole conversation, and also shot bursts of video with a pin-head camera on my shirt collar. It might not make any difference, or it might make all the difference. I burst through the office front door, looking for my team, and froze.

Emerging from Lundy's office was the last person I expected to see there.

Ellie Winslow.

My mouth hung open. She glanced at me, then walked past without speaking, without even slowing down. In a blink she was through the front door and outside.

Lundy appeared in the doorway. "So, Mr Moro, you've deigned to turn up."

I stared at him, then at the door Winslow had just left through. I was momentarily lost for words.

"Another urgent client install?" he prompted, scratching his neatly trimmed beard.

I shook myself. "Have you had any complaints?"

"So few it makes me suspicious."

"Who was that you just met with?"

"That's no business of yours."

"Yes, but—"

"Get on with your work, Jake. I want your paperwork in the system by lunchtime. Now, I have things to be getting on with. As do you."

I nodded. "Of course." I turned and made my way into the open plan area. Meg, Sid and Daniel were at their desks.

Meg looked up. "How did it… what's the matter?"

"Server room, now," I replied.

They followed me in. I watched Daniel close the door. As usual he said nothing.

"Did you see that woman who was meeting with Lundy?"

"Kind of," Meg said. "Why?"

"That was none other than MI5 agent Ellie Winslow."

"What?" Sid shouted. "Why was she here?"

"I've no idea," I said. "She just walked out, without explanation. Lundy wouldn't discuss it."

"Was she here to intimidate you?" Sid asked. "Or to speak with him?"

"Take your guess," I said. "Just as I take one step forward, something else happens to confuse things."

"One step forward? Did Prebble provide anything useful?"

"In a manner of speaking. There was certainly an interesting development." I removed the camera from my lapel and plugged it into Meg's laptop. I quickly selected an image.

"What the heck?" Meg said. "Is that—"

I nodded. "He's got the Picasso on his damn wall."

She peered closer. "Are you sure?"

"As sure as I can be. Prebble discussed it openly: says he bought it. His story checks out – at least it fits what we know so far."

Sid shook his head. "Isn't it odd that Prebble didn't detect your camera? Didn't he swipe you down? For someone so cautious with his security it seems out of character."

"This just cannot be a coincidence, the painting being in Prebble's office," Meg said. "There's a connection here we're not seeing. Why would MI5 want to recover a Picasso? What could possibly be so important about it?"

"I'd prefer," I said, "to focus on our chances of getting it out of there."

Sid coughed. "Short of asking him to hand it over, they're very low. I've been conducting some investigations on the security in Prebble's building, particularly the protection for that office. The vault at the Bank of England would be easier to access."

"What about the painting's previous owner, Reginald Monday?" Daniel asked. "Why don't we go speak to him?"

"I agree," Meg said. "Maybe he wants revenge? Regardless of whether it was actually stolen, he certainly seems aggrieved and he might be able to help."

"What about the fact that the painting wasn't insured?" Sid said. "We should ask him about that. People who can afford original Picassos aren't usually dumb and incautious, however good they think their security is."

"This whole thing stinks in a hundred ways," I said. "Meg's right: this can't just be a coincidence. I'm fed up of being given the run around." I pulled out my phone and dialled a number I had recently programmed in.

"Who are you—" Sid began.

I raised a finger to my lips. The phone was answered on the first ring.

"Jake," Ellie Winslow said, "what a pleasant surprise."

"Don't mess with me. What were you doing here?"

"Not your concern. The world doesn't revolve around you, Jake."

"Fine, play games. I'm calling to tell you the deal is off. I found the painting. But I have no doubt you knew that. In fact, I'm sure you *always* knew where it was."

Winslow gave a sniff. "We were fairly certain Prebble had it somewhere. We were aware he had reached out to you. How do you think we knew to be on the Eurostar?"

"You bugged me?"

She laughed. "We bugged *him*."

"So you know where it is," I said. "Great. You're the government. Go get it."

"No, Jake. You're going to do that for me."

"You want me to take it from his penthouse in one of the most secure company buildings in the country? I'm used to taking on private residences: low level stuff. If it looks too tricky, I walk away."

"You don't have that option here, unless you want to be arrested right now."

"I don't get why you won't do it yourself. You could go in the front door."

"If the government were linked to the operation, Prebble would throw every ounce of his media empire into destroying us. If we went in *officially*, we'd need a warrant and, in the time it took to get one, Prebble would remove the painting. You, however, don't have a rule book to comply with."

"What can possibly be so important about this work of art? Prebble said it wasn't even one of the best Picassos. How can anything about it relate to national security?"

"That's above your pay grade."

"Did you know that the painting isn't even stolen?"

She raised an eyebrow. "Told you that, did he? He's playing you. When he realised you'd noticed the painting, he came up with a story. Jake, you'll be doing the right thing getting the painting back for us. After all, you have one unique advantage: VIP access to his penthouse. You got inside once. You can get inside again. Now stop asking questions and making excuses, and start thinking about how you're going to get this done."

FIFTY-TWO

I stared at the phone after Winslow disconnected. Something didn't feel right.

"I'm sure of only one thing," I said. "We're not being told the full story. Could this get any worse?"

"Sure it could," Sid said. "Calum could turn up and insist we give the painting to him."

"Then thank everything that we finally found the bugs." I shook my head. "We have to turn this around. We have to fight back. I'm not giving up." I turned to the others.

Sid cleared his throat. "I'm not ready to lose just yet."

Daniel shrugged. "I'll go with what Meg does."

"So," Meg said, "shall we work out what we're actually going to do?"

"I have a couple of ideas," Sid said. "First, I don't care if this Winslow checks out. We should run some deeper checks. We need to know what else she's doing."

Meg frowned. "I don't think that's a good idea. We're trying to get her off our backs, not piss her off."

"Maybe," Sid said. "But we need to know what we're dealing with."

I nodded. "Do it. Just carefully."

"Of course. And second, I do agree with Meg. That we need to get Winslow off our backs."

Meg folded her arms. "Yeah, well I have a habit of saying things that make sense—"

"But it's too risky to take on the theft of the painting ourselves," he interrupted. "We need help from someone with expertise in the criminal sphere." He paused and smiled. "Someone like Rouse."

"I don't understand," I said.

"Get him to help you."

"Help with the picture? Or help manage the MI5 team?"

"Either," Sid said. "Both, now that you mention it."

"What exactly are you suggesting? That he whacks Winslow? I think you overestimate my relationship with Rouse and what he's willing to do to help me make him money."

"Better that he finds out about Winslow from you than from someone else."

"I agree," Meg said. "Go to him. If he wants you to continue on his team, he won't want you in jail."

I nodded reluctantly. "That does, somehow, make sense."

"It's not like you can make things any worse. Although try not to upset him enough that he puts you in a block of concrete."

"I will certainly keep that in mind."

FIFTY-THREE

I reached out to Rouse by phone. While he sounded surprised, he agreed to meet me the next day at his club; clear in the tone of his voice was the message that this had better be something that required a face-to-face meeting.

Rouse's club was the famous Huntingdon, on the banks of the Thames, near Putney Bridge. The converted stately home was surrounded by five acres of perfectly manicured lawns: this close to London, it was an obscene waste of space. When my car swept between the gate posts, I was directed to a space where a number of large, suited men were waiting to conduct a security search. They looked disdainfully at my car, then searched me physically and electronically. My phones and watch were taken from me. Then they escorted me past a line of cars even Kieran would have respected, including two Porsches, a grey Ferrari 458 (which I recognised after my visit to Kieran's showroom), a Bentley and an Aston Martin DB8. From there we went up a set of private stairs to a penthouse suite looking south across the gardens towards the river.

Rouse sat on the balcony, staring at the view. Next to him on a silver tray was a large silver tea pot and fine-bone china cups. He didn't turn to face me. "If you ever come here again, you'd better not embarrass me by bringing that car. If I didn't want you to leave promptly, I'd get my men to push it into the Thames."

"Perhaps if I didn't have to pay you all the money I earn, I'd be able to buy something nicer. That said, when I'm working, the goal is to stay unnoticed. An unremarkable car doesn't turn heads."

"Here, *every* car turns heads. Yours turns stomachs." He narrowed his eyes. "So, Jake, what is this about? And I've not been having a good day, so make it quick."

"I have a problem," I said. "I seem to have attracted some unwanted attention."

"Then you should have been more careful." Rouse lifted the lid of the tea pot and gave the leaves a stir.

"And I've been forced into doing a high-risk job."

Rouse turned to face me. "You work for me - I think we can acknowledge that is how things are. Nobody else is going to force you into any job."

"The new party is quite insistent."

"Who is it?" he asked. "I can have a word with them."

"Perhaps you should. It's MI5."

If Rouse was surprised, he hid it well. There was no fear in his expression, just a heavy frown. "What do they want you to do?"

I drew a deep breath. "To steal a Picasso."

"My, my." He put the lid back on the pot. "Which one?"

I blinked. It was an unexpected answer. I'd thought he wouldn't believe me. "*Le pigeon aux petits pois*. Are you an art buff?"

He shrugged. "Sure, if there's money in it. So what's the problem?"

"They don't want to pay me. And I don't know if I can do it successfully, but they're not giving me a choice."

"Fascinating. Why are you telling me?"

"After our last discussion, I thought it was in both our interests that I keep operating as I am. This job threatens that."

"I don't see the connection."

"If I turn the job down, I'll be arrested. If I'm in jail, I won't be able to keep paying you. I do need your help. Resources, manpower."

"And what makes all this so challenging? Who does this painting currently belong to?"

"Bernard Prebble."

Rouse's brow creased, then he poured a cup of what smelt like earl grey into one of the cups. "Never been fond of that man. I imagine his security will be sophisticated. It will be a fascinating test for you."

I hesitated. "What do you mean?"

"Do the job. And I will have the painting."

"What? How does that help me?"

Rouse leaned forward and inhaled the aroma from his cup. "I wasn't aware my role was to help you."

"And, presuming I'm able to obtain the painting, what am I supposed to tell MI5?"

"Whatever you like. Except anything about me."

I glared. "And what will you pay me for getting you the painting?"

He raised an eyebrow. "Let it not be said that I am not fair. I'll pay you the same as MI5 were going to."

My fingers tightened into fists.

A heavy hand fell on my shoulder. I spun and saw Vince, a fixed expression on his face. "Your time's up," he said. "Mr R, your guests have arrived."

Rouse picked up his cup of tea and appeared to forget about me. "Best get the vintage Cognac ready. He'll only bitch if we try and give him the cheap stuff."

"I'll tell the staff."

Vince steered me back through the corridors and down a set of back stairs. As we descended, he spoke in a low voice, "Particularly difficult meeting coming up. Your timing wasn't the best."

"Oh? Who is it?"

"Let's just call him *the Russian*."

I swallowed hard. I suspected I knew who that was.

"For what it's worth, I thought you conducted yourself well."

I blinked. "Sorry, what?"

"You thought things through. You made a reasonable request. You had Mr R's interests in mind, as well as your own. You showed him respect."

"Yet it got me nowhere."

Vince shrugged. "I'm not the boss."

"If you were, you'd have handled it differently?"

"There have to be rules and standards. Or we're all just pigs wrestling in the mud."

"So what should I do?"

"What the boss asks. This painting seems to have piqued his interest."

"But what about MI5?"

We reached the bottom of the stairs and Vince

opened a fire door. The alarm did not go off. A few paces away sat my decidedly undesirable car. Vince shrugged. "They can only arrest you, whereas Mr R has… no such limitations."

I climbed into the car, noting my watch and phone on the passenger seat. "Winslow is scary in her own way. Could you try and appeal to Rouse?"

"He's not one to receive appeals well. Do you remember I mentioned someone stealing a wedding ring from an elderly woman?"

I nodded.

"That was actually my own mother. It was about three years ago, and I asked Mr R to look into the theft. I gave him photos: everything he could have needed." Vince pulled his phone from his pocket and tapped away, then handed it to me.

I looked at the image of an engraved rose-gold ring. "It's…", I searched for the right word, "…wonderfully traditional."

"Made in 1948 by Clacton's Jewellers in Covent Garden." Vince gave a brief smile. "I'd never asked Mr R for a favour before."

"And?"

"He asked how much it was worth. When I said it had only sentimental value, but to my mother it was priceless, he told me to stop wasting his time."

I gave a quiet sigh. As an afterthought I tapped my phone and captured his screen image, then handed his phone back to him. "I'm sorry I asked for his help."

Vince nodded. "So was I, Jake. So was I. Sometimes you have to accept that the only person who is going to help you," he tapped me in the chest, "is you."

FIFTY-FOUR

The meeting with Rouse at the Huntingdon Club had not move things forward as I had hoped. As I drove back, I considered my options. They were not good. None of it was good.

I parked outside my house and let myself in, still distracted, so I didn't register the barely-audible footsteps behind me as I closed the door. Not until it was too late.

Strong arms locked around mine. There was a whisper in my ear, "You're getting sloppy, Jake." Then I was shoved forward, away from my assailant. I spun around and saw Calum grinning at me.

"What the heck?" I shouted, rubbing my arms, aware how much stronger he was.

"Thought we'd pay you a visit with your first set of instructions."

"You broke into my house to do that? Your phone not working?"

"We're going with the personal touch."

"You and Meeks? You think you can trust him?"

"I trust him to do what is good for business. He's looking to make money, so am I. It's simple."

"What exactly do you want? Or are you just trying to intimidate me?"

"Whatever works. And what we want is the Picasso."

I blinked. "What do you mean?"

"The one you discovered in Prebble's offices. The one that MI5 asked you to steal. Agent Winslow, wasn't it?"

My mouth fell open. "How the hell do you know about that?" How was Calum doing this? Had we missed a bug somewhere? I shook my head: those questions would have to wait.

"You'll give us the painting if you don't want us to shop you to the police or the drug dealers, depending on which seems funnier on the day."

I knitted my fingers together. "Why would I give it to you instead of Winslow?"

"Because we'll actually cut you in on the action. It's only fair, since you'll be doing all the work."

"You are something else."

Calum smiled. "We are *three* steps ahead of you. At the least."

I stared at my former colleague. At his smile.

And something inside me snapped.

"You know what, I'm done with you idiots. You do whatever you have to do. I can't operate with you blackmailing us. I'd rather just take the consequences. I really don't care anymore. So do your worst."

"That's not very smart, Jake."

"I couldn't give a toss what you think. And if you've nothing else to say, I'd like you to leave."

"You'll see sense." Calum stepped towards the front

door and put his hand on the lock. "We'll be back in touch."

"I won't hold my breath," I said.

He pulled the door open and began to walk through it, then stopped and turned. "Next time we speak," he said, "you *will* see it differently."

IT WAS THE STRAW THAT BROKE THE CAMEL'S BACK. The tipping point. If Calum knew about the painting and Winslow, then somehow they were still hacking or infiltrating my operations. I had run out of ideas and time. I couldn't give everyone what they wanted. The words of a song my father used to play on vinyl echoed in in my head.

Know when to hold 'em. Know when to fold 'em. Know when to walk away.

Know when to run.

I sat on the sofa and tried to think clearly. So much had happened so fast. I now had at least four different groups messing with my life. Prebble wasn't threatening me with anything, but the others were an immediate danger to me and I could not possibly pacify them all. And, if Prebble found out that I was planning to steal from him, I was pretty sure I could also place him on the danger list.

I knew what I couldn't do, and I knew what I could.

But before anything else, there was one thing I had to make sure of.

FIFTY-FIVE

The taxi pulled up at the end of the driveway, stopping in the shadow of the large oak tree. I tipped the driver enough to make him smile, but not enough to make him remember me. If I could have got here any other way, I would have done, but using my own car, which was probably bugged, or hiring one, which created a digital footprint, were out of the question.

There was no sign of anybody suspicious, so I turned and walked down the drive. Nobody came out to meet me, as I had instructed. There was a key under a particularly sad-looking garden gnome. I used it to let myself in.

Kieran sat at the kitchen table, his expression unreadable. Liam beamed at me, running up and giving me a hug. "Uncle Jake!" He squeezed me tightly. "Did you bring me a present?"

I hugged him back. "Not this time."

"Can you go and play in the other room, Liam?" Kieran said through tight lips. "If, that is, it'll be safe there." He glared at me.

"Why?" Liam asked. "Are you on a covert mission?"

I raised a finger to my lips. "Someone might be listening."

He hesitated, then tapped the side of his nose. "Understood, Agent Jake. I'll go keep watch. If I see anything I'll call you on my special phone." He reached into his pocket and pulled out the handset I'd given him. "I always carry it on me."

"Good work. You do that." I watched him run out of the room, then turned back to my cousin. He did not offer me a drink. For several moments he just stared at me. Finally he spoke. "What is going on, Jake? It's almost like you believe you really *are* a secret agent." He placed his hands flat on the table. "We can't up and leave. We only just moved, and I can't unsettle Liam again."

"I never meant for this. I was so careful. I've always tried to keep you out of my... complexities." I hesitated. "Even while trying to save you from your own."

"What are you talking about?"

"I know about your gambling."

"Huh?" He looked confused. "Of course you do. I told you about it the other day."

"I know about *all* of your gambling debts to the Rouse organisation."

He blinked. "What?"

"That day you got a broken nose. You claimed it was an accident, but I saw the man who did it. I followed him out of your house. And I later tracked him to Rouse's HQ. I offered to take on the debts for you."

"You offered to pay two million quid? How could you even pay a fraction of that? They must have laughed you out the door."

His reaction stung me with disappointment: after years of building up to finally coming clean, I was expecting something far more explosive, but he seemed more resigned than surprised. "I haven't paid it all back yet. But I've made good progress. The problem is, things have got even more complicated recently."

Kieran stood and walked over the window. "You never even told me you knew."

"Didn't you wonder why Rouse stopped asking for the money?"

"I was just grateful for the respite. Look, this is all a bit much to grasp. How are you paying him back? Did your father leave you money in his will?"

"If only. I've developed a freelance business."

"Doing what? IT? Are you a hacker?"

"Not exactly. I recover stolen items for a fee. I have a lot of tech that helps me trace things. Digital breadcrumbs are everywhere these days."

Kieran nodded. "Look, that is very cool. But I never asked you to do this. Why are you telling me today? What's changed?"

"I can't keep up the payments. And if I can't make the payments, you are in a lot of trouble. You have to leave." I reached into my bag and produced a folder. "This contains Eurostar and plane tickets. Get as far as Paris, then take a bus somewhere random. Pay in cash. I've included some fake IDs for once you're on the continent, although I doubt they'll pass a full border check. Don't try to contact me once you're away. It will only make tracing you much easier, because they'll definitely be watching my comms."

"Why don't you simply keep doing what you've been doing? Ask for a bit more time."

"Because it's not only Rouse. There are other parties involved, and I can't please them all."

Kieran's brow furrowed. "Then go to the police."

"Believe me, I'd do that if I thought it would solve matters. You should have asked who Rouse was before you got into debt to him. Let's just say he has a large interest in poured concrete. And if he doesn't get his money, you and I might end up with a lot of it poured on top of us."

"That isn't funny."

"Do I look like I'm joking? Your new debts have made everything impossible."

"I'm sorry. But like I said, I never asked you to do this, Jake."

"What was I supposed to do? You've always looked after me. And you've had enough bad shit for several lifetimes."

"I don't know what to say. Your father would be proud of what you've done. Except that it's me, and I know he never liked me."

"Oh, I don't know if that's true."

"Well, we both lost our parents well before their time. I appreciate that you're doing your best so that my son doesn't. How long do we have?" he asked, glancing around.

I was about to answer when the phone on the kitchen wall rang loudly.

Kieran frowned. "Should I answer that?"

I shrugged. "They probably have a lot more than your number."

He stood up and grabbed the phone, listening to the person on the other end. Looking puzzled, he handed it over. "It's for you."

I took the phone.

"Hello, Jake," Calum said.

I swore. "How did you know I was here?"

"I'm resourceful. And I have one of your friends with me."

I felt a tightening in my chest. "What do you mean?"

"Rumour is that you're thinking of skipping town. So I thought I'd re-balance your decision-making." I could almost hear him smiling.

There was a pause then a second voice spoke into the phone. "Don't worry about me," Meg said. "I'm going to hurt Calum in places he won't want hurt. I don't need your help with any—"

Meg's voice cut off and Calum spoke again. "Are we on the same page?"

"If you so much as—"

"Don't be stupid, Jake. And don't for a second think that I won't do whatever I have to do."

I wanted to scream. I wanted to reach down the phone and take Calum by the throat. "What do you want?"

"Come back to town and do what we asked of you."

I ground my teeth. "I need Meg back if I'm to do the op."

"Sorry, but that ship has sailed. You're just going to have to improvise." He paused. "Don't try anything, Jake. Remember what I told you: we're always three steps ahead."

The line went dead. I put the phone back on the cradle, then stared at the wall.

Kieran moved next to me. "What's happened now?"

I puffed out my cheeks. "I'm going back to do what they want."

"Have they got a friend of yours?"

I blinked. "Someone I work with. Someone I don't want them to hurt."

"Is there anything I can do to help?"

"Stay here, and stay out of trouble. If you don't hear from me in forty-eight hours then leave and do what I told you."

"What are you going to do?"

"I'm going to get my friend back."

FIFTY-SIX

THE ANSWER TO HOW I COULD FIND MEG HAD SUDDENLY sprung into my mind, and it was Calum who had made me think of it.

He'd obviously been watching me for months and knew where I'd been. Until now I'd been reacting to his moves. That had to stop. Instead of doing what Calum demanded, I had to take away his leverage. I had to get to Meg. Using the tech I had developed with Sid, I could use the GPS database once to track someone or something. Although Sid had warned that the phone companies' intrusion detection systems would mean we could probably only do it once, this was the time to do it.

I found an internet cafe and used my laptop to activate the external database that Sid and I had set up; this prompted it to start pulling historical location data from an unsuspecting mobile-phone service-provider. We'd created it as a security measure to ensure that we could find anyone on the team at any time in case anything ever went wrong with a recovery. Although

Calum and Meeks' people would not have let Meg keep her phone or any other device, and obviously I could not use the system to track Calum's new phone, I could still back-trace something less obvious.

If you are holding someone prisoner, it has to be in a private site you have control over: somewhere you've visited before, likely several times, as it isn't something you can set up securely in a hurry. New tenants or purchasers prompt attention, so renting something specifically to hold a prisoner is always risky; better to adapt somewhere that you are already using for some other purpose.

Calum might have visited such a site without his phone, but I had to hope he'd been careless: he couldn't have gone off-grid that frequently or we would have started to notice. And if he had been careless, as he must have been, then a pattern would develop.

I sipped a large latte, loaded with sugar, and began looking at the data. It seemed that Calum had got around. He had roved across London. Many of the movements correlated with our operations. There was too much to make sense of, so I stripped out city locations. That helped. Calum had been a fan of Arsenal and there were a number of visits to the Emirates Stadium; I removed those too. I also removed data from trips to Heathrow, Gatwick and Stansted airports.

I cast my eye over the remaining possibilities and one site caught my eye. It was in the middle of nowhere, just south of the M40 in Oxfordshire, perhaps an hour's drive out of London. Using Google maps, I zoomed in and found it was a lone warehouse or barn on an abandoned farm. Calum had been there more than a dozen times but, from the background checks I'd previously run on him, I knew he had no relatives in that area.

I pulled out my phone. It was time to arrange a rescue.

FIFTY-SEVEN

The SUV was a rental: black paint, darkened windows, big enough for seven, though currently it held only three. It was nearly 10pm when I parked it in the narrow country lane, switched off the headlights and turned to my two passengers. "You guys ready?"

Sid looked at me. "Are we still sure this is a good idea?"

"Anything that gets Meg back is a good idea," I said.

"I agree," Daniel replied, stretching his arms. "But we don't know what we're walking into."

"They don't know that we're walking in at all."

Sid shook his head. "You keep assuming the element of surprise. What if you're wrong, like you were about us being bugged?"

"How could they know? I only came up with the plan a couple of hours ago." I climbed from the car. "Now let's do this."

Sid and Daniel joined me as I opened the boot. Inside was a large black canvass holdall. Unzipping it, I removed a taser, baseball bat and shotgun.

Daniel immediately selected the firearm and inspected it with an expert eye. "Are you sure, Jake? Isn't this crossing a line?"

"They crossed the line when they took Meg. Besides, I've loaded it with rock salt. We just need to make it look like we mean business."

Sid examined the taser. "I think this is more my thing." Then he patted his backpack. "Along with the toys I brought to the party."

I shrugged. "Just don't hesitate." I picked up the baseball bat.

Daniel looked around. "Did you bring torches?"

I smiled. "Much better than that." I produced three sets of night-vision head-gear that would enable us to see in almost absolute darkness.

Sid slipped his on, pulling his ponytail through the straps. "Very natty."

"At least attempt to be serious," I said.

"I'm trying. This is all scaring me. Isn't it scaring you?"

"I'm too angry to be afraid."

Daniel put his goggles in position and started adjusting them.

I handed over three super-bright LED mag-lites. "And these are just in case. Now let's do this before Meg gets impatient and decides to rescue herself."

We climbed over the barbed-wire fence and made our way through the muddy field. The barn was a shabby wooden building with a corrugated iron roof. It had several windows, though all but one were boarded up. We stopped fifty metres away and listened. We could just make out conversation coming from inside.

Sid dropped to a knee and opened his backpack.

Inside was his latest variant of the camera drone, equipped with four rotors to provide vertical lift. He pulled out a complex-looking remote-control then pressed a button on the drone and threw it into the air. There was a whoosh then the aircraft took off towards the barn, lost from sight in moments. On the remote control a fifteen-centimetre display lit up, showing what the drone was seeing, enhanced for night-vision. Daniel and I removed our goggles and leaned close to watch. A grey image of the barn swelled on the screen as the craft approached the remaining window, slowing to provide a view inside.

"A figure, probably female, sitting on a chair," Sid said. "Her hands are tied behind her. She's wearing a hood, but it's Meg's height and build." Sid adjusted the controls and the image swung to the left then the right. "Two guards. No guns visible. Wonder why they've got her wearing a hood?"

"Calum?" I asked. "Johnson?"

"Not in sight."

I turned to Daniel. "What do you think?"

"I guess it's her."

"You think we've stumbled on an entirely separate hostage situation in a random barn in the middle of nowhere?"

He blinked. "Just tell me what to do."

"Sure you don't want me running tactical?" Sid asked.

I shook my head. "You're our taser guy, remember?"

We moved to the main entrance. I crouched and reached for my lock-pick kit. Pulling out one of the tools, I slid it into the lock then stopped. The mechanism was already open.

"Maybe they got sloppy?" I whispered, but it felt wrong. "You take the one on the left; I'll take right. Sid, you cover the room in case anyone else appears."

I kicked the door open and rolled through the door to the right, bringing my baseball bat up. Daniel rolled left, and brought up the shotgun, pointed it at the ceiling and fired.

The noise, in the interior of the barn, was stupendous. I staggered back. Sid, who had followed behind Daniel, dropped the taser and covered his ears.

I turned to the three figures, two standing, one cuffed in the chair, and immediately knew something was off. None of them had moved. They were like statues.

"Hands in the air!" Daniel shouted, lowering the shotgun from the ceiling and aiming at the figure nearest him.

I cursed and walked over to the figure standing on the right, giving it a shove with the end of my baseball bat. It toppled backwards and clattered to the floor. "It's a dummy," I said, turning to the figure on the chair and lifting the hood. It was another mannequin.

Daniel jabbed the barrel of his weapon at the remaining figure. It, too, fell to the ground.

"I think we'd better get out of here—"

On one wall a large dusty TV screen flickered on. It showed an extreme close-up of Calum's smiling face. "Guys, why don't we have a chat," he said, "before you run off?"

I ran over to the screen, bat raised. "Where is Meg?"

"I knew you'd follow the trail of digital breadcrumbs: that you'd feel you could solve this. But there is no actual trail, Jake. Three steps ahead, remember?"

"Just answer my question. If you've hurt her—"

The image pulled back, Calum's face taking on an expression of sympathy. "It's OK, Jake. Meg is fine. And if you continue to do as we ask, she'll continue to be fine."

"I want to speak to her. Or the deal is off."

Calum shouted something over his shoulder. There was some grunting and two large men dragged Meg in front of the camera.

She looked tired, unkempt. And very, very angry. "Hello, boys," she croaked. "I see you're having a party without me."

"Well, you haven't been returning our calls," I said, trying to keep my anger in check.

"Seem to have mislaid my phone."

Calum pushed her aside. "So, Jake, stop messing about and get on with your job. There'll be no more warnings."

Meg pushed him back. "Don't do it, Jake. I can rescue myself."

"You couldn't find her if you wanted to. We found the new tracers. High quality stuff. Government-level, maybe."

"What tracers?" Sid asked. "We don't have any—"

"Yeah, right," Calum replied. "Now get on with recovering the painting or…" He pulled out a large, serrated dagger. The screen went dark. I stared at it in fury.

"So what do we do now?" Sid asked.

I closed my eyes. "We do better."

FIFTY-EIGHT

It was cold and quiet in my house as Sid, Daniel and I walked into the kitchen. I placed the three takeaway pizza boxes on the table, and a large bottle of Coke that the pizza place had insisted on giving us free. "Plates?" I asked.

In answer, Sid and Daniel grabbed a box each, and started eating. I shrugged and did the same.

"So what is this?" Daniel asked, between mouthfuls. "The last meal of three condemned men?"

"Or," Sid said, "is this when we accept we have to do what they say?"

I looked at them, then I shook my head. "No, gentlemen. This cannot be the moment we give up. This has to be the turning point."

"Haven't we said that before?" Sid asked.

"Yeah," Daniel said. "We still can't take a step without being anticipated."

I leaned closer. "We have two choices. The first is to go to the police."

"And how is that going to work?" Sid asked. "Rouse

won't worry about them. Meeks and Calum well, they'll probably drop us in it further, just for the hell of it. And as for Winslow, maybe she'll pull strings and the police won't respond."

"Even if they do," Daniel said, choosing a slice of Hawaiian, "this isn't going to play out like an episode of 24. The police won't suddenly send in a SWAT team without a lot more information. And even if they do, they probably won't be fast enough."

I nodded. "I agree, which means we go with the second choice – we solve this. And for that we need a new plan, and fast. But before we blindly go ahead, let's think this over." I paused. "What did Calum mean by having found a tracer on Meg?"

"Who knows?" Daniel asked.

"He described it as government-issue," Sid said. He snapped his fingers and stared at me. "Are you thinking what I'm thinking?"

I closed my eyes. "That Winslow is bugging us? We scanned ourselves. Several times. I simply don't believe it."

"Maybe Meg wasn't thorough enough?"

"Look," Daniel said, "we're never going to know. All these what ifs aren't getting us anywhere. We need to do something."

"You're suddenly talking a lot," I said. "But you're right. The crux of the issue is that we have too many different problems and we're flying blind. MI5 want us to do a near impossible job. If I don't, they will arrest me. If I don't give the painting to Rouse, he'll kill me. If I don't give the painting to Edgar and Calum, they'll hurt Meg. And if we do any of this, we're stealing from someone who is supposed to be a client. It's a no-win situation."

"That's an unfortunately accurate summary," Sid said. "We're not set up to operate in what feels like a goldfish bowl. We always assumed we were the ones working in the shadows, taking advantage of other people's ignorance. But recently quite the reverse has been true. And I still don't understand how. We replaced all the drives."

"I agree, it's impossible." Then suddenly it struck me. "Unless—"

"Unless what?" Daniel asked.

I couldn't believe I'd overlooked it. It was suddenly so obvious. "Unless the chips were already compromised."

Sid looked confused. "But weren't they brand new from your supplier?"

"*Abigail*," I said slowly. "And yes, I thought they were brand new. I was told they were brand new."

Sid looked alarmed. "I didn't check the new chips. I just assumed… I mean they were all shrink wrapped…"

"So if someone puts something in a plastic bag, you lot switch off your brains?" Daniel asked. "They clearly had to get up early in the morning to outsmart you."

"Hey, shut up," Sid said. "It's not like anyone else thought of it before now."

"Look," I said, "this was a plan with layers, but suddenly part of it makes sense."

"So what do we do?" Daniel asked. "I mean what do we do with this Abigail? We have to get her and question her: find out who she is working for," Daniel said. "Surely it's Meeks."

"Why would she tell us?"

"I can be persuasive."

I shook my head. "If you're suggesting what I think you're suggesting, then we are not doing that."

"She crossed the line. She deserves wherever it takes."

"We need to do something we haven't done so far."

"Which is?" Daniel growled.

"We have to make people do what *they* want to do: it's a hell of a lot easier than the reverse. If we just grab her, they'll immediately respond, likely with some other trick. If we spread a bit of *misinformation*, we might be able to engineer an advantage."

"So we do what?" Sid asked. "Buy *more* gear from her?"

"Perhaps. But there must be some element they don't control. Some factor they didn't consider." I gave a smile. "And the answer has just come to me."

"What?"

"Not what." I picked up my glass and took a sip. "*Who*."

FIFTY-NINE

THE NEXT DAY I SET OFF FOR MY MORNING RUN WITH more than the usual degree of anticipation, activating the newly-installed phone-tracking app. It showed my target near Wimbledon Common. I glanced at my watch: I was perfectly on time.

Turning onto the common, I began following the gravel footpath around the edge. Next to a signpost stood another jogger, counting her pulse. As I went past, she coughed, then started running, and easily caught up with me before sprinting past, green Lycra and trainers flashing with reflective strips. Straining, I managed to get level with her. "See," I said between breaths, "I knew you could have run after that bag snatcher yourself."

Susan Statham glared at me. "Don't let the fact that I am awesome mislead you. I *detest* running. I never do it unless there is no alternative. I'd rather be soaking in a hot tub with a couple of mimosas." She spread her palms. "But you turn your hand to what you have to in this business."

"You've certainly committed to the hi-vis look." I pointed at the reflective strips on her shoes.

"Jake dear, all the runners like to be seen these days." She raised an eyebrow in my direction. "I assumed you'd be the kind of guy who was up to date."

We took a detour around a particularly large clump of trees, then I signalled for her to slow down. "If we're going to speak, I'd prefer a jog rather than a sprint."

She eased her pace. "OK, but why *are* we meeting?"

"I need your help."

She gave a laugh. "How the mighty have fallen."

I stopped running. "I'm serious. Meg's been kidnapped."

"That girl in your team? By whom?"

"A difficult client. I can't involve the police."

"That's less than ideal. Presumably your client wants you to do something; why not just do it?"

I sighed. "It's a *very* complicated situation."

"How many complications are we talking?"

"Give or take forty million of them. Which is why I need your help."

She blinked. "I'm not sure if you've forgotten, but I'm not in this for the money."

"And that's why you're the person I called."

"OK, you've got my interest. Explain."

We walked as we talked. I gave Susan as much of the background as I could. She listened without saying much, then finally shook her head. "This is majorly screwed up. How'd you get yourself into this mess?"

"It seems to have just happened."

"In my experience there's usually a reason. Perhaps you'd better try to work out what it is."

"Does it matter?" I asked. "How can we possibly give them all what they want?"

"Then we have to think creatively. Either we change what they want, or we make them think they've got it, when they haven't."

I sighed. "Even if I could come up with a solution, I don't have any systems that I can use anymore: not without being monitored, or letting them know I know."

"Which is why you need me. You really should have been more… diverse with your equipment sourcing. Having a single point of failure with your IT supplier is a big mistake."

"Next time I'll do things differently."

"If you get a chance at a next time. You came to me so I could dig you out of this mess, so my question is 'what's in it for me?' I may not be in it for the money but that doesn't mean I just help anyone, for any reason."

"Then what do you want?"

"A dinner where you don't actually walk out: one where we talk about what we can do to change the world. In however small a way."

"How could I refuse?"

She laughed. "Quite, given that you have at least three serious players after that painting and your deal to find the daughter will disappear if your client discovers you're planning to steal from him." Susan reached into a slim pouch clipped round her waist and removed a small calculator-like device slightly larger than a credit card. She handed it to me. "A new comms unit for you. Use it to route everything you send me."

I turned the ugly unit over in my hand. "From the design-free end of the '90s?"

"Looks can be deceiving. And it has one feature that

your current kit does not: the bad guys won't be able to monitor it. Now, we need to get busy."

I ARRIVED AT THE TECHFIXED OFFICES, FEELING hopeful. That hope was quickly dashed.

As I walked in Sid looked up, an agitated expression on his face. Without a word he nodded towards the server room and, sensing his mood, I followed him. Once inside he locked the door.

"What's the matter?" I asked.

"You know I said we should look into Winslow? Well look what I uncovered as part of our other surveillance efforts – one camera feed in particular that you asked me to monitor." He pulled open his laptop and tapped on a video file. It began playing, showing a house in a quiet street. It could have been anywhere in Britain, but I recognised it at once. It was from a hidden camera I had placed recently.

I watched Ellie Winslow approach Kieran's front door. She knocked sharply and, almost immediately, the door was opened. A beaming Kieran appeared, they spoke briefly then he beckoned her inside.

I stared at the screen then tapped to rewind the video. We watched it again.

"What is going on here?" I asked finally.

"Isn't it obvious?" Sid said. "Your cousin is cooperating with MI5."

"To do what? Look, is the footage real?"

"Of course it's real. It's from one of our systems, and there are no tags or artefacts that suggest it's been manipulated."

I rubbed my temples. "Why would she be meeting with him?"

"He doesn't look surprised. She doesn't show him any ID. They must be working together. Most likely it's something to do with you."

"Kieran doesn't know what I do. Or he didn't until very recently. Maybe she misrepresented who she is?"

"Do you really believe that?"

"I don't know," I said, pulling out my phone. "But I'm going to find out."

SIXTY

The venue for the meeting was a first-floor cafe at Paddington Station, overlooking the concourse. Kieran stood up and gripped me by the shoulders. "Is there any news about your friend?"

I pulled back from him and indicated that we should sit. "I think it's time we were *completely* honest with each other." I watched his reaction but there was none. If he was this good at hiding things, it was a wonder he ever lost at cards.

"Of course, Jake. But what do you mean?"

I pulled out my tablet computer and called up a photo of Winslow. "Do you know who this is?" I slid the tablet across the table.

He glanced at it. Again no reaction. "Why?"

"Dammit, just answer the question." As I raised my voice, I noticed a large man sitting a few tables away seemed to glance in my direction. He immediately stared down at his newspaper.

"Look, if we're being honest," Kieran said, "maybe it's… safer if I don't answer."

"I know you've met with her. Likely more than once."

"How could you… oh never mind. Her name is Ellie Winslow." He leaned closer. "She's an MI5 agent."

I swallowed. "Why were you meeting with her? Was she asking about me?"

He glanced around. "It wasn't the main reason we spoke."

"Then what was?"

"Jake, you have to know that I would never have lied to you, not without very good reason." He sighed. "She was quizzing me about an old MI5 case."

"Why would she do that?"

"Because I used to work there. She used to be my boss."

I stared at Kieran. "You're having a laugh. You've always been in sales."

"My cover. Well, until Carol died. The car showroom is a real job."

"What did you do at MI5?"

"I'm not supposed to talk about it. Official Secrets Act and all that—"

"So what, you were an assassin?"

He gave a snort. "I was a desk jockey. A research assistant. Very boring, even though it was intimately linked with national security."

"And you never told me? You lied to me all these years?"

"Jake, it comes with the territory. Why are you so interested in Winslow?"

"She's got me working on a case for her. She hasn't given me a choice."

"Oh. Look, I can't say I'm shocked. Her reputation is… She's the reason I couldn't stay there any longer."

"It's funny, my father always said you were lying about something." Out of the corner of my eye I saw the large man with the newspaper stand up, glance in our direction, then walk out. Almost immediately another large man walked in and took the same seat.

"Yeah, well, in my defence," Kieran said, tapping the table, "I had a good reason."

"Why is Winslow talking to you now?"

"Like I said, an old case."

I folded my arms. "To do with Bernard Prebble?"

"How would you know that?"

"Because he's intimately involved with what she has me working on."

"Which is what?"

"Kieran, I came here to get intel from you. Not the other way around."

"Look, if I'm going to disclose classified information I'd really like to limit it to what you truly need to know."

I knitted my fingers together. "She wants me to steal a painting from Prebble's penthouse suite: an original Picasso."

Kieran whistled. "That must be worth… millions."

"Forty of them, in sterling, so I'm told."

"Recovering a painting isn't MI5's thing. Why is she involved?"

"She won't say."

"And is she paying you for this service?"

"If only. She's paying me with information about my father's murder."

"Info that the police don't already have?"

"Yeah, I thought that was odd. But I suppose MI5

might have their own data repositories. She said my father worked for her as a consultant. Would you know anything about that?"

He frowned. "Just that it sounds pretty unlikely. But she was a field-agent. I was only an analyst. I wouldn't have known if he was doing some work for her."

"So basically you can't help me? I don't know who I can trust. Or if I can trust anyone."

Kieran nodded. "That's always a good question to ask."

I stared at him. "Are you saying you don't trust Winslow?"

"She's very good at what she does. And she got that way by knowing how to get around the rules. In my experience you can trust her to have her own agenda."

"Then what does she want from me? Is it really just the painting?"

"Could it have something to do with whatever your father was doing for her?"

"Don't you think I've asked myself that question?"

"I mean he worked with Maxwell Rouse. Bernard Prebble. Winslow… That's a lot of potential for trouble."

"So what? You're suggesting my father was up to something criminal? He wasn't like that."

"No offence, Jake, but you can't say that. Not with certainty."

"He was my father."

"Parents aren't perfect."

"Except your father."

"Well he did sacrifice his life to save mine, but maybe my mother wouldn't agree."

"I'm sure she would have made the same decision:

you over your father and her own life. It's what parents do."

"Then you didn't know my mother at all, Jake."

"That's a conversation for another time." I shook my head. "If there's a link to my father, I'm just not seeing it. Rouse hinted once that my father might have stolen, but he never went into details. I always presumed it was just fishing after some unfinished business."

"Yet three years after his death, Winslow is clearly still actively interested in whatever your father was involved in."

"Maybe it's not to do with me. Maybe it's to do with you and that's why she approached you. Maybe you're the centre, and I'm on the periphery."

Kieran closed his eyes, an odd expression on his face. Was it frustration? "No, Jake. It's not me she's after. It's you."

"How do you know? And how do you know Rouse?"

"I really am sorry for the mess that I've got you caught up in with him. If there was anything I could do to sort this out—"

"I think it's gone way beyond your capabilities." I reached forward and gripped his arm. "No more lies, Kieran. Tell me about Rouse."

"It won't help you. I don't know where Winslow comes into all this but there is one thing you should know. She's no longer part of MI5."

"Huh? That makes no sense."

"Oh she can certainly make it look like she is with contractors to staff her new operation, but she was fired two years ago. I assume it was for some type of misconduct. Now she's seeking to profit from the intel she gathered while in her post. I don't know what the connection is with your father, Prebble and Rouse, but if the painting is worth what you say it is…" He shook his head. "You should take it to the authorities, only…"

"She'd hurt you if I did?"

"Not just me. She'll do whatever is necessary. And she won't hesitate."

"So what should I do?"

"In the end, you have to make your own choices. But if it was up to me, I'd give her what she wants or things are going to end very badly for all of us."

SIXTY-ONE

My meeting with Kieran had made one thing clear: before I did anything else, I had to find out just what was so special about this painting, beyond its apparent monetary value. I crouched in the darkness, waiting for our target. It felt good to be running a mission again, even though I didn't have my usual tactical support. Sid was focusing on alternative methods to track down Meg. Instead it was Susan's voice that buzzed in my ear. "He's coming up the stairs."

Reginald Monday lived in a spacious penthouse apartment. Penthouses were often easy to access physically, at least from the top, if you didn't mind climbing. It wasn't my favourite activity, but it usually paid off. With Susan's remote support, I had disabled the alarm system and gained entry. But instead of recovering an item and leaving with all haste, I checked out my exit options, then selected a position in the shadows and waited.

"Now," said Susan.

I heard a key turning in the door, then it swung

inwards. A tall bony figure, with beady eyes, stepped through and typed a code into the alarm keypad. It gave an error beep, and he hesitated. Then he walked over to the fireplace and spoke loudly. "Are you here to hurt me or steal from me?" The voice sounded intensely familiar, but I was having trouble placing it.

"Neither," I said. "I just want to talk to you."

"Then get out. I don't talk to anyone without an appointment." He hesitated, then raised his head to the ceiling with a sigh. "Jake Moro?"

I swallowed. "How did you know—"

He spun and my question was answered.

I did know Reginald Monday. Except I knew him as my boss at TechFixed: Bill Lundy.

"OK," he said, "I presume you have a team member listening in. Invite them up. I think we're all going to need a drink."

We sat on three of Lundy's expensive leather armchairs, drinking cognac. Susan stretched out like she owned the place.

I began by stating the obvious. "So *you* are Reginald Monday? That makes no sense at all."

"It's a business identity. I've used it for so long I suspect it survived your verification process."

I shook my head. "Is this some long con I've completely missed?"

"There's no need to feel bad. I offered you this job very shortly after your father passed away and before you started your consulting business. You've changed a lot since then, learned an enormous amount. I doubt I'd catch you out now."

"You know about my other business?"

"Not in detail, but I did investigate enough to work what you kept going off to do. I'm not a complete old fool."

"*You* conned *me*. I suppose that makes me a *young* fool."

"I'm not conning you, Jake. Quite the reverse."

Susan stifled a laugh.

"This isn't funny," I said.

She reached out and jabbed a finger in my ribs. "Oh come on. Mr Lundy here clearly wishes you no harm. He didn't give you brandy under duress."

"All these years I've been working for someone who isn't real."

Lundy shrugged. "William Lundy is my real name. The business is real, even if I did set the whole thing up for tax reasons, to offset expenses at the art dealership."

"But why me? You could have hired anyone."

"Because your father asked me to keep an eye out for you, and I said I would."

I frowned. "You knew my father?"

"I was one of his clients. He made me a great deal of money over the years. I trusted him and hoped I could learn to trust you too. In the three years you've worked for TechFixed, I've certainly never had any reason to doubt the work you do for me."

"When did he tell you to watch out for me?"

"In the weeks before he died. He said he had a serious problem – one he wasn't sure he could resolve. He said he was planning to leave."

"We *were* going on holiday. I was at the airport on

the day of the bomb. Why haven't you told me all this before?"

"Because he asked me not to drag you into it. But now you've dragged yourself in, and I didn't even realise it was happening. Why are you here tonight, Jake?"

"I met with Bernard Prebble recently. He has *Le pigeon aux petits pois*. Claimed he bought it from you. Yet your official position is that it was stolen."

Lundy's eyes narrowed further. "And?"

"I've been asked to unsteal it. As you know, that's what I do in my little side business."

"Well, you're going to find that rather hard in this case."

"Yes. I've seen Prebble's security."

"That's not the real issue. If Prebble has a picture, it isn't genuine."

"How can you be so sure?"

"Because," he said, with a smile, "I still have the original."

"You reported a painting stolen when you still had it, even though you weren't involved in an insurance scam?" I asked.

"I said *a* painting was stolen. I was very specific in the wording. I'm not a liar."

"If the painting in Prebble's office is a fake, wouldn't he know that?"

"Perhaps." Lundy scratched his nose with a bony finger. "But he's never made any claim to that effect, public or otherwise, to my knowledge."

"So how did my father come into this? And why did you report a painting stolen then imply it was that one?"

"I was experiencing a… cash-flow problem. Your father came to me with a proposal that was too good to refuse. I got to keep my painting, and he paid me a lot of money. All in return for access to the original. Of course there's only one reason people ask for extended private access to a rare painting: to make a forgery."

"And you reporting it stolen added credibility that it was the original."

"I'm sure that was the intention. I then had to make sure I kept the original far from view. But since I never wanted to exhibit it publicly that really wasn't a problem."

"So where is it now?"

Lundy laughed. "In a Swiss bank vault. You can't get to it."

"Now that sounds like a challenge," Susan said.

I frowned at her, then turned back to Lundy. "Have you got any idea why my father did all this?"

He shrugged. "He didn't share his plan with me. All I know is that he spent several weeks on the forgery, and almost the same amount of time getting the perfect frame hand-crafted. I have to say the finished result was pretty stunning."

"You're saying he painted it himself?"

"Apparently your mother was something of an artist and she taught him. He said he never had much imagination, but he did have the technical ability to replicate a work almost exactly. Only far more slowly than most forgers: anyone else could have made two paintings in the same time."

"No forgery would fool every expert. Not the type Prebble can afford."

"That wasn't my problem. I presumed Prebble found out he'd been deceived, and I wondered for a while if he had something to do with your father's death. But the idea that he'd murder someone, even for forty million, seems unlikely. Bearing in mind that this is a man who allegedly stole a billion from his own pension fund, I doubt he would get out of bed for the price of a Picasso.

"So you just went along with the plan?"

"Of course I did. I needed the money and I made sure my part was low-risk. I kept well out of the rest. Your father was in with a rather 'bad' crowd – I presume you know who he had been dealing with – but that wasn't my problem. Maxwell Rouse would murder you for the change in your wallet. Well, more accurately, he'd *have* you murdered. He doesn't get his hands dirty any more, much as he'd like to. In fact he's got a lot more risk averse since taking a big financial hit around the time your father died."

"Someone else I know suggested my father might have been involved in Rouse losing money – or at least something valuable."

"Your father didn't seem like a man driven by monetary gain. Perhaps he was just in the wrong place at the wrong time when he died. All I know is that he was working on getting out of whatever he was involved with. It felt like the least I could do to offer you a job to keep you afloat after such a sudden loss."

I stood. "I appreciate you talking to us."

Lundy nodded. "I wish you all the best, Jake. It's always been good knowing that if anyone ever does steal something from me, I'd know who to call."

SIXTY-TWO

We left Lundy's apartment, this time using the lift, and walked quickly to where Susan had parked her van.

"So," she said, as I climbed in, "I'm not clear exactly where that leaves us."

I shrugged. "With more questions." We called Sid and Daniel on speaker-phone and briefed them about what had just happened.

"Lundy?" Sid coughed. "What a dark horse!"

"You're not wrong," I said.

"So I guess," Susan said, "that you're going to tell your various patrons that the painting is a fraud."

I looked at her. "That's the last thing I'm going to do."

"But if the painting isn't real, why are we stealing it?" Sid asked. "Or are we not doing that anymore?"

"Look, it's obviously never been about the painting. MI5 would never get us involved for something like that."

"So you think Winslow knows it's a fake already? Why ask you to steal it if it's not really what she's after?"

"I think she's trying to provoke Prebble into something."

Susan shook her head. "Then why doesn't she just tell you what she actually wants you to do?"

"Maybe it's classified. Maybe she just doesn't trust me. It would be fair enough: I don't trust her either. Some further information came my way that might explain things: I'm not sure she's as 'on the books' as she claims."

"What about your father? It seems he was trying to defraud Prebble, not that Prebble doesn't deserve it, but if Winslow knew I doubt she liked it."

"Maybe my father didn't trust her either and was doing his own thing to try to get away from Rouse."

"So who do you think killed him?"

"I don't know. Both Rouse and Prebble had more reason to keep him alive in the short term."

"You're presuming they behaved rationally." She shook her head. "Not that it changes things for the moment. What's the plan?"

"First, we get the painting from Prebble's penthouse."

"Of course. We just walk in and take it."

I smiled. "Something like that."

Susan laughed. "OK, just supposing you can pull that off, what then? You can't give the painting to all three."

"We aren't going to give them the painting. We're going to give them what they want. But we still need to find out where Meg is, because I don't trust Meeks and Calum to honour any deal we may make."

"Surely you have some trick up your sleeve?"

"I had one – accessing old GPS logs – but it was a one-shot deal. All the other stuff Calum knows about already."

Susan nodded. "What about that tech supplier? Maybe she could help us use their techniques against them. I can help you with that. All you need do is use your charm to set up another meeting."

"Well, I do owe her money, so that won't be hard. Except… I might need to borrow some funds."

Sid coughed again. "Don't look at me."

Susan sighed. "You mean me, don't you?"

"And there's one other thing you could help me with." I pulled out my phone and sent her an image.

She looked at her phone's screen. "Doesn't look expensive. I doubt anyone's going to pay much to retrieve that."

"They're not going to pay anything. I'm looking into it on spec, but I have a hunch it might prove important."

"You want me to try and trace it?"

"Actually I already know where it is: someone's selling it on eBay. I'll ping you the listing. I just want you to buy it. Add it to what I owe you."

"When I said I wasn't in this for the money, I didn't mean I was in it to give other people money. Not even you, Jake."

"I'll make it up to you."

"You'd better."

SIXTY-THREE

I sat on a bench, high on Richmond Hill, looking down across the meadows to the grey sweep of the River Thames. A cold wind was blowing so I drew my collar up. Abigail was on time as always, on this occasion clad in a grey overcoat and skinny trousers. She nodded as she walked up, her expression fixed and wary. I smiled briefly towards her, then looked back down at the river. "Thanks for seeing me on such short notice."

"I hope you're not after more gear on credit." Her tone was flat, not really annoyed, but nothing like it usually was. She was clearly not in sales mode.

"Actually no, that's not why I called."

She shrugged and sat next to me, wrapping a scarf around her pale neck. "So?"

"How long have I known you, Abigail?"

She turned and stared at me. "Good God, you're not asking me out, are you? I know I flirt a little, but that's just—"

I tipped my head. "No, I'm not asking you out, but thanks for the put down."

She coughed. "Oh, well, sure. Sorry." She drummed her fingers on the bench. "I suppose we've been doing business nearly three years. Why do you ask?"

I swallowed. "You've always come through for me. I rely on the very best tech and you always deliver it."

She shifted on the bench. "It's just good business."

"No, I think it's more than that. You've," I paused, smiling to myself, "gone beyond what I could have expected on a number of occasions."

She looked at me oddly. "Of course, Jake. You're one of my best customers."

"While I'm not going to go into any of the details, I'm having a particularly difficult time at the moment."

"I'm sorry to hear that, but I don't—"

"I wanted to recognise your support as someone who has been there for me." I reached into my pocket and produced a white envelope. "This is what I owe you, including the bonus."

She took the envelope, glanced inside, then placed it in her own inside pocket. "I thought you were short on funds."

"I moved things around. It was unfair to impose on you any longer. I know your other contacts need to be kept happy too."

"Of course." She blinked. "Thanks."

I stood up and she followed suit. "Well, I'd best be going," I said. "Good to see you." She nodded, but before she could turn away, I reached forward and gave her a hug. I felt her tense, but she didn't pull away. "Thanks, Abigail. I couldn't have done this without you." I squeezed her shoulders, then stepped back. She nodded, then walked away. I watched her for thirty seconds, then turned and walked in the opposite direction. My phone rang. It was Sid.

"How did it go?" he asked.

"According to plan."

"Great. And I have an update for you."

"You've found Meg?"

"Not yet. But I have found the second person on our most wanted list."

SIXTY-FOUR

It took us nearly four hours to drive to the location Sid had identified. The thatched cottage was deep in Exmoor, itself in the remoter reaches of Devon. We turned off a tiny road onto a track between tall rough hedges, more than a mile from the nearest home.

"In our own country and still practically off the grid," Sid said, holding up his phone to indicate the lack of any mobile signal. "I only made the trace because it flagged on an ATM camera we'd overridden."

Susan raised an eyebrow. "You hacked bank cameras?"

"It's not actually the bank that operates them. They outsource the ATM units, so it's a little easier. And it's a great way to look for people: who doesn't need cash every now and then?"

I ran a hand over my debit card in my pocket, then put both hands quickly back on the wheel as we hit yet another pothole. "These days," I said, "I usually try to avoid carrying real money. It's not exactly secure."

Sid gave a laugh. "Because when money's in our

bank account there's no way it can be messed with, as we've recently seen." He shook his head. "If you're trying to stay out of sight, cash has its advantages." He paused. "Except that's how we found her. Maybe she should have stuck to using Bitcoin."

We turned off the road and negotiated a long, unmade driveway, before parking next to a battered old Land Rover.

"So, what's the plan?" Susan asked.

"We introduce ourselves," I replied. "If it was going to be any more complicated, we wouldn't have left Daniel behind."

We climbed out and I knocked on the heavy wooden door. From inside there were footsteps, then a woman in her early twenties appeared. Her hair was different from the photos I'd been shown, and she had a couple of extra piercings, but there was no doubt who it was. The family resemblance was clear.

"Good afternoon," I said, putting a friendly expression on my face.

She gave me a fixed smile. "Sorry, I don't buy from door to door salesman so—" She trailed off as she saw Susan and Sid standing behind me.

"Ariadne?" I said. "We're here on behalf of your father."

Her smile vanished in an instant. "Oh crap."

It was not the reaction I was expecting. "Your father hired us to find you," I said. "He thought you might have been kidnapped and he wanted to know where—"

"How the hell did you find me?" She folded her arms. "You weren't supposed to be able to."

"We're specialists in locating things," I said then

stopped. "What do you mean we weren't *supposed* to find you?"

She shook her head. "I knew this wouldn't work. What a waste of time."

"You *knew* we were looking for you?" Susan asked, taking a step forward. "How?"

Ariadne rolled her eyes. "You can all leave! I'm not having anything more to do with this."

I cleared my throat. "Your father has spent a lot of money trying to find you. If you just come back with us to London, I'm sure it will all make sense."

"I'm *not* going back with you."

"Did you know about us, Ariadne?" asked Susan.

She shook her head. "How much did he promise you? Wait, I don't care. You're crazy if you think he's going to pay you anything." She turned and spat on the ground. "He gives me an allowance to stay out of his life. Then a couple of weeks ago I get the order to move here and stay completely off-line for the foreseeable if I want to keep getting the money." She looked around with obvious distaste.

"He told us he was worried your boyfriend might have taken you against your will."

"What boyfriend? And I suppose he implied that I'd been kidnapped and locked up in a basement?"

"Something like that." I held up a hand, palm open. "Clearly there's been a misunderstanding. But could you just—?"

She took a quick step back into the house then reappeared holding a baseball bat, with a determined look that might have made Vince hesitate.

"I've said all I'm going to say," she said forcefully. "Now, get out of here."

We drove back the way we'd come, although my foot was somewhat heavier on the accelerator.

"What the hell just happened?" Sid asked. "We nearly got hit by a baseball bat. You know, maybe she's the one who abducted her boyfriend, locked *him* up in the basement."

I shook my head. "If Prebble didn't want me to find her, what *did* he want? Was it just an excuse to get close to me?"

Susan rubbed her temples with her index fingers. "Do you have something he wants? Do you know someone he needs to get to?"

"No disrespect, Jake," said Sid, "but given he's a billionaire, it seems pretty unlikely you'd have anything that he'd want or need."

I thought back to what I knew, overlaying it with what Lundy had told me. Suddenly a memory flooded my mind. I smacked my hands on the steering wheel.

"What?" asked Susan.

"There's a place I need to look."

"For what? Where are we going?"

I smiled. "To find something my father left hidden for me."

SIXTY-FIVE

We drove without stopping, and without much regard for the speed limit. Three hours later we were parking in Wimbledon. I marched into my house, Susan and Sid following close behind. Daniel was already waiting in the kitchen. Stacked next to him on the floor were a number of battered plastic and steel boxes with heavy metal clasps.

"I brought every power tool I could find," he said, "including a disk cutter. What exactly are we going to do with it all?"

I walked over to the store room, the one my father used to keep locked, and pulled the door open. Inside, on the neat metal shelving was the usual collection of tinned cans and cleaning products. Quickly, I slid them aside and stared at the walls. They were plain, unmarked. Was I letting my imagination get the better of me?

"What's going on, Jake?" Susan asked, standing behind me. "There's nothing in here."

I closed my eyes, remembering the smell that time

I'd returned home early from school and found my father coming out of this cupboard. *Oily*, but not oil: oil *paints*.

After my father died, I had high expectations of finding something interesting in this space, but the boxes had just been filled with old clothes and cleaning materials. I had shrugged and cleared it all with Kieran's help, then used it for my own supplies. But what if we hadn't been thorough enough?

"Prebble's daughter gave me an idea. She asked if we thought that she'd been locked up in a basement. It set me thinking that there might be one here." I stamped my foot on the bare wooden floorboards. They sounded similar to the rest of the house. "Just very well hidden."

Sid poked his head inside. "Why don't we try something with a little more science behind it?" He pulled out a handheld device. "I'll scan for electronics in the wall and floor: see if there's some mechanism concealed." He pushed past me and started running the device slowly over each surface. He stared at the display and shook his head.

I blinked. "Nothing at all?"

"Absolutely *nada*. Sorry, Jake."

My face broke into a smile. "Don't be sorry."

"What?"

"Nothing means something in this situation. There should be wires in every wall of this house, or pipes."

Susan snapped her fingers. "It's shielded. Maybe lined with lead."

Sid nodded. "I admire your logic. But how do we find out where?"

I coughed. "There are days for subtlety." I turned to Daniel. "And there are days to use a disk cutter."

The floorboards we sliced through in minutes. Suspended below them was a heavy metal plate, in the middle of which was an airtight door with a keyhole. I knew of no key that would fit it, so we kept cutting; it took nearly an hour of grinding, screeching and sparking to get through. Suddenly the plate dropped away, clanging repeatedly as it fell. Below was a set of stairs, descending into darkness.

"What lies beneath?" muttered Susan.

I started down the stairs. The place reeked of my father, and I suddenly felt closer to him than I had in more than three years.

SIXTY-SIX

THE NIGHT BEFORE MY FATHER DIED HE'D BEEN IN A really good mood: the best in a long time. We had dinner at the kitchen table: Thai takeaway, our favourite treat. "I think we should go on holiday," he said, through a mouthful of prawn satay. "Somewhere warm and relaxing. I'm about to close a really big deal, so have your bag packed." He turned and looked at a painting that hung on the wall to his right: a stereotypical idyllic beach scene, with powder-white sand and palm trees. "Takes your breath away, doesn't it? Always leaves me speechless."

"Looks OK," I said. "What's the wifi like, though?"

He snorted. "If I ever die, I want you to go somewhere like that: somewhere *exactly* like that. Picture postcard perfect, you might say."

I frowned. "What brought this on?"

He reached across and put a hand on mine. "You never know what the world will bring."

I turned to look more closely at the watercolour

painting. I'd seen it so many times, it was almost invisible to me. "Is it valuable?"

"I've told you many times that there's a lot of money in art: something you would do well to remember. But in this case, I doubt it. I've no idea who painted it. It's the place that's important." He paused. "Although it does have a particularly nice frame, made from driftwood. The right frame always makes the picture worth more."

"So you often say. But that scene could be anywhere."

He smiled. "It's a beach on an island off Thailand. Somewhere not really discovered by the tourist industry, at least not yet." He waved another stick of satay. "I went there with your mother the year before she passed."

"While I was on that school trip. Was it something to do with her treatment?"

"Not specifically. Well, maybe in a holistic sense: it certainly made her smile. We made a plan to go back every year." He blinked. "The issues with the treatment… Someday I'll tell you." He shook his head. "It's taken me a while to figure out what I should do about it."

"You mean it was someone's fault?"

"Not that anyone could ever prove it, but I need to put things right: make sure the world knows what really happened." Suddenly he smiled. "But not tonight."

"If someone did something bad, you should go to the police. Or the newspapers."

"Some people operate at a level above that." His eyes glistened. "Which is why it's taken me a while to find a way to deal with everything. And as part of that I have a surprise for you. We're going to take that holiday, and we leave tomorrow."

"Sorry, what?"

He reached into his pocket and removed an airline ticket. "This is yours. BA009 to Bangkok – Business Class. Also I've booked a fab hotel at the far end."

"Really? How can we afford this?"

"You don't need to worry about that. Now the flights were really hard to get, so unfortunately I'm going to be on a later flight. I'll see you there the day after tomorrow."

"It's not much time to pack. How long are we going for?"

"A couple of weeks. Just take a few changes of clothes, and some swimwear. Anything else we can pick up out there. Look, I know this is sudden, but it's really important. *Nothing* must get in the way of it. We need some time away together, having fun. Whatever happens, I promise I will see you there."

SIXTY-SEVEN

Halfway down the stairs to the hidden basement I found a light switch and flicked it on. Yellow light hissed into being below, illuminating a room about four metres square. It had the cold, stagnant odour of somewhere that had not felt fresh air in some time.

But there was another smell: oil paints.

I descended the remaining steps and looked around. Susan and Sid followed me down. "Can't believe the lights still work," she said.

I pointed at the ceiling, where there were nine bulb placements, five of which were lit.

"Redundancy - very prudent," said Sid. "He thought like an engineer, even if he wasn't one."

Against one wall was some steel racking: on the top shelf were two black folders I immediately recognised from my father's office. They bore the handwritten labels BC and BP. I picked up BC, which contained a large amount of research on Bitcoin and other cryptocurrencies; it was a lot fuller than I remembered seeing it previously. The BP folder was, now that I thought about it, perhaps obvious. Bernard Prebble.

I started flicking through printouts of web pages and copies of company documents. There were statistical reports about a drug trial. I checked the dates and swallowed. Suddenly I knew why my father had made the file, and why he had hurried to hide it that day in his office.

On the second shelf were two boxes. One was almost a cube, while the other was wide, long and flat. The second box was the right dimensions for what I was expecting to find. My father had dropped all these clues and I hadn't picked up on any of them. Until now. I moved over to the box, pulling my Swiss army knife from my pocket and slicing through the tape, but I couldn't bring myself to open it.

Susan moved past me and tapped the first box: brown card, printed with red writing and a faded biohazard warning sticker. "What's this?" she asked.

I looked up and frowned. "A course of cancer treatment. I presume it's what my mother took."

"Did it make a difference?"

"Yes. It made things worse."

She looked down. "I'm sorry, Jake."

"So am I."

Sid gestured at the box. "Isn't this company owned by Prebble? It came up when we did the background research on him."

I turned back to the long, flat box and gently lifted the lid. Inside was a flash of colour and I heard myself gasp.

Sid stood next to me. "That is an intriguing development."

Susan nodded. "Did you know it would be here?"

"I suppose there were clues. I guess my father believed in having a backup." I closed the box and picked it up, turning to Susan. "Did you get that item off eBay? Did you pass it on?"

"I did. He was most pleased to get it back: said he owes you one."

"That's what I was hoping. Anything else I need to know?"

Susan turned to Sid. "I ran my own analysis on the bugs you removed from your systems: the strange thing is that they weren't functional. It's hard to make something that small and impossible without some form of relay, like I used with that business-card bug. These were designed to make it look like you were bugged, not to actually bug you."

"And you didn't spot it?" I asked Sid. "That's not like you."

"I knew we were being monitored so when I found bugs I assumed they were working." Sid shrugged. "Susan knows more about this stuff than I do."

"Maybe," Susan said, "but I agree it doesn't make any sense."

I stared at them both. "You know, maybe it does. Maybe it's the final piece in the puzzle. Are you familiar with Occam's Razor?"

"The simplest explanation is usually the best?"

"I think it applies here. Now, I have several phone calls to make. Then we need to get ready."

"For what?" Sid asked.

"Payback."

SIXTY-EIGHT

It has always amazed me how you can walk half a mile north from Park Lane and find yourself in a different city entirely: suddenly you are on dark, grimy streets teeming with people who, in the middle of the night, were probably going about less than savoury purposes. Tonight I was one of them.

I'd arranged to meet Kieran at an all-night cafe that, even at 2am, was relatively packed. He slid into the booth opposite me, not even glancing at the paper cup of coffee I pushed in his direction. His eyes looked tired. "Jake, I know I said I'd help you in any way I can, but this wasn't quite what I had in mind. Do you have any idea how hard it was to arrange an overnight babysitter on such short notice?"

"I wouldn't have asked if it wasn't very important."

"I'm sure, but this is all a bit clandestine for my tastes."

"I wanted to talk to you about the 458."

He blinked. "The Ferrari?"

"I need to take it for a spin."

"Sure, let's go get the keys now." He smiled, then hesitated. "You're not joking?"

"I have a very important meeting to go to. And I need to create the right impression or the people involved will probably kill me."

"Jake, this is crazy."

"I realise that."

Kieran sucked in his lower lip. "The main showroom doors are time-locked: once everyone goes home for the night, you can't open them before 7am. Plus the Ferraris all have an additional manufacturer tracking system; it can't be deactivated until the car is purchased, with all the associated paperwork. Within fifteen minutes they'll be after you. I'm guessing that won't be long enough."

I sighed. "No. And the police turning up at the meeting won't be conducive to my goals. Can the tracking system be hacked?"

"Not according to Ferrari. They're always going on about how it's military grade, so I wouldn't pin your hopes on it. Likely easier to steal a police vehicle."

"What about the other cars?"

"Similar systems. The motorbikes would be easier, but I imagine that wouldn't create the visual impact you're after."

"Might another dealer be less rigorous with its security?"

Kieran shook his head. "Not for anything worth that amount. And if you're after the 458, we're the only UK dealership that carries it."

I blinked, remembering my visit to the Huntingdon club and the cars parked outside. "So if someone bought one, they bought it from you?"

"If it's UK registered, then yes."

"Did you sell one to Maxwell Rouse?"

He nodded. "I first met Rouse as a customer. Of course he was a real arse when he was in the showroom."

"You say the tracker system is turned off upon sale. Can you turn it back on?"

"We've never been asked to, but I suppose it's theoretically possible. Why?"

"So I can confirm where it is. Do you keep a spare set of keys?"

"We might. But you're not going to—"

"I need to borrow them."

"If you're borrowing his car, this meeting isn't with Rouse. When you said someone might kill you, I assumed it was—"

"Best if you don't ask. Best if you stay well out of this."

"It's not the Russian?"

I raised an eyebrow. "How would you know about him?"

"Another old case that Winslow said she was investigating." Kieran took a sip from his coffee. "So I'm going to help you steal a Ferrari to meet a Russian drug dealer. Anything else?"

"I'm glad you asked. About those motorbikes…"

SIXTY-NINE

"You haven't driven until you've driven a car with a V8 engine. Be careful not to get carried away. And stay under the speed limit at all costs. Police cars will want to stop you, so don't give them an excuse."

I'd had a very busy few hours, but Kieran's final words still hung in my mind. Because of him I now had an opening, but there were so many things that could go wrong. I sat in the bucket seat of the grey 458 and opened the throttle. When I was nearly pushed through the seat and into the engine with the force of the acceleration, I decided perhaps I should heed Kieran's words and eased back. Ten minutes ago, I'd sent a message from my phone and received an immediate reply: *Come now. No tricks.*

I pulled up outside the apartment block. Four large men greeted me, making grudgingly admiring comments about the car. They conducted a rigorous search of my person, then escorted me to the waiting elevator.

It was not the first time I had been here, nor the first

time I had seen the face of the man I'd come to meet. It was, however, the first time he had seen mine. I had to hope it would not be the last.

I entered the apartment and the bullet-proof door was closed behind me. Andre Coralov stood and nodded. He did not offer to shake my hand. "You said you had information about stolen property of mine." His accent was pure Eton, not a trace of Russian. "Who are you?"

"I'm Jake Moro. I work for Maxwell Rouse. I know you wouldn't have let me up here if you hadn't already checked that." I paused. "What do think of my car?"

He shrugged, but I saw the tic in his cheek. "It's a Ferrari. What's not to like?"

"I believe you're on the waiting list for one of your own."

"How would you know that?"

"I know a lot of things. Who stole your diamond necklace, for example."

The tic in his cheek became far more pronounced. "Who?"

"Me."

There was a moment of stillness, then four of his bodyguards produced guns and trained them on me. Coralov appeared not to notice. "Why?" He shook his head. "And why come here and tell me?"

"I was lied to. I was told it'd been stolen and needed to be recovered."

"So you came into my home and took it?" He sighed. "You were brave to come here tonight. Brave, but stupid. Did you bring the necklace with you?"

"No."

"Do you still have it?"

I hesitated. "I do not."

Coralov blinked. "Then do you have any last words?"

I cleared my throat. "I'm here on Mr Rouse's behalf. He is deeply embarrassed that one of his team should have encroached on your territory. He has tasked me with helping you get the item back. He also wants to talk again about opportunities to work together."

"The last time we spoke, Mr Rouse did not seem of that mind-set. In fact, he seemed rather distracted."

"I can assure you that's in the past. And, as a gesture of good faith, Mr Rouse is going to leave his car in your care." I threw the keys to Coralov.

He caught them sharply. "And my necklace?"

"As I said, I don't have it. But I know where it is."

A flicker of a smile played across his face. "What do you want from this meeting, Mr Moro?"

"Just a chance to put things right."

"And the person who has my necklace? Will you not have to answer to him?"

"Perhaps you can help me with that."

SEVENTY

The lift rose smoothly from the underground car park. I clutched the oversized art binder in two hands. Bernard Prebble met me at the lift, as before, and beckoned me into his office. The painting still hung on the wall behind his desk. For just a moment too long, I stared at it.

Prebble cleared his throat. "You have news on my daughter? I had to move an important meeting to be here."

I nodded, tapping the folder. "Some significant new information. Can I show you?"

He pointed to the surface of his desk. "Be my guest."

I unfolded a huge map of the world, spreading it flat with both hands. It was marked with coloured dots of different sizes. "The green dots represent the best quality sightings. The yellow, those that we think are questionable. The orange, those we consider likely to be false."

Prebble frowned. "She could be anywhere."

"It's as specific as I can get without putting bodies on

the ground. We need to activate local resources to follow up."

"You're asking for money up front?"

I tipped my head and smiled. "Yesterday that would have been the case."

"I don't follow. Has something changed—"

"Yesterday I found her. And it turns out all those sightings were faked – deliberate attempts to misdirect me, when you knew exactly where she was all along. In fact you moved her so I would find it harder to find—"

"What the blazes are you talking about? These are lies! I just want to know where she is."

"If that were true," I said, pushing the map aside, "it's certainly not because you love her and miss her, is it, Mr Prebble? No, there's something else you need from me."

"And what would that be?"

I shrugged. "We'll discuss that another time. For now, I'll be taking the painting." I pointed behind him.

"Of course. Would you like it gift wrapped?"

"No need. It will fit in this case."

He frowned. "You're actually serious?"

I removed a taser from my pocket. "I'm taking the painting one way or another. I'd prefer if you gave it to me without a fuss, but it makes no difference."

"You're crazy."

I produced plastic zip-lock cuffs. "Are we going to be civilised about this or do you want to struggle?"

Prebble muttered then held up his wrists. I quickly put the cuffs in place and locked a second loop around the leg of his desk. He looked at me. "*Why* are you doing this?"

UNSTOLEN

"It's stolen, so I'm taking it back: that's what I do, remember? I *unsteal* things."

"I paid good money for it."

"I doubt any of your money is *good*."

He gritted his teeth. "I'm fascinated to see what your plan is."

"As you wish." I walked over and picked the picture off the wall. For a moment, nothing happened. Then the alarms sounded all around. There was a whirring sound and steel shutters slid into place over both doors and all the windows. There was no way out.

Prebble shook his head. "And all this time I thought you were capable."

"Sorry to disappoint you," I replied, placing the painting in my art binder, but leaving the zip open.

"Clearly I misjudged the situation. But nothing like you have."

I shrugged and waited. It didn't take very long.

The police arrived unbelievably quickly, let into the room by Prebble's security team, who were waiting outside to raise the steel barriers. They remained there while the team of officers entered. Prebble nodded to the policewoman in charge, who immediately walked up and cut his plastic cuffs.

"Get this idiot out of my sight," Prebble said. "Call my office when you're ready to take statements."

"Very good, sir," said the woman. She nodded to her team, who cuffed me. They each took an arm and started guiding me away. The policewoman walked over to the folder and lifted the painting out. "I trust you'll be happy enough for us to take his bag as evidence, provided we don't take the painting too."

Prebble muttered assent, but he was already looking

away. As the policewoman turned to the wall to re-hang the painting, I reached with my cuffed hands and unhooked a small black object from my belt, throwing it to the ground. A blinding white flash filled the room, combined with an overpowering smell of burning. There were cries and shouts as people desperately tried to cover their eyes. It would take them thirty seconds or more to recover their vision.

But the two officers continued to hold me tight. I was going nowhere.

Prebble swore loudly, blinking furiously as tears rolled down his cheeks. "You little bastard!" He walked over to me, his face red. "What a waste of time. It got you nowhere."

I shrugged. "Worth it to see the look on your face."

"We'll add it to the charge sheet," said the policewoman, blinking furiously herself as she reached to put the painting on its hook. "At least I didn't drop it."

"Quite," said Prebble. "It would take close to a thousand years on your salary to pay me back."

She looked about to say something, then checked herself, gave a nod and turned to me. "Let's get this piece of work out of here."

SEVENTY-ONE

I didn't say much as we drove away from Prebble's building, heading west. As we approached Knightsbridge police station, the car slowed then sped up again, passing the building by. I looked over my shoulder then back to the driver. "Hey, you guys aren't the police, are you?"

"What gave it away?" asked Susan, laughing as she pulled off her police hat. She ran a hand through her hair.

"After all that fuss, I see you had no trouble re-routing the alarm in time."

Sid bowed in my direction as Daniel grinned and leant over to undo my cuffs. A few minutes later, Susan pulled over. Sid and I jumped out and quickly removed the police decals and fake roof-lights.

Susan flashed me a smile as we climbed back in. "The old tricks are the best."

I eased back in my seat. "Now for part two."

The drive took an hour. We dropped Sid and Daniel off when we were nearly at our destination. They nodded towards me, then walked quickly away, knowing what they had to do. Susan and I drove on, and a few minutes later we arrived in the small area of woodland, dusk gathering around us.

My car was waiting, fully prepped. We transferred the large folder into the boot, but before I could close it, Susan gripped my hand. "Can I have a look?" she asked. "I didn't really get a chance as I made the switch. Too much flash bang and all that."

"Isn't one fake as good as another?" I shrugged. "Be my guest."

"Something about this one is special," she said as she slid open the zipper, easing the picture into view. "So that's what this is all about? Can't say I get the picture, but it's a beautiful frame."

I laughed. "Yes, it is. My father always said the frame makes the picture."

"You sure you don't want me to come with you on the next part?"

I shook my head. "It's not about manpower now. I just have to remember what they're trying to do, and use it against them."

"Well, if you need me, give me a call."

I hesitated. "Why are you doing this?"

"Because tonight you're the one in need of help." She gripped my shoulder and stared me in the eyes. "And I'm going to keep bugging you until that isn't the case."

SEVENTY-TWO

I drove on alone to the barn — the one we had raided before when looking for Meg. I parked a hundred yards away, under the cover of trees, then made my way on foot. Already there were an S-Class Mercedes and an Audi A8 parked next to the barn. The door stood open, a figure in a bowler-hat silhouetted within the frame.

"Do you have it?" asked Meeks, as he folded his arms.

"Do you have Meg?" I called back.

"She's waiting for you." He turned and vanished inside.

I walked back to the car, opening the boot and retrieving the folder containing the painting. When I returned to the barn, I saw two men, carrying automatic weapons, standing on either side of the door. "Are the goons necessary?" I asked, as I walked inside.

"Calum said you'd do as you were told, but I'm not so sure," Meeks said.

I put the folder on the top of a rough wooden table.

"I'm smart enough to know when I have no choice. Now, where is Meg?"

"First, I see the painting." Meeks reached for the folder and flipped it open. The painting from Prebble's office lay within. He shone a torch on the ornate frame, squinting. "You actually did it. This is impressive, Jake."

"That obviously means a lot to me," I drawled. "Meg?"

He removed a device from his pocket and pointed it at the wall. The television turned on. This time it displayed a video-feed of Meg, looking very unhappy. Calum stood next to her. "Evening, Jake," he said, grinning. "How are things?"

"What is this?" I said. "This is supposed to be an exchange. Why is she not here?"

"If you think," said Meeks, "that I'm going to hand her over before I've had the painting verified, then you have another thing coming."

My phone vibrated in my pocket: a particular pattern. I smiled at Meeks. "And so have you, if you thought we wouldn't find where you were keeping her."

There was a shout from the TV screen and Calum suddenly vanished from view as somebody jumped on him.

Then Daniel appeared on the screen.

"Are you going to untie me?" hissed Meg.

"Getting right to it," Daniel replied. "You're good, Jake."

"You made a mistake," I told Meeks. "You wanted to take advantage of my team, but you forgot how good we are. I found out about Abigail and bugged her. When she made contact with you and Calum, we were able to trace the call."

He shook his head. "So you got your girl back. It makes no difference. I still own you." He leaned forward and picked up the painting. "I also have what I wanted, though I'm not quite clear why you brought this if you knew where she was."

"In part it's because you *do* still own me. And if I don't do something about that now, it's going to go on and on. So it ends here. And not just with you. With everyone who thinks they're pulling my strings."

Meeks laughed. "I'll just call the Russians, shall I?"

"Actually, that's a good idea. In fact, I'll save you the trouble." I tapped some buttons on my phone and the wall screen flickered and shifted. A face appeared.

"Ah, Mr Meeks," Andre Coralov said.

Meeks took a step back. "What?" He cleared his throat. "I mean… who are you?"

"Come now, you know exactly who I am. And I certainly know who you are, after Jake… reached out. It was a fascinating conversation."

Meeks glared at me. "What have you done?"

"You should be thanking him. He's put things right. You're lucky that he cleaned up your mess." On the screen Coralov held up a diamond necklace. "He was kind enough to tell me where I might find this. And he said you might be distracted with this meeting, so I could go and fetch it." Coralov licked his lips. "Mr Meeks, if Jake or I have any more trouble from you, then… Well, you know who I am, don't you? Now I want you to leave, and don't attempt to take that painting with you. I understand Jake is going to need it. As for me, I'm going for a drive."

Meeks snarled at me then walked away, surrounded by his guards. I tapped my earpiece. "Sid?"

"I'm some distance away and the connection isn't good, but you can call if you need the cavalry and I'll hear."

"Is one horse really the cavalry?"

"It's one horse more than no horses."

I was about to reply when I heard a car pull up outside.

SEVENTY-THREE

I nodded to Maxwell Rouse as he walked through the doorway, flanked by four large henchmen. He did not look like he was in a good mood. "Vince passed me your message," he said. "I hope this is going to be worth my while."

"I think you'll be happy," I replied, pointing at the table. "Although you seem a little distracted."

Rouse hesitated. "I've had a personal item of some value taken from me today, so forgive me if I'm a little distracted."

"Your Ferrari, by any chance?"

His expression was one I wish I could have captured. "How do *you* know that?"

"Because I'm the one who took it."

Rouse sighed. "If this is a joke, you've picked the wrong day to make it."

I folded my arms. "I took it from your private storage, and I gave it to Andre Coralov."

The silence lasted several moments, as I watch

confusion and anger tousle on his face. Finally he spoke. "Why?"

"To cement a new deal between you both."

Rouse tipped his head, eyes suddenly calculating.

"There's a shipment coming in two days. Three containers. If you move it according to the terms he says you discussed before, then he will return your car to you. There may be a few miles on the clock, but he said he'll try to avoid any scratches on the paintwork. As to why… I needed to show Coralov he could trust you, and to show you that you could trust him."

"If this is an attempt to deceive me, I will kill you."

I shrugged. "You've mentioned that before. So, are you going to have a look?"

Rouse glanced at his bodyguards, then walked slowly forward, his eyes widening. "Is this another trick?" His fingertips ran over the frame.

"This is the painting from Prebble's office that Winslow asked me to steal."

"How did you get it?"

"Let's just say it wasn't easy."

Rouse cleared his throat. "Perhaps I underestimated you. You've done me a great service—"

"Of course," I said, "this isn't just about the painting. You've been waiting for a chance to get back at Prebble, haven't you?

Rouse stared at me.

"When I explained that Winslow wanted the painting, I saw a flicker of reaction. You already knew about her, so I looked deeper and do you know what I found? She was the agent who investigated the theft of the one billion from Prebble's company pension scheme.

She questioned you. It's on the record. I'm good at finding records."

"That money was never found. Prebble lost it, but I certainly don't have it."

"You had a plan to steal it though, using someone who had access to Prebble's premises: my father."

A smile spread across Rouse's face. "You just keep on demonstrating why I have to keep you on my team. I was hoping you knew where the money was, but clearly that's not the case." Rouse shook his head sadly. "A billion pounds, Jake. A man will do a lot for a billion pounds."

"It wasn't your money."

"That's how stealing works. Your father was brokering a deal with Prebble over the painting. While he was delivering it, he was meant to hack the accounts and transfer the money. It seemed he succeeded, because the money disappeared from Prebble's accounts, but it never appeared in mine. I was on my way to meet with your father, to ask him about that, when he was killed. At least getting this painting gives me some small sense of revenge."

There was a cough at the doorway. "It would if you were going to keep it."

We both turned and saw Bernard Prebble standing there.

SEVENTY-FOUR

Before I could respond, there was a shout from the doorway and several black-clad men swarmed through it. They all carried silenced semi-automatic weapons. They surrounded Rouse's men and pushed them to the ground. One of the attackers searched Rouse; removing a knife and a pistol, he shouted, "Clear!"

Bernard Prebble strode in, his suit for once less than immaculate, his tie loose around his neck. He swung his gaze around the room, passing over Rouse then settling on me. "I'm disappointed in you, Jake."

"You're disappointed?" I asked. "We had a deal that I look for your daughter, yet you had no interest in finding her or ever paying me the money you promised."

Prebble pursed his lips. "You were clever, Jake, but not clever enough. I put locator tags on all my property. I simply followed you here."

I shrugged. "You have to appreciate the bigger picture. I had to do something. I've been under some pressure." I nodded at Rouse. "I'm sure you know who that is."

"I know who *everyone* is," Prebble replied. "Good evening, Max."

"I presume you're planning on killing me," Rouse said, his heavy brows furrowing, "because if you don't I'm going to dissect you while your children watch."

Prebble extended a hand towards one of his men, who immediately placed an automatic pistol in it. Prebble checked the magazine, chambered a round, then pointed it at Rouse. "I'd be careful with those threats."

Rouse's eyes narrowed. "You don't have the balls to pull that trigger."

Prebble raised an eyebrow. "Even if that were true, I have plenty of people who would do it for me." He released the safety catch. "But it's not true."

"Look," I said, "can we just remember why we're all here? If I hadn't stolen the painting, Winslow would have got someone else to do it."

Prebble snapped his attention to me. "Winslow?"

"Are you going to deny you know who she is?"

"Of course not. She spent weeks hounding me after the pension fund incident. Why would she want to know about the painting?" He frowned. "Were you working for her? I thought you worked for Rouse?"

"It seems I'm working for everyone these days. And I've given a great deal of thought to why Winslow wanted the painting, which I'm not even clear was actually stolen: it isn't really a matter likely to involve her agency. I can only think of one good reason. I figure you've come to the same conclusion she did, given how much energy you put into pursuing the painting tonight."

Prebble raised his hands. "It *is* a Picasso."

"Yeah, it sure looks that way," I said.

Rouse frowned. "You mean it's a forgery?"

Prebble took three steps towards me. "You knew? Then why bother stealing it today?"

"For the same reason you've been watching me. This isn't about forty million: it's about a billion – the money that disappeared from your pension fund."

A hush came over the room.

Prebble stared at me for several long moments. "Your father took the money."

"I think you're right," I replied.

"But I've been watching you for years, and you haven't accessed it – not even to pay back Rouse. So where did your father put it? It shouldn't be possible to hide a billion pounds without any trace."

"And yet I expect that was exactly what you were trying to do when you originally stole the money from the pension fund. Tried using cryptocurrency, didn't you?"

Prebble frowned. "He told you that, but not where he put the money?"

"No, I'm just putting the pieces together. I remembered one of the last things my father said to me: 'there's a lot of money in art.' He was being literal." I smiled. "I think I know where the money is, but I need to know a couple of other things before I tell you."

Prebble sighed, pointing his gun at me. "Let's not screw around any longer. Tell me or I will shoot you."

"Then you won't find out."

"I don't have to shoot to kill, at least not to begin with."

I folded my arms. "How *did* the money leave your pension fund in the first place?"

"There was an accounting error," Prebble said, "which moved the funds to a temporarily unmonitored account."

"And then instead of reversing it, you decided to steal the money, so you had it converted into a cryptocurrency called eBond, similar to Bitcoin, and placed on a secure server. With a cryptocurrency, the file or rather the 'wallet' containing the currency *is* the money: it doesn't need to be held in *any* account."

"But what's to stop you copying a file or 'wallet' so it's impossible to lose?" Rouse asked.

"For technical reasons, there's actually no such thing as an eBond, even in file form: there's just a list of transactions that have taken place on the eBond network. You can copy the list to another drive, but that action will automatically delete the original list. And you have to have the list to prove to the network that you own the eBonds."

"And if you lose the computer drive?"

"Then," I replied, "you've lost the money. And it seems that is what happened here."

"But that's ridiculous. Why would anyone take such a risk?"

"Someone wanting to make sure the funds were completely untraceable."

"I was told they would be secure," Prebble said. "The eBonds were stored on a standalone server – one not connected to any network - while I planned my next step. Then suddenly they weren't there anymore. Once I learned of Rouse's connections to your father, I assumed Rouse had taken them."

"I never saw the money in any form," Rouse replied. "Charles died before he could give it to me."

"You killed him because he didn't pay up?"

"No. I wanted my money. With him dead I never saw a penny."

"So it was you," I said to Prebble. "You found out what he'd done and had him murdered."

"Not my style, Jake," he replied.

"Then who?"

"Who knows? One billion pounds creates a lot of enemies. What I'm more interested in is where the money is now. Why don't you tell us your theory?"

"I think my father took the money then hid it somewhere he thought safe. I'm guessing he made a deal with Winslow to recover the funds. It had to be somewhere incredibly secure that would leave no paper-trail."

"And where was that?" Prebble asked.

"Don't you see? He left it with you."

"What? Don't be ridiculous."

"He smuggled it into your office, so you would keep it safe."

"I would have found it. I sweep my offices daily."

"Oh you're well aware of it." I smiled. "The painting isn't a clue. Remember what he said about there being a fortune in art? The money is *in* the painting."

Prebble looked at me and blinked. Then he looked at the painting. I could almost see the cogs turning. He walked forward and picked it up. "Where?"

"When I was younger, I invented a special bug: a solid-state drive I called a 'leech': low powered, tiny, almost impossible to detect. The eBond can't be copied, but it can be moved – and that's what happened. I suspect the leech drive was hidden in a special slot in the frame and then the eBonds were moved onto it. It has to be why my father did the deal with the painting. He wanted the Picasso, fake or otherwise, hanging in your office, inside your firewalls, so the leech could quietly acquire those eBonds."

"But how did he plan on getting the painting back?" Rouse asked.

"That's why it was a fake. My father expected Mr Prebble here to discover that then demand he be given the real one."

"Except I decided to hang on to the painting," Prebble said, "because I liked it and knew no one could tell the difference."

"Of course then my father died in the explosion, which neither of you two crooks will admit to arranging."

Prebble let out a laugh. He looked at the frame then carefully slid the pieces apart. I watched as he examined them, stopping with the bottom section. He held it up to remove a metal cylinder, perhaps four centimetres long and half a centimetre wide. "That's it?" he asked.

"Were you expecting gold plating?" I said.

"I suppose not, although I'm confused. You've clearly done a lot of planning, yet now I have the money in my hands."

"It might seem that way," I said, "but you have to see it from my perspective. I had several people who wanted it, but the money wasn't the thing that mattered to me." I blinked at Prebble. "I knew about the tracker in the painting: I wanted you to follow me here. I knew that the only way to deal with my situation was to get you all in the same place at the same time then let you fight it out." I paused and looked around.

Prebble raised an eyebrow. "Well, it won't be much of a fight."

"That's right," said a voice from behind them, "it won't. Now drop your weapons."

Red dots erupted all over the room, several on Prebble and Rouse, and on each of the guards. Those guards still holding weapons looked at each other then carefully placed them on the floor. A SWAT team swarmed into the room, shouting instructions, wielding zip cuffs. It was all over very quickly. There was a moment of silence, when everyone stared at each other, wondering what was going to happen.

Then Ellie Winslow walked in, grey hair neat and sharp, her eyes glistening behind her wire-framed glasses. "Good evening, gentlemen."

SEVENTY-FIVE

The SWAT team moved quickly through the barn, cuffing everyone except me.

"This is a good day, indeed," Winslow said, her face breaking into an odd smile. "Didn't even need to resort to the gas grenades." One of her team walked over and whispered in her ear. The smile cracked slightly. "Fine, fine. Escort them," she gestured toward Rouse and Prebble's men, "to the collection point, then secure the perimeter. Oh, and can you make sure our VIPs don't wander off."

The SWAT team used additional restraints to tie Rouse and Prebble to one of the barn's supporting pillars. Then they shepherded all the guards away, leaving just the four of us in the barn. I watched as Winslow closed the doors firmly behind the last of her people.

Prebble strained against his cuffs. "Don't you think you need your protection squad?"

"I'm sure I can cope. Good work, Jake. Rouse and

Prebble are huge busts, and it's not even what I asked you to do."

I shrugged. "They brought it on themselves."

Rouse glowered at me. "Just how many people did you tell about tonight?"

"Quite a parade," Prebble said, who was turning an unpleasant shade of beetroot.

"You guys gave me no choice," I said. "There was no other way out."

"You think we'll let you get away with this?" Rouse said.

"I might as well strike from a position of strength," I replied, "rather than waiting for you to strike at me when I'm weak."

"You have a point about Rouse," Prebble said, "but what have I done to you, Jake?"

"You used me to try to get your stolen money back. And I'm still not convinced you didn't kill my father."

"Well, that certainly wasn't me," Rouse said. "If I was going to finish him off, I'd have done it *after* he paid me."

"Not me either," said Prebble. "I prefer detonating people's characters in my newspapers. I don't much like things getting messy."

"You mean," said Winslow with a half-smile, tapping one of the discarded guns on the floor with her foot, "apart from commanding an unlicensed armed team to do what exactly?"

"They weren't working for me," Prebble replied. "And you won't find any evidence to prove otherwise."

"Handling stolen goods, then?" She nodded to the painting, which was now lying apart from its frame.

The cords stood out on Prebble's neck. "That

painting isn't stolen, other than from me. I paid for it in a legitimate deal. I suggest you speak to Reginald Monday again about that false allegation."

She tipped her head on one side. "How about the fact that it's a forgery?"

He raised an eyebrow. "I haven't attempted to pass it off as genuine. The insurance is in line with its actual value. I've committed no crime as regards that painting. Like I said, I don't like it when things get messy. If I wouldn't even commit insurance fraud, why would I kill a man?"

Winslow walked over to the table and reached underneath it, pulling out a small silvery object. "True. But there is still this to consider."

Prebble glared but did not reply.

"It's a military-grade bug. I've been outside for the last hour, monitoring every word. I heard you confess to the theft of one billion pounds from your own pension fund."

Prebble shrugged. "My lawyers will shred you and your inadmissible surveillance devices. If Jake has the money, all that proves is that Charles Moro stole it. Maybe that Jake was involved in the plan from the start. You've got nothing." He turned to me. "And you are getting away with nothing."

"No," said Winslow. "You're getting what you deserve." She turned to me. "So where is the money, Jake, because I don't believe you left it in the frame for one of these crooks to find."

"Somewhere safe. I've worked out what my father was doing involved with all this. He was doing what I do." I stood up straight. "He was *unstealing.* So I'm going to finish what he started. I'm going to pay it back."

Winslow nodded. "I'd expect nothing less, Jake, but procedure demands that I process the transfers."

I looked at her. "After what happened to my father, I deserve that moment."

"You do, but my hands are tied." Her eyes narrowed. "Jake, I'm sure you understand my position. There can't be any risk here. Not with this much money."

"The real question is 'Can you trust her?'" Rouse said.

"The thing to remember," said Winslow, "is that, thanks to your help, I can put these two both away for many, many years. You can draw a line under this whole, terrible matter."

"Or we could just split the money," Rouse said. "Two-hundred and fifty million each, or are you all *really* that virtuous?"

"For the benefit of the recording," said Prebble, "that was Maxwell Rouse's suggestion."

"I don't know about all of us being virtuous," replied Winslow. She held up a remote control and pressed a red button. "That's enough recording for today. Because after what you have both done over the years, I think it's long past time that you both saw a little justice." She reached into a shoulder holster and withdrew an automatic pistol.

"And here we go," Rouse sighed loudly. "She's going to take the money. That's always what this was about."

Winslow frowned. "That was a really stupid thing to say. You think I've pursued this money for over three years just to take it for myself."

"Yes, that's exactly what I think."

She raised the gun and pointed at him. "Then why wouldn't I just pull the trigger?"

Prebble laughed nervously. "You'd have to kill all of us. How would you explain that?"

"I can explain anything. After watching you lie for a living, I've picked up more than a few tips." She walked forward and flipped off the safety catch. "I suppose I should thank you. Or," Winslow swung and pointed the weapon at Rouse, "perhaps I should finish you off first? Heaven knows you'll never get the justice you deserve within the system. You own too much of it."

"Agent Winslow," I said, "you don't need to do this. You've won."

Her hand tightened around the gun. "I know. But I *want* to do it. It's the right thing to do. So many people will applaud it. As would so many more, if they knew the truth." She swung back to pointing the gun at Prebble, holding the barrel inches from his face. "Isn't that right, Bernie?"

A bead of sweat trickled down his brow. "Whatever you say. You seem to be holding all the cards."

I swallowed. Kieran had warned me about Ellie Winslow. But he hadn't prepared me for this.

Winslow nodded. "Do you know how many times I've done this in my dreams? How many times I've watched your expression of horror and pain. And do you know what I've learned?"

Prebble blinked.

"I've learned that it was over too quickly." She whipped the gun back into its holster. "So, I'll pass. Tempting as it is."

"Why you—"

Winslow launched a fist and struck Prebble in the face. He rocked backwards, eyes rolling into his head.

"Love it!" Rouse cried. "With a right hook like that you should—"

She turned and punched Rouse even harder. He fell silent, doubled over, cuffed hands reaching for his bleeding nose.

"Now, Jake, I want the money. And don't make me draw my weapon again."

I took a step back, glancing at the outline of Winslow's shoulder holster. "You have quite a temper."

She blinked. "Usually I manage to keep it under control."

"But not the day my father worked out what you were up to. That's why *you* killed him."

"Me?" Winslow gave a snort. "Look, I don't have time for this. It's taken more than three years to unravel the mess Charles left behind. I'm not going to fail now." She walked over to the painting and picked up the piece of frame where the leech had been secreted. "Where is the money?"

I swallowed. "Why would I tell you? Are you going to threaten to kill me too?"

"You're going to tell me because it's the right thing to do. We've been over this."

In the distance, I heard a faint whining noise, almost inaudible.

I sighed. "Fine. I'll show you."

She tapped her jacket where the holster bulged. "No tricks now. I know full well what you're like."

I glanced at my watch as we left the barn and headed towards my parked car.

SEVENTY-SIX

It was dark outside, a cold fog rising from the ground and lurking between the trees. "Where are your team?" I asked Winslow. There was not the sound of a single footstep around us.

"They're at the perimeter with Rouse and Prebble's goons."

"A bit odd to send them all away."

"I received word of a possible incursion. Hard to know just how many men either of those bastards have at their disposal."

"So you're on your own?"

"I can take care of myself."

"And me, presumably."

"I'm not underestimating you, Jake. I never will."

"After everything you've done, can I trust you to keep your word? I've done everything that you asked."

She frowned. "My word? Sure. But the law is a somewhat more binding framework, and there's nothing ambiguous about what I'm doing."

"You think?"

She stopped and looked at me. "What exactly do you mean?"

"Let's just say that I have a source of intel that made me think otherwise."

"I don't have time for this. And if you think what I just did to Prebble and Rouse was wrong, well it was no more than they deserved. I'm sure your father would have agreed. He was in it to get revenge against Prebble, after all. One of Prebble's subsidiaries developed the cancer drug that killed your mother. Apparently the testing was flawed: clear health risks had been flagged and they knew it. But delayed release would have tanked the company's share price, so Prebble did what he had to do."

"And it's not likely that he will ever pay for it." I swallowed. "What I don't get is why is this all happening now," I asked. "If you were monitoring me for three years, why wait until now to set the ball rolling?"

"I'm a patient woman, but even *my* patience was running out."

We reached my car. I walked to the boot and went to open it.

"Slowly now," she said. "Don't try anything smart."

I gently raised the lid and stepped back. "There you go."

She peered inside. It was clearly empty. She reached into her jacket and pulled out her gun. "Don't mess me around. You know, for twenty years I kept catching criminals and getting nothing for it. They did a few years in prison then came back out to enjoy their ill-gotten gains. There was no real justice, no restitution. My brand of justice is going to stick. All the people the money was taken from are going to get a call they did not expect. Except that's not going to happen if you don't give me the money." She aimed carefully at my chest. "Give it to me now."

"I'm sorry, I can't do that."

In the distance came the sound of an engine revving.

Winslow stepped back, looking uncertain. "What's that?"

The noise got closer, then suddenly crescendoed as a driver-less motorbike burst into the clearing. We both leapt back out of its path, as it careened into the side of my car.

"Drop the gun," barked a voice, "or I will drop you." A bright torch shone from behind a nearby tree, glinting off a gun barrel.

Winslow glared and let her pistol fall to the ground.

"You cut things fine," I said.

Meg walked into the circle of light from my torch. "That bike is fast, but it's not a helicopter."

I stared at the tangled remains. "That bike *was* fast. Kieran is going to kill me."

Meg sighed. "You're welcome." She walked over and picked up Winslow's pistol. "I presume this means you found the money?"

"Hidden in the painting, in a digital drive. It's a long story. She was trying to force me to tell her where it is."

Meg nodded, hefted Winslow's gun and handed it to me. "Just in case she tries anything. So where is it?"

I looked around. "It's safe."

"Come on Jake, this is me."

I hesitated, weighing the gun in my hand. "A compartment in the engine block."

Meg strode over to the car and popped the bonnet.

She leaned forward and ran her fingers over the engine. "Got it." She held up a small silver object.

"Handle it carefully: there's no backup."

Meg pulled a small object from her pocket and held it up to the drive. I watched her let out a quiet gasp. "It's really here." She turned to look at Winslow. "It's actually here."

I frowned. "Why do you have a scanner like that? Where did you get it?"

She slid the drive into a pocket and smiled. "I'm sorry, Jake, this is going to come as a real shock."

Then she held up her gun and pointed it at me.

SEVENTY-SEVEN

I stared at Meg in the torchlight. "You're working with Winslow? How is that possible?" It was still all but silent in the clearing, with just a faint whine hanging in the air. If you weren't listening for it, you probably wouldn't even notice it.

"You spend your life tricking and deceiving people, Jake, so I can see it must be somewhat galling that someone's done it to you."

"But we've worked together for nearly three years. We've been through so much. We're friends."

She shook her head. "I was just playing a role."

I blinked. Anger fired within me. "You're forgetting that I have a gun too. Or are you that confident you're quicker?"

"Go ahead and shoot me," said Meg. "I'll let you go first."

I weighed the gun in my hand. "It's not loaded, is it?"

"Not anymore," replied Winslow.

I popped the clip then checked the chamber,

confirming that the gun was indeed empty. I threw the gun to the ground and clenched my fists. "What did she do to turn you? When did it happen?"

"She didn't turn me. I've always worked for her."

"You're ex-MI5?"

"I'm not ex. I'm still on the books, under deep cover: did my skillset and contacts really not give me away?"

I shook my head. "I trusted you. And you were no better than a common criminal."

Meg shrugged. "Coming from you, that's rich."

"We return the things we steal to the rightful owner." I shook my head. "What about Meeks? Was he part of your little crew? Was the kidnap a fake?"

"That was an unexpected complication."

"What about Daniel? I suppose he's MI5 too."

"Very astute. Calum's departure provided the opportunity I needed to expand my control of the team."

"I still don't understand why now. My father died three years ago. What has changed? I don't believe either of you just got impatient."

Winslow cleared her throat. "We came to the conclusion that the painting was key and that your father was cleverer than we'd given him credit for."

"Well he must have worked out what you were doing or he wouldn't have kept things from you. And guess what?" I said. "I worked it out too."

"A bit late, Jake."

"Your bugs, the ones embedded in the microprocessors: we realised they weren't functional. So that meant we almost certainly had a bad operative in our midst. I didn't want to believe it."

Meg tipped her head. "You knew? And still you didn't plan accordingly?"

"I planned for a lot of things today. I just didn't expect you to be part of it."

"We have the money," Winslow said. "That's all that matters."

"Do you?" I said. "Are you sure about that?"

Meg frowned. "What's he talking about?"

Winslow shrugged. "He's clutching at straws. Now let's tidy up and get out of here."

Meg raised the gun. "What if we don't have the money after all?"

"You just checked the device," Winslow said, rolling her eyes.

"Perhaps I should re-check it?"

As they spoke, I heard the whine pick up above me.

Meg took a step back and ran the scanner again. Her face filled with alarm. I had to fight to keep the smile from mine. "It's gone!" she shouted.

"What?" Winslow strode forward and wrenched the gun from her hand, pointing it at me. "Explain!"

"Meg may have mentioned a drone Sid has been modifying. He's got it to run almost silent. It's been hovering above us for a while now, leeching the eBonds."

Winslow scowled. "If you don't land it right now I'm going to shoot you."

"One thing about that," I said. "Whose gun do you have?"

Winslow frowned, her eyes flickering to Meg. "Why?"

"Do you know who gave it to her? It was Daniel. Given that I trusted Sid and Meg with my life, I figured he had to be the mole. Of course I was wrong, but giving him a weapon full of blanks has proven unexpectedly advantageous."

Winslow swore and pulled the trigger. There was a dull click.

I turned to Meg. "You said I shouldn't trust anyone. I think it was the only time you were honest with me."

Meg shrugged. "I don't need a gun to take you out."

Above us, the whine increased in volume. Winslow and Meg looked up. The tiny black craft was just visible in the darkness. Something small dropped from it and hit the ground, but I didn't see it because my eyes were already closed.

SEVENTY-EIGHT

I crouched, turning away from the flash-bang grenade, covering my ears as it tore the night apart with an explosion so sharp it could shred eardrums and a puff of white so intense that, had my eyes been open, I'd have been blind for minutes.

Groans from Winslow and Meg suggested it had worked as I'd hoped. I pulled out my phone, ready to make a call, but oddly there was absolutely no signal. From the dark between the trees came the sound of booted feet. A large figure approached and crouched next to me.

"Everything OK, Jake? I couldn't get here any sooner."

I blinked my eyes open and made out Vince's surly face. "Could be worse. Thanks for coming."

He whistled loudly. Two dozen or more figures, clad in black, appeared from the shadows. They cuffed Winslow and Meg with plastic ties, then searched them thoroughly before forcing them to sit in the middle of the clearing.

"I see my intel about another group was correct," Winslow said, her eyes dark and angry. "Not that it did me any good."

"We needed to flush out your people," Vince replied. He held out his hand and pulled me up. "Appreciate your help, Jake."

"No problem."

"No, really. Getting that ring back meant the world to my mother," he said with what, for him, passed as a smile. "I'm glad I could return the favour. That's how good business is done."

"Don't get too comfortable," Winslow growled. "My team will be back any second."

"Actually," Vince said, "I wouldn't count on it."

I walked over to her. "This is over for you. The police will be here soon."

Her expression was one of utter confusion. "*You* called the police?"

"Of course. Did you think this was going to go any other way?"

"But… after everything you did? After what you did to your own father—"

"What?" I said. And then I realised what she meant. "You think I killed him? Why would I have done that?"

"I didn't need my source to work that out: obviously you did it to get the money."

"But I didn't get the money. Not until today. I didn't even know about any of it until this last week!"

Meg frowned. "He's not going to confess. He never once broke cover in all the time I was there. Not a single mistake."

"Because it's not a cover! This is ridiculous," I said. "Why do you believe this?"

"Our intel isn't wrong," Winslow replied.

"Just admit what you were doing. You were trying to steal a billion and *you* killed my father." I turned to Meg. "As for you, I thought I knew you. I trusted you. I cared about you."

Meg shook her head. "You've got this all wrong, Jake. Winslow is on the level. I'd stake my life on it."

"Be glad," I said, "that you haven't had to do that."

"I don't understand," Winslow said. "Jake, if I was acting illegally, do you think I would have had the SWAT team with me?"

I shrugged. "As I mentioned, I've got an inside source. One beyond reproach."

"Really. Because I have one as well. And he told us, you were the mastermind behind everything: the billion was stolen using tech of your design, after all. And you killed your father because he got in your way."

And suddenly I knew. We were all wrong. Because we had the same source: someone who had been lying to me for a long, long time.

There was the sound of a throat being cleared. "Mind if I cut in?"

We all turned as Kieran walked into the clearing, flipping a coin in his left hand and holding a gun in his right. He wore his signature straw boater, although it no longer looked amusing.

"You!" exclaimed Winslow.

My world crumbled.

"Me!" Kieran said with a smile.

SEVENTY-NINE

I stared at Kieran, my heart racing. "This can't be real."

He grinned at me. "I can't believe how well you've done. I mean I've always known you had talent but, seriously, what you pulled off tonight? Incredible."

I reached quickly into my pocket, feeling for my phone. It was time to call in one last favour.

Kieran pointed at me. "Don't waste your time with the phone. I've got a broad-spectrum jammer blocking all cellular signals in the vicinity. It's based on your own design, so thanks for sharing."

I pulled the handset out. There was indeed no signal. But there was the sound of approaching footsteps. Sid ran into the clearing, clutching his drone control. He looked around, confused. "I tried to call but there's no signal. What did I miss? Why is Kieran here?"

"I'm afraid," I said, "that this has all got rather complicated."

"That would be an understatement," Winslow said.

"Yes," Kieran said, screwing a silencer onto his

handgun. "So let me make it very simple. Give me the drive, Sid. I know you have it. It was on the drone."

"Wait, what?"

"I'm going to give you three seconds to do what I've asked or I'm going to shoot you."

Sid's face took on a sarcastic expression. "Oh right. Because you're actually going to do—"

Kieran fired.

There was a muted retort, and the bullet struck the ground, inches in front of Sid. He fell back, screaming.

Kieran moved forward and frisked him roughly, removing the pen drive from a pocket. He pulled out a phone-sized device and plugged the drive into it, then began tapping on the screen.

I whispered urgently to Vince. "Aren't your men armed? Do something!"

"I'm sorry, Jake, but that wouldn't be appropriate."

I turned and stared. My lungs felt devoid of air. "You're working for him? That makes no sense."

Vince shrugged. "It's just business."

"I recovered your mother's ring."

"And I thank you for that."

Kieran laughed. "Don't get mad at him. Vince is the epitome of loyalty." He unplugged the drive. "All verified and correct."

"But he… he beat you up when you couldn't pay the gambling debt."

"C'mon, Jake, do you still not get it?"

I shook my head. " I don't understand what the hell is going on."

He puffed out his cheeks. "Fair enough. If anyone deserves an explanation, after everything, it's you. Follow me." He nodded to Vince. "I'll be fine. Just keep an eye on our friends from the Security Service. Get my laptop set up with the encrypted tunnel: everybody else stays offline. Oh yes, and send someone to check on our other friends in the barn."

Vince nodded and started barking orders.

Kieran beckoned to me. "Come on, Jake. It's time you heard the truth."

EIGHTY

We walked a short distance through the trees, out of earshot of Meg, Winslow, Sid and Vince.

I stared at Kieran. "Tell me this is when you admit this has all been some trick to help me out. Or to get justice for your parents' death or... something."

He smiled. "Ah, Jake. Ever the optimist."

"Then tell me how this makes any sense. What happened to you?"

"That's a big question. But if I were to distil it, I think the bottom-line is that I decided not to take crap anymore."

"So you thought you'd implicate me in a criminal conspiracy?"

"Jake, a billion pounds is a lot of money."

"I've spent the last three years of my life earning money to protect you. At least I thought I was."

"Perhaps that was your driver. But you've found something you were really good at. That you wanted to do. In fact in a sense I've made you the man you are today."

"That's… ridiculous."

"Is it? I've guided you. Shaped you. Helped you become a better man."

"And you'd know all about that, naturally. What made you like this?"

"Do you not get it? I haven't changed: I've stayed exactly the same. You just haven't noticed. Although I have, out of necessity, misled you a great deal. And I wanted to apologise for that." He paused. "Of course let's not forget that you lied to me too. About what you've been doing. I can't believe you didn't just confront me about the gambling debts three years ago. That was certainly what my plan predicted."

I frowned. "You engineered the whole situation? You made it look like you owed money when you didn't?"

"Rouse wasn't a party to it, but I had Vince in my employ from the start. We put on a little show for you, to see what you would do: how far you would go. And I must admit, you went far beyond the call of duty."

"But why do it at all?"

"I knew your father had taken the money. I needed you to locate it. Except of course you really didn't know where it was either. But you found out eventually. Quite remarkable."

I kicked at a tree.

"If I could have extricated you from the whole thing earlier, I would have. But I needed you. You're a useful guy, Jake."

"Yeah, I get that. Rouse feels the same."

Kieran laughed. "Oh, yes. Rouse. What a card. Likes to think he's in charge. I learned a lot about his operations while I was at MI5. You wouldn't believe the valuable information I picked up there. And information truly is power. It's just that, working within the confines of the law, you can rarely do anything with it. Then I learned of the money Prebble had stolen. He thought he'd been smart: that he'd got away with the near perfect crime. But when there's blood in the water, you attract sharks. And that's when Rouse got involved and brought your father into his plans. Unfortunately for Rouse, your father had his own agenda. But for Prebble the outcome was the same: he lost his ill-gotten gains. Stealing something that's already stolen is the best kind of crime, because the second victim can't even admit what's happened. It's why you do what you do."

I shook my head. "It's not the same at all. I un-steal to give things back."

"Yeah. For a price."

"If I could afford to do it for free, I would."

"Oh don't be such a sap. There's nothing wrong with being paid for something you're good at. I tell my son that every day."

"So what happens next?"

"Either we become friends again. Or I kill you."

"You expect me to believe you'd do that?"

"Jake, in the end none of us know what's going on inside anybody's head except our own. In many cases we don't even fully comprehend that."

I nodded slowly. "Then let's be friends."

"Excellent." He clapped me firmly on the shoulder. "Of course, just in case, there's going to be a small test. With so many lies flying around, I thought a moment of absolute clarity would be beneficial."

"So what's the test?"

He smiled. "It's more of a present really. Come with me."

EIGHTY-ONE

We walked back to the clearing. There, hands cuffed behind their backs, were Bernard Prebble and Maxwell Rouse.

Prebble looked up. "What the hell is going on? Why is Winslow tied up? Who is in charge?"

Rouse scowled. "If someone doesn't untie me fast, I'm going to bury you all in concrete. And what is he doing here?" He nodded at Kieran. "Vince, what the hell is going on?"

Vince just shrugged.

Kieran smiled. "Mr Rouse. So good to see you again. Except with the shoe on the other foot, so to speak."

"Why you ignorant punk, I'll—"

Kieran aimed his gun at Rouse's face. "Let's be clear. You have no idea who I am. But I know exactly who you are. Now, shut up while the grown-ups talk." He turned to me. "Jake, these two men have caused you so much anguish. So my present to you is the opportunity to punish them."

"I don't follow."

"It's quite simple: you get to kill them. Revenge, not just for you, but for everyone else they have wronged. Justice for all!" He flipped his coin in the air and caught it. "Don't tell me you haven't longed for this moment."

"It won't bring my mother and father back."

"I guess not. But depending on what you believe, it may give them peace. It should give *you* peace. Now you need to choose your method." He held out his gun towards me, while his other hand slid a dagger from his belt, an ugly black-bladed weapon, which he flipped and offered hilt first.

"Can it be both?" I asked.

"Excellent! Embrace the shadow, Jake. Show them you will not be bullied any longer. Show them who's the boss."

Rouse cleared his throat loudly. "Look, Jake, crazy time is over. We'll make a deal."

"We could," Kieran said, "but you were a dead man before I got here."

"What are you talking about?"

Kieran pulled out his phone. He held it up to show BBC News running footage of a major car accident. The vehicle was an unrecognisable mess.

"Why do I care?" Rouse asked.

"Because it's a Ferrari. A 458 to be specific. Driven by a Russian of our mutual acquaintance."

I gasped. "You're joking."

"A bomb was triggered when it went over ninety miles an hour. I did tell you to stick to the speed limit, Jake."

"You knew who I was going to meet? You planted a bomb in the car, and used me to deliver it?"

"Coralov has proved a pain to deal with the last couple of years. You provided an excellent means to remove him. Naturally they're going to blame you, Mr Rouse. It was your car. You loaned it to the victim."

Rouse scowled. "I had nothing to do with—"

Kieran smiled. "Come on, Jake. You may as well get the pleasure, before Coralov's men arrive to do it for you. You deserve it."

I laughed. "You're just trying to get me to do your own dirty work. Would you do this, if you were me?"

"Do you not know me at all? Rest assured, there's nobody I wouldn't kill if they got in my way. If they got in the way of my son." He paused. "*Nobody.*"

Winslow gasped. "You killed your wife."

"What?" I said. "That's absurd."

"Is it?" she replied. "We always suspected there had been foul play. There was no evidence of anyone being there except Kieran. He made the 999 call. What if she discovered what he was up to and tried to stop him?"

Kieran shrugged. "There can be such a thing as too much truth, don't you think?"

Rouse looked up at the sky. "I think we're all dead."

Kieran held out the weapons to me again. "So, Jake, it's time to make a choice."

EIGHTY-TWO

I stared at the dagger and the pistol.

"It gets easier after the first time," Kieran said. "I promise."

"I'll take your word for it. But I don't care how much they've done, I don't think I can kill them."

"Don't you want your revenge? They both deserve it." Kieran frowned. I sighed and picked up the pistol. It felt heavy. "Of course now I have a loaded gun, I could do anything I wanted with it."

Around me were the rapid sounds of more than a dozen automatic rifles being lifted in to firing position. "Excellent point," Kieran said. "Do go on."

"Touché."

"We need to help each other. Two orphans up against the world. We have to, because nobody else will."

"So this is all for the money?"

"C'mon, a billion pounds – that's not a chance that comes up even once in most lifetimes. What do you want to do here, Jake?"

"Give it back. Like I'm sure my father intended."

"Think the best of him – I won't argue. But would you really?"

"The thing is, this isn't just about the money. You seem to be a crime boss in your own right."

"I saw the opportunity. I had the vision and the capability. And nobody saw me coming."

"Now you hide in plain sight. Rouse had no idea who you really were. He's like a dinosaur, and you're… some new virus taking over the system."

"Well I don't know if I like the metaphor, but sure. I'm constantly evolving."

"So what are you going to do with a billion pounds, Kieran?"

"I have a few plans."

"Not plans your wife agreed with, if Winslow's right."

Kieran puffed out his cheeks. "She found out, and I had no choice. Liam will have every opportunity open to him. I can't have it any other way."

I looked around me. "You confident you've actually got the eBonds?"

He blinked. "Very funny. We checked the drive."

"No really. Do you think I wouldn't have taken multiple layers of precaution?"

"You had no idea about me."

"No. But I assumed I didn't know the full picture of what was going on. So I prepared for everything. I wasn't going to let anyone take the money."

Kieran turned to his men, snapping his fingers. "My laptop, now."

One of the men dressed in black rushed forward,

removing it from a backpack and holding it out. Kieran flipped it open and started rattling on the keys.

"So you still have a network?" I asked.

"I've tunnelled through the firewall that's jamming you."

"Something you learned from me?"

"In this case, I went elsewhere for the code. Couldn't very well have you thwarting it. And if this doesn't work, I'm going to shoot you now. Right after I shoot Meg and Sid." Kieran's eyes narrowed as he entered a series of three long passwords. There was a pause then a soft chime. He snapped the laptop shut. "Transfer complete. Just in case you were worried." He handed the laptop back to the man in black. "Now where were we?"

I closed my eyes. Kieran had countered every trick in my bag. He knew me too well. I crossed my arms and gripped my shoulders, and felt a tiny bump under one palm.

I'm going to keep bugging you.

"You were suggesting I kill Prebble and Rouse. I think I'm ready now."

Kieran smiled. "OK, Jake. Make me proud."

EIGHTY-THREE

I walked over to Rouse and Prebble, hefting the gun in my hand.

"You're not going to do this," Prebble said. "You are not a murderer."

I shrugged. "It's not like I'm being given much choice. Or rather I am – it's my friends or you."

"Yes, but—"

"And why do you deserve mercy? You sold drugs that you knew could kill. But you didn't care. I bet you care now."

Prebble swallowed. "I'm sorry."

"I'm surprised you know the word."

Kieran cleared his throat. "Hilarious and compelling viewing as this is, can we get on with things?"

I turned to Rouse, raising the gun. "Maybe you should be first?"

"This is bull-crap," he spat. "Let me out of these cuffs and I'll—"

"Just do it, Jake," Kieran said.

"I presume," I said, "that you've got cameras set up to record me."

"Isn't that how you do things? I copied the whole set up from you in fact."

"How did you get hold of the stuff?"

"You're not Abigail's only customer."

I nodded. "And you're not concerned the cameras will record you?"

"I'll be editing out anything… *unhelpful*."

"Still, the footage will exist."

"I'm the only one who will ever see it."

"There's one thing, though. Given that I thought Winslow was 'bad', I set up my own cameras to record this scene."

"I had the area swept." Kieran reached into a pocket and threw three small cameras onto the ground in front of him. "These what you mean?"

"Of course this time I needed extra redundancy. Just in case one or two were faulty…"

Kieran threw three more onto the ground. "Yeah, I thought you might. But why bring it up? If I hadn't found them, you'd have an advantage now?" He narrowed his eyes. "What are you doing? Stalling? Hoping someone will somehow overhear on an unsecured channel?"

"You might be incredibly smart, but you don't know tech. You didn't fully think this through. I might not be prepared for you, but I am prepared for the unexpected. I plan for it. And I have people on my team who are both great, and also don't do what I tell them."

"What?"

"I have a new team member, and I told her to stay out of it. She didn't. I found something on my jacket. A bug better than even the ones that you planted. I'm sure there are several more on my car and on Sid. Possibly elsewhere. Even with specialist equipment it would take you hours to find them. And they're not only cellular."

Kieran marched towards me, his gun raised. I held my hands up, then spoke into my watch. "Contact Agent Liam."

He frowned. "What?"

"The irony is, I sent someone to protect you. And your son."

"Uncle Jake!" said Liam's excited voice, squawking from my watch's speaker. "My phone does work!"

"Cool, huh? Are you OK?"

"Of course. Your friend Daniel is here. He said you ordered him to protect me."

"That's right, Liam. I'll check back in with you in a few minutes. Over and out." I tapped my watch to disconnect the call.

"How did you get through?" hissed Kieran. "You're being jammed."

"It really is a sat phone."

"So you're going to threaten my son?"

"No, Kieran. I'm going to protect him. And if you don't surrender right now, I'm going to tell him what his father really is."

"You have no proof."

"I have another twelve cameras and recording devices hidden around this clearing."

Kieran clenched his fists. "You're bluffing."

"I don't bluff. There's no mileage in it. I think Liam deserves the truth, but that's up to you."

"Really? I believe you'll find I still hold all the cards."

I laughed. "You always thought you were such a

great player – I know it must have been hard for you to even pretend that you'd lost. But today, even though you think you have four aces, you *are* going to lose."

Kieran lowered his gun. "I still have the money. That will buy me more lawyers than you can count. Why are you so confident?"

"You have two big problems: first, I have more evidence than you know. I planted leech devices around your home the last time I visited. I wanted to make sure I wasn't being compromised, and that you weren't being threatened. Of course they'll have picked up a lot of useful detail about your operations. So you see although I only planned to protect you, I'll beat you because I care."

He lowered his gun, his shoulders slumping. "You always said you'd beat me one day. I never believed it."

I raised my gun. "After everything that's happened, maybe I should just finish this."

"Maybe you should."

"I also said I would protect Liam. I just didn't realise it would be from you. Which brings me to your second problem. You don't have the money."

Kieran laughed. "We both just witnessed the transfer. It's moved on a dozen times since then, via various tax havens. Good luck finding it."

"Yes, that's what we saw on your device. But what you didn't see was the funds bouncing somewhere else."

"I don't care where else you put your leeches; they can't have been anywhere near my computer."

I shook my head. "I wasn't sure what to expect. So I made a plan where it didn't matter who ended up taking the eBonds. The code was on the drive itself. It's a trick I learned from one of my former clients. The thing about being outsmarted is you can learn from it."

Kieran's jaw grew hard, and the hand holding the gun at his side twitched.

The bug buzzed quietly again. Morse code.

N - O - W.

I smiled. "You can go quietly, or you can go loudly. But either way it's over."

All around us appeared red dots from laser sights. The real cavalry was here.

I closed my eyes.

And someone threw a gas grenade onto the ground between us.

EIGHTY-FOUR

THREE DAYS LATER

ONCE AGAIN, I WAS DRESSED ALL IN BLACK, ALTHOUGH this time it wasn't for camouflage. The cocktail party was in full swing, but I took a moment to step into the house's private gallery. I brushed my fingers over my bowtie and self-consciously straightened my dinner jacket. Next to me, resplendent in a new frame and illuminated with LED lights, was *Afternoon Sun on the East Wing*: the small oil painting Gerald Meeks had hired me to acquire.

"I think it looks just perfect hanging there," Susan said, her heels clicking as she walked up to me, slipping her arm through mine.

"I'm glad we could do the right thing," I said, "and *un*-unsteal it for the person who actually owned and wanted it."

"I quite agree," said Rodney Bickerstaff from the

doorway. "It's nice that you could come back, without a face mask this time."

I turned to him and nodded. "I really am sorry for what happened. I thought I was providing restitution."

"You made it right, Jake. That's what matters." He cleared his throat. "It almost makes me feel bad about pointing a shotgun at you the last time we met."

I shrugged. "It was fair enough under the circumstances."

"And what about our mutual friend?"

"Gerald Meeks? I hear from the police that his problems are only just beginning."

"Win-win." Bickerstaff gave a nod. "Take your time here. Join us in the drawing room when you're ready." He turned and left us alone.

Susan rested her head on my shoulder. "So, what's next, Jake?"

"I haven't thought beyond surviving the last week. My eyes are still smarting from that gas grenade."

"Maybe I should have left you to it."

I inclined my head. "I believe I've already said thank you. And I'm grateful that, aside from when you were demonstrating your skills, you've always been straight with me."

"You're still upset about Meg."

"She lied to me for nearly three years."

Susan shrugged. "It was her job."

I folded my arms. "Then she should have done her job better. She and Winslow actually thought that I was behind stealing the money. They thought I killed my father when he got in the way."

"Winslow built their case around what she thought

was an unquestionable asset. Kieran was a former MI5 operative: one of their own. And remember, for the last three years they've watched you become a professional thief, albeit one with quite high morals. It did reinforce his story."

"I suppose."

"And of course Kieran had you fooled too," she said, though she winced sympathetically. "You believed what he told you about Winslow."

"I always thought Kieran was the one helping me: that I owed him. But he just made it feel that way. He manipulated everyone till we were all playing to his tune."

"And by constantly pointing fingers elsewhere, somehow nobody suspected him."

"My father always had his doubts," I said. "Sadly he didn't act on them."

"Well, Kieran's plan has finally collapsed thanks to you. You even managed to resist shooting Prebble and Rouse when given the opportunity." She smiled. "You proved yourself the better man."

"Maybe it was a mistake. Prebble won't go down easily: he has a lot of lawyers."

"But he will go down. Rouse too, although there are rumours about him trying to make a deal to get into witness protection."

"I'm not surprised," I said. "I think he'd say anything to stay out of sight of Andre Coralov's people, given that they think he killed their boss. Although I get the feeling Winslow won't allow Rouse any quarter while she's still breathing."

"What about Kieran?" Susan asked.

I sighed. "They're still building the charge list. There's a lot to unravel. He took what he learned at MI5 and he used it like a well-informed parasite. Nobody knew what he was doing, but he knew everything so he was free to do things that people couldn't fathom or anticipate. And whenever something did happen, there was always a simpler logical explanation."

Susan shook her head. "The finger of blame never pointed anywhere near him."

"Like when he killed my father." I turned away. "I know he must have been the one who set the bomb: what he did to Coralov shows he likes to kill that way. And yet…" I swallowed.

Susan raised a hand and squeezed my arm. "I don't think he did it, Jake. Kieran didn't want Charles dead any more than the others did. He wanted the money. He only killed his wife because she put the billion in jeopardy."

I frowned. "You're suggesting someone else was involved?"

"I'm suggesting we still don't have all the answers. And there's something I wanted to show you." She began rummaging in her purse. "You were at the airport, the day you heard about the bomb, right?"

"We were going on holiday."

"But you were travelling on different days? Why?"

"My father said the flights were full."

"He had you in business class. The flights are almost never full, so I checked it out: availability on those days was good. Did he say anything odd to you?"

"He said I should get on the flight whatever happened."

"But you didn't?"

"I didn't think 'whatever' included him being killed in an explosion."

Susan pulled a postcard from her purse. "I found this on your doormat when Sid and I dropped off that gear for you earlier."

I took it. And hesitated. It was the same picture of a white sandy beach, palm trees and a small beach cafe in the distance that I received regularly. "This just arrived?"

She nodded.

I flipped it over. As always there was just my address, neatly printed. As always the message was blank. "It's a mistake. Some printed machine sending a postcard to the wrong address. I get one every other month."

She blinked. "Did you ever consider it might *not* be a mistake?"

I frowned and flipped back to the picture. As I stared at it, I realised that I'd never really looked at it properly. If I had, I've have realised I saw the place every day. It was a different angle on the scene, but it was definitely the same place as in the picture on the wall in my kitchen.

The subtlest of messages. The merest of hints. From someone who had outsmarted everyone. I turned to Susan, finding it hard to form words. Could it really be true?

"Are you coming to the same conclusion I have?" she asked. "That's good, because I thought maybe I was tripping out."

"You think this is from… That's impossible." I felt the room start to spin. "There were witnesses. DNA evidence."

"Your father managed to steal and hide a billion

pounds, while outsmarting MI5, Rouse and Prebble. You think he couldn't do a simple thing like fake his own death?" She tipped her head to one side.

"But why?"

"I'm going to hazard a guess that it was to keep you safe. He might have known there was someone else involved, but he hadn't worked out who it was and didn't want to risk them going after you. Once he was 'dead', he knew you'd be safe."

I waved the postcard again. "So this is a message? Sent with a code that I've not had the perspective to understand?"

Susan reached into her purse again and pulled out two airline tickets. She handed one to me. "Why don't we go and find out?" She paused. "Unless you've got something more important to be doing?"

I laughed a little shakily. "Not that I can think of."

"I thought not, particularly after I saw a story breaking on the news about an hour ago. Apparently Bernard Prebble's spokesperson has announced the repayment of nearly a billion pounds to his company's pension fund. When reached for comment, he looked more than a little irate about the whole thing."

"Is that right?"

"Given the jail time he's facing that really is saying something. Of course it was nearly a billion that was repaid, rather than the whole amount, but I don't think anyone's complaining."

"Well, I'm a nice guy, but with any restitution job there is the issue of a reasonable commission. As my cousin told me, there's nothing wrong with being paid for something you're good at. The difference is I plan on doing something good with the money."

Susan raised her glass. "So, Jake, are we going to change the world?"

I clinked her glass with mine.

ACKNOWLEDGMENTS

My thanks for choosing to read **Unstolen**. If you did enjoy it, do consider leaving a quick review on Amazon or Goodreads - as an author, reviews are absolutely critical in getting noticed, and are always hugely appreciated. As a thank you, you can also get a FREE short techno-thriller - use the following link: http://www.tonybatton.com/free-story-from-interface.

I owe a great debt of gratitude to the many people who have encouraged and supported me through the long process of bringing *Unstolen* to completion. A special thank you to my *beta team* who so willingly read (and re-read) the manuscript and provided feedback and criticism - it was invaluable in making the book better: *Jin Koo Niersbach, Imogen Cleaver, Paul Cleaver, Chris Turner, Christine Lane, Johan van Wijgerden, Maurice Murphy, Elli Murphy, Alex Bott, Joshua Allarm, John Nicholson, Mary Seear, Tania Williams, Patrick Wijngaarden and Judy Bott.*

As you may have noticed, this book has been written in British English. I fully appreciate other English-speaking nations have different preferences in the spelling of certain words - I make no value judgement as to which is 'best', but I had to pick one! I hope it hasn't spoiled your enjoyment of the book.

If you have any comments, questions or feedback I'd love to hear from you. I can be reached via my website www.tonybatton.com, and on Facebook and Twitter.

Best regards

Tony Batton
London 2018

ALSO BY TONY BATTON

Interface

Resurface

Artificial Inheritance (a short story)

ABOUT THE AUTHOR

Tony Batton worked in international law firms, media companies and Formula One motorsport, before turning his hand to writing novels. He is passionate about great stories, gadgets and coffee, and probably consumes too much of each.

Tony's novels explore the possibilities and dangers of new technology, and how that can change lives. When not writing, or talking about gadgets, Tony likes to play basketball, guitar, and computer games with his two young sons. He lives in London with his family.

Unstolen is his third novel.

You can connect with Tony online at his website: www.tonybatton.com or on Facebook and Twitter.

Printed in Poland
by Amazon Fulfillment
Poland Sp. z o.o., Wrocław